SALVATION

THE PROTECTORS #2

SLOANE KENNEDY

Salvation is a work of fiction. Names, characters, businesses, places, events and incidents are either the products of the author's imagination or used in a fictitious manner. Any resemblance to actual persons, living or dead, or actual events is purely coincidental.

Copyright © 2016 by Sloane Kennedy

Published in the United States by Sloane Kennedy
All rights reserved. This book or any portion thereof may not be reproduced or used in any manner whatsoever without the express written permission of the publisher except for the use of brief quotations in a book review.

Cover Images: ©Zaretska Olga, © artofphoto

Cover Design: © Jay Aheer, Simply Defined Art

ISBN-13:
978-1532926389

ISBN-10:
1532926383

CONTENTS

Salvation	v
Trademark Acknowledgements	vii
Trigger Warning	ix
Acknowledgments	xi
Series Reading Order	xiii
Series Crossover Chart	xvii
salvation	xix
Prologue	1
Chapter 1	5
Chapter 2	12
Chapter 3	20
Chapter 4	31
Chapter 5	38
Chapter 6	53
Chapter 7	60
Chapter 8	69
Chapter 9	75
Chapter 10	81
Chapter 11	88
Chapter 12	96
Chapter 13	104
Chapter 14	107
Chapter 15	114
Chapter 16	125
Chapter 17	131
Chapter 18	137
Chapter 19	144
Chapter 20	151
Chapter 21	158
Chapter 22	171

Chapter 23	177
Chapter 24	190
Chapter 25	199
Chapter 26	206
Chapter 27	213
Chapter 28	218
Epilogue	224
Sneak Peek	231
Prologue	233
About the Author	239
Also by Sloane Kennedy	241

SALVATION

Sloane Kennedy

TRADEMARK ACKNOWLEDGEMENTS

The author acknowledges the trademarked status and trademark owners of the following trademarks mentioned in this work of fiction:

Tetris

TRIGGER WARNING

Listed below are the trigger warnings for this book. Reading them may cause spoilers:

This book contains flashback scenes that reference rape/sodomy with a foreign object.

ACKNOWLEDGMENTS

Kylee and Claudia, what can I say? Your little bit of crazy has kept me sane. My new ultimate goal in life is to someday earn the title of honorary soul sister.

SERIES READING ORDER

All of my series cross over with one another so I've provided a couple of recommended reading orders for you. If you want to start with the Protectors books, use the first list. If you want to follow the books according to timing, use the second list. Note that you can skip any of the books (including M/F) as each was written to be a standalone story.

Note that some books may not be readily available on all retail sites

Recommended Reading Order (Use this list if you want to start with "The Protectors" series)
1. Absolution (m/m/m) (The Protectors, #1)
2. Salvation (m/m) (The Protectors, #2)
3. Retribution (m/m) (The Protectors, #3)
4. Gabriel's Rule (m/f) (The Escort Series, #1)
5. Shane's Fall (m/f) (The Escort Series, #2)
6. Logan's Need (m/m) (The Escort Series, #3)
7. Finding Home (m/m/m) (Finding Series, #1)
8. Finding Trust (m/m) (Finding Series, #2)

9. Loving Vin (m/f) (Barretti Security Series, #1)
10. Redeeming Rafe (m/m) (Barretti Security Series, #2)
11. Saving Ren (m/m/m) (Barretti Security Series, #3)
12. Freeing Zane (m/m) (Barretti Security Series, #4)
13. Finding Peace (m/m) (Finding Series, #3)
14. Finding Forgiveness (m/m) (Finding Series, #4)
15. Forsaken (m/m) (The Protectors, #4)
16. Vengeance (m/m/m) (The Protectors, #5)
17. A Protectors Family Christmas (The Protectors, #5.5)
18. Atonement (m/m) (The Protectors, #6)
19. Revelation (m/m) (The Protectors, #7)
20. Redemption (m/m) (The Protectors, #8)
21. Finding Hope (m/m/m) (Finding Series, #5)
22. Defiance (m/m) (The Protectors #9)

***Recommended Reading Order** (Use this list if you want to follow according to timing)*
1. Gabriel's Rule (m/f) (The Escort Series, #1)
2. Shane's Fall (m/f) (The Escort Series, #2)
3. Logan's Need (m/m) (The Escort Series, #3)
4. Finding Home (m/m/m) (Finding Series, #1)
5. Finding Trust (m/m) (Finding Series, #2)
6. Loving Vin (m/f) (Barretti Security Series, #1)
7. Redeeming Rafe (m/m) (Barretti Security Series, #2)
8. Saving Ren (m/m/m) (Barretti Security Series, #3)
9. Freeing Zane (m/m) (Barretti Security Series, #4)
10. Finding Peace (m/m) (Finding Series, #3)
11. Finding Forgiveness (m/m) (Finding Series, #4)
12. Absolution (m/m/m) (The Protectors, #1)
13. Salvation (m/m) (The Protectors, #2)
14. Retribution (m/m) (The Protectors, #3)
15. Forsaken (m/m) (The Protectors, #4)
16. Vengeance (m/m/m) (The Protectors, #5)
17. A Protectors Family Christmas (The Protectors, #5.5)

18. Atonement (m/m) (The Protectors, #6)
19. Revelation (m/m) (The Protectors, #7)
20. Redemption (m/m) (The Protectors, #8)
21. Finding Hope (m/m/m) (Finding Series, #5)
22. Defiance (m/m) (The Protectors #9)

SERIES CROSSOVER CHART

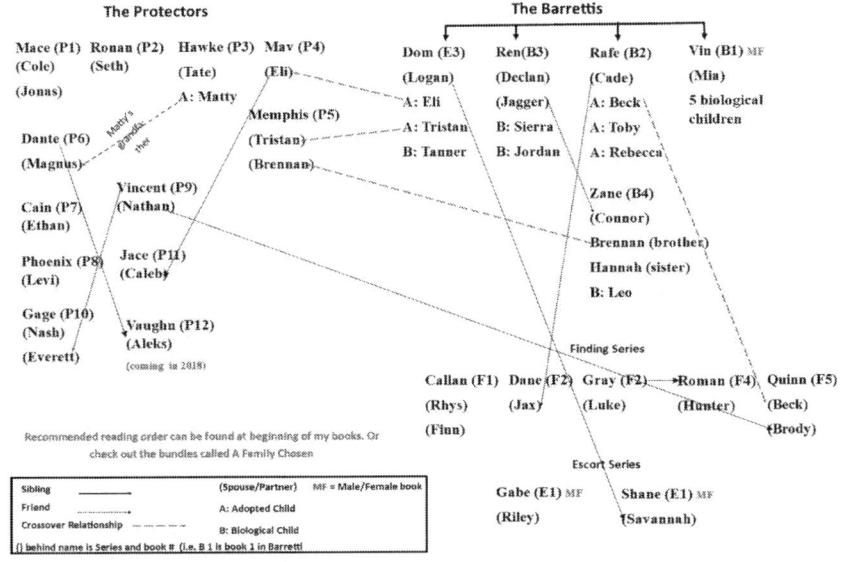

SALVATION

noun sal·va·tion \sal-ˈvā-shən\

The act of saving someone from sin or evil

PROLOGUE

RONAN

I ignored the sleek German Shepherd running towards me and kept my eyes on the house that sat up the slight hill several hundred yards away. I'd thought the grove of trees would hide my presence, but I'd been wrong because I'd seen the shadow of the man staring in my direction from his bedroom window, minutes before the back door of the house had opened and the dog had darted through it.

I'd been wrong a lot lately.

Wrong in trusting a man who'd sworn his loyalty to my cause, only to throw it away for a lucrative payout that would have taken an innocent man's life.

Wrong to think my efforts to save a man I'd come to think of as a friend had done anything other than lead him further into the pit of despair he'd so desperately been trying to escape from after suffering an insurmountable loss.

Wrong to think that I could stay away from the young man who was forever tied to my past...a past I wanted nothing more than to forget.

Did it work for you, Ronan?

A simple question from someone who'd reminded me a lot of the man in the house. It had come in response to my insistence that my choice to pursue justice outside the limits of the law had provided me with an alternative outlet for the hatred that consumed me. I hadn't answered Jonas Davenport when he'd asked me that. It was a question that, even now, I still refused to answer. Because it didn't matter. It had stopped being about me the first time I ended one life to save another.

I could hear the dog snarling as he neared me but, as soon as he crossed into the trees, the growling ceased and I put out my hand in greeting and he began whining excitedly. He sniffed and licked my hand repeatedly before settling down next to me and leaning against my leg. I let my hand stroke over the dog's lush coat. I hadn't seen the animal in several years, but I wasn't surprised that he remembered me since I'd been the one who'd picked him out of the litter of eight well-bred puppies and watched him grow up alongside the teenage boy I'd gifted him to.

I looked back up at the house and felt my gut clench at the sight of the open door leading from the expansive patio into what I knew was the kitchen. The invitation was clear.

It wasn't the first time I'd watched the young man from a distance; it wasn't even the first time I'd stood in these very woods waiting to see a glimpse of him as he passed by a window. Some days I never even saw him.

Being near him was a need I couldn't explain, but one I'd given up trying to deny. My only consolation was that I'd been strong enough not to act on the desire that had consumed me on that fateful day when I'd stopped seeing him as a boy and started wanting him as a man. One feather light brush of his mouth over mine and he'd become so much more than the little brother of the man I had been planning to spend the rest of my life with.

My only saving grace, the only reason I hadn't taken what he was offering, was the promise I'd made to protect him. But I'd known as soon as he kissed me that what he needed protection most from was me.

Until now.

I gave the dog a final pat and began walking up the hill. Because it was time to keep my promise...no matter what it cost me.

CHAPTER 1

RONAN

"How long?"

I heard the words the instant I stepped over the threshold into the dimly lit den, but I didn't respond. Instead, I let my eyes settle on the young man sitting on the leather couch that was facing a set of glass doors leading to a porch overlooking Puget Sound. His back was to me, so all I saw was the back of his head and his wider-than-I-remembered shoulders.

He'd been easy to find because all I'd had to do was follow the dog through the large house. But it wouldn't have mattered either way because I knew the place like the back of my hand. Not only had Trace and I spent several of our leaves together here in the year that we'd met, but I'd also made countless trips after his death to check on his younger brother. And even though it had been three years since I'd seen Seth Nichols, I wasn't ready for this moment. I'd never be ready...

The dog trotted around the couch and I saw Seth's arms move, presumably to caress the animal. I took my time walking towards the couch in the hopes that I could get control of my churning gut. It was a sensation I fucking hated.

I actually paused just behind the couch so I could get a hold of myself and settled my gaze on Seth's honey blond hair that fell in soft waves just above his ears and nape. I could see the baby fine hairs along the back of his neck and cursed the urge to reach out and feel their softness beneath my fingers. Trace had had the same color hair and one of my favorite things to do as he'd lain on top of me after we'd made love, was to run my fingers through the short strands so I could watch the light play with the different colors that threaded through them.

That brief memory of Trace was quickly tainted by my final memory of him...one where his beautiful hair was soaked in blood while the green of his eyes started to fade, his pupils growing larger, their inky blackness glazing over as his last breath left his body.

The thought of Trace and how he'd been taken from me was enough to obliterate all of my anxiety and replace it with the familiar, bitter cold that settled in every part of my body. I welcomed it like an old friend and then walked around the couch. I'd already read the police report so I knew to expect the bruises, but words on paper weren't the same as seeing them firsthand.

"How long?" Seth repeated, his eyes still on the horizon even as I stepped up to him and put my fingers under his chin. He stiffened slightly, but didn't resist when I tilted his face up to examine the black and blue mark on his left cheek, another on his lower jaw and the small gash next to his left eye. His forest green eyes connected with mine for a moment before shifting away as he pulled free of my hold.

In so many ways he looked exactly the same as I remembered him, the damage to his face notwithstanding. But as painfully young as he still appeared to me, there was something missing that I couldn't quite put my finger on. He'd filled out in the three years since I'd last seen him but he'd never be a large guy. I knew him to be a couple inches shorter than Trace, which meant he was at least three or four inches shorter than me. Fortunately, the few features he shared with Trace, like the eyes and the hair, weren't strong enough to make it feel like I was looking at a younger version of my dead lover. But that fact only heightened my desire to put my fingers back on his warm skin.

"How long what?" I asked as I stepped away and sat down on the coffee table in front of him. I was both glad and annoyed that he refused to look directly at me. But the thought was short-lived because his eyes shifted to me before he answered.

"How long have you been watching me?"

I debated playing dumb but decided against it. It was beneath me... and him. "Off and on," I answered. "How did you know?"

Seth shrugged and then reached next to me on the table for an icepack. He pressed it gingerly against his cheek. "I'd get this feeling once in a while like I was being watched." Seth nodded towards the dog that had settled at his feet. "He'd always start acting funny, too... agitated. Thought I was going crazy for a while," he muttered.

The thread of anger I heard in Seth's voice didn't surprise me but it bothered me more than it should have. Not that I didn't deserve it because I did. I'd even steeled myself for it but a small part of me had hoped he'd still look at me the way he used to when he was younger... like I was his hero or something.

"What happened?" I asked as I motioned to his face. I already knew what had happened but I wanted him to tell me.

"What are you doing here, Ronan?" Seth asked. "And don't tell me some bullshit about you just stopping by for a visit. We both know you can't stand to be around me."

I flinched at that. I'd never explained my reasons for walking away the day he'd kissed me. I hadn't even said a word, just as I hadn't looked back, even when I'd felt his hopeful gaze boring into my back as I'd walked to my car. He'd called and sent texts over the first few weeks but I'd steadfastly ignored them. I'd nearly broken when I'd heard his final voicemail, his voice heavy with unshed tears, as he'd told me how sorry he was and begged me not to leave him. I'd had my finger hovering over the call back button for several long minutes as I'd listened to it over and over again. But then I'd done the right thing and deleted the message because I wasn't the man Seth wanted...I'd never be that man again.

"What happened?" I repeated, but when Seth's jaw hardened, I felt a shimmer of lust roll through my belly. He'd always been so meek and innocent as a child. And as much as I hated to think he'd lost some of the gentleness that had made him so different than his brother, the darkness inside of me responded to the challenge of bending his show of strength to my will. "I've kept tabs on you," I finally admitted. "I was…made aware of the police report you filed."

Curiously, Seth seemed unsurprised by my words because all he said was, "Then you already know what happened. Next time use the front door," Seth said as he stood. "Code's the same."

I grabbed his wrist before he could walk away from me and I heard him gasp at the contact. I had no doubt it was because he was feeling the same rush of electricity and heat that I was. My dick hardened even more in my pants and I was supremely grateful that I was sitting down. I gently tugged Seth until he was once again sitting but all his anger had fled and was replaced with unadulterated arousal.

"I want to hear you tell me," I managed to say as I forced myself to release my hold on him.

It took Seth a moment to collect himself and his eyes quickly shifted away. "I was mugged," he finally said. When I remained silent, he continued on his own. "I was walking to my car in the garage underneath my office building when this guy came up behind me and demanded my wallet and keys. He hit me a couple times, took my wallet but left my keys and ran when he heard someone coming. The cops found my wallet in the alley next to the building. All my cash was gone but everything else was there."

"Did he hit you before or after you gave him what he wanted?"

Seth dropped his elbow to his knee so he could rest his jaw against the icepack he was holding in his hand. "Before, I guess. I already had the keys in my hand and I was getting my wallet out when he punched me the first time."

"Did you lose consciousness at any time during the attack?"

Seth shook his head.

"The doctor should have given you stitches for this," I said as I carefully turned his face to examine the cut next to his eye. It wasn't a particularly deep injury but a stitch or two would prevent scarring. The fucker who'd hit Seth must have been wearing a ring of some kind…

"I didn't see a doctor. I refused medical treatment when the cops showed up."

"Why?" I asked as I let Seth pull away from me again. A few years ago he would have welcomed my touch.

"I'm tired, Ronan. I need to lie down for a bit. Have a safe trip back to wherever the hell it is you live now," was all Seth said as he once again stood.

I was about to reach for him again when the dog jumped up from between us, a low snarl emanating from its throat. It tore out of the room at the same time that a voice called out Seth's name.

I had my gun out long before the man rushed into the den, the dog at his heels. "What the hell?" he said in shock at the sight of me and then his eyes shifted to Seth whose jaw had dropped at the sight of my weapon.

"Jesus, Ronan," Seth whispered as he stepped into the line of fire. "He's a friend," Seth said, though his eyes never left my gun even after I lowered it and let it hang loosely by my leg. Fuck, now I'd have even more explaining to do.

"Seth?" came the shaky voice from directly behind him.

Seth stepped away from me and went around the couch. His friend was still watching me but as soon as Seth neared him, his face went slack. "Oh my God," he murmured as he reached his arms out and wrapped them none too gently around Seth. I didn't miss the way Seth winced at the contact and I bit back the urge to order the little shit to let Seth go. But it wasn't just because his hold was too rough… it was because he was holding Seth at all.

I let my eyes scan the man as his attention was on Seth. He was in his mid to late twenties and was actually a pretty decent looking guy in a sweater-wearing, pocket protector kind of way. His height and build were average and his brown hair was carefully styled. His clothes looked expensive and everything matched so well that I had no doubt he was the type who spent a lot of time in front of a mirror getting his look just so.

"I came as soon as I got your message," the man said as he pulled back enough to get a look at Seth's face.

"I told you that you didn't need to come," Seth said. "I know you had patients to see..."

The man made some type of dismissive grunt and then he was pulling Seth back into his arms. "My favorite patient needs me, I'm there," the man insisted.

Patient? The guy was a doctor? What the hell was Seth seeing him for? And what the fuck kind of doctor acted so familiar with a patient?

"I knew it was too soon for you," the man said with a shake of his head. "I wish you would have heeded my advice...you know I only want what's best for you."

When the man finally released Seth after running his hands up and down his arms for a ridiculously long time, his beady eyes shifted to me. "Who's your friend?" he finally asked. I didn't miss the way he swallowed hard as his gaze fell to the gun I had yet to put away.

"Barry, this is Ronan Grisham. He's an old friend of the family," Seth said.

I was pleased to see the man made no attempt to shake my hand. In fact, he actually moved back a couple of steps as I came around the couch and approached both of them. I barely hid my smile at that.

"Ronan, this is Dr. Barry Fields," Seth murmured. "He's been helping me work through some things," was all he offered in way of an explanation.

Barry laughed and reached out to pat Seth's arm. "Now, now, Seth. You know we've come to mean much more to each other than just doctor and patient," he said jovially.

Seth shifted uncomfortably at either the words or the intimate contact but he made no move to extricate himself from the other man's lingering contact. Since I couldn't rip the fucker's arm off his body, I settled for stepping forward until Barry was forced to move back enough that he couldn't maintain his hold on Seth.

"Time for you to go, Barry," I said coolly.

"Well, uh...I think it would be better if I stayed," Barry stammered. "Even you should be able to see that Seth needs a doctor," he added arrogantly.

"He has one," I interjected. "A real one."

"Ronan…" Seth warned but I ignored him.

Barry's mouth was opening and closing like some kind of fish gasping for breath. "I don't know who you think you are, Mr. Grisham, but Seth is my patient-"

"You're right, Barry," I said calmly as I put my gun into one of the double shoulder holsters under my jacket. "You don't know who I am." I fisted my hand in his expensive sweater and shoved him back against the wall. "And believe me, you want to make sure it stays that way. Now get the fuck out!"

I held him there for several seconds as he squirmed to break free of my hold and when I finally did release him, he gave Seth a quick glance as he straightened his sweater. "Seth, I'll call you later to see how you're feeling." The man straightened as best he could and then nodded at Seth and slowly left the room as if leaving was his choice.

It wasn't until I heard the front door slam closed that I turned my attention to Seth. I was surprised when he pushed past me and said, "It's your turn, Ronan. Get the fuck out."

CHAPTER 2

SETH

I wasn't expecting Ronan to put his hands on me. And I definitely wasn't expecting the rush of the lust that went through me when he shoved me hard against the wall and held me there with his body. My anger was supposed to have made me immune to the need I'd had for him from the time I was old enough to realize that's what the emotions churning through me were, but it hadn't. My fury, my hurt – all they did was ratchet up the intensity of what I was feeling.

I should have done a lot of things as he held me there.

Pushed him away.

Cursed him.

Admitted that he'd destroyed me when he'd walked out on me three years earlier.

But all I could do was stand there and relish the feel of his strong fingers wrapped around my wrists, pinning my hands to the wall. I welcomed the heat that wafted off his big body and warmed me in a way that nothing else could. I drank down the sound of every one of his rough breaths, the only proof that he wasn't completely unaffected by the contact, because his hard eyes gave nothing away. And when I dropped my eyes to his lips, lips I knew from experience were softer than they looked, I felt the slightest shudder roll through his body.

I didn't know how long he held me there for and, in truth, I didn't care. I'd wanted for so long for him to see me as something other than his boyfriend's pesky, desperate little brother, that I needed to get as much out of this one moment where he was seeing me as a man that I could, because I suspected it would have to sustain me for a very long time.

I'd met Ronan for the first time when I was thirteen and my brother, Trace, had brought a then 28-year-old Ronan home to meet our parents after they'd met at the military hospital where Ronan was completing his residency. Even at my young age, I'd been fascinated by Ronan. He'd had a certain cool confidence to him that had drawn me in, but it was the way he'd laughed and joked with me that had had my hero worship turning into something more within a couple of visits. I'd fought to keep the fact that I was falling for my own brother's boyfriend a secret, but Trace had easily picked up on it and hadn't wasted time in teasing me every chance he got with jokes about not trying to steal his boyfriend out from underneath him. And he'd never failed to make sure Ronan was around when he'd made the comments. I'd known that my brother's ribbing was meant to be harmless fun, but my feelings had run so deep that every joke he'd made had caused pinpricks in my soul, because I'd known I'd never have what he had. Because despite my mother's assurances to the contrary, I'd known even then that I'd only ever want Ronan and any man who might come my way in the future would always pale in comparison.

Maybe it would have been easier if Ronan had shared my brother's penchant for making light of the way I felt. But he'd only fanned the flames of my burgeoning want by protecting me from my brother's unintentional cruelty, and he'd never allowed the awkwardness to change the way he'd treated me. He'd always been kind, interested and encouraging. And he'd promised me that someday I'd find that lucky someone who would change my life the way Trace had changed his.

And then everything *had* changed. In less than a year my parents were gone, my brother was gone and the Ronan I'd fallen in love with was gone.

I managed to remain perfectly still as Ronan held me against the wall, afraid that any movement would break whatever reverie we'd both fallen into. I wanted so badly to lean forward and brush my lips over his, to once again taste the sweetness that was so unexpected and so intoxicating, but I'd learned my lesson the first time around. And as much as I wanted Ronan to leave, I couldn't bear the humiliation of him choosing to walk away from me again instead of enduring my naïve, painfully inexperienced kiss.

Ronan finally pulled back and released his hold on me, but just one of my wrists. "You have a first aid kit somewhere?" he asked as he tugged me forward.

"My bathroom," I said.

I followed him silently to the main part of the house and didn't try to read too much into the fact that he still had a hold of my wrist. My dog, Bullet, came with us, but I didn't miss how the animal stuck right next to Ronan's side. Since the German Shepherd was my perpetual shadow, it should have bothered me more that he'd abandoned me for Ronan. But it didn't. It was just a reminder of how easy it was for man and beast alike to gravitate to the big, quiet man.

Ronan led me to the bathroom and turned me so my back was against the counter. He glanced at me and I automatically said, "Bottom drawer" since I knew what he was looking for. He found the first aid kit and opened it and pulled out a couple of butterfly bandages before running a washcloth under water. His touch was surprisingly gentle for such a big, scary looking guy and I wondered how many of his patients were shocked by the contradiction. At 6'5, Ronan towered over most men and he had the bulk to back it up. He wasn't bulging everywhere, but he had a rock hard body that even now rippled beneath his clothes. His stormy gray eyes were typically shrouded in mystery, but I'd seen them both joyful and haunted and everything in between.

I wished for the thousandth time that I could reach out and touch him because every time he shifted, my eyes were drawn to a spot on his upper chest where he'd left the first button of his shirt open. I could see bronzed flesh and a smattering of black hair that I desperately wanted to experience beneath my fingers. Would it be soft like the silky, coal black hair on his head or would it be wiry and rough? I'd seen enough naked men when my curiosity about sex had gotten the best of me and I'd checked out gay porn sites, but the life I'd been living hadn't afforded me the opportunity to experiment hands-on and, unlike Ronan, I was utterly lacking in the chest hair department.

Ronan finished cleaning the injury and then closed it with two butterfly bandages. But once he secured the last bandage, his fingers didn't leave my face right away and I held my breath as the rough pad of his thumb grazed my cheek.

"Better?" he asked, though his voice was a strange, hoarse whisper I'd never heard before. That, combined with his touch, stoked the nerves in my already swollen cock and I swallowed hard as I tried to shift my body so he wouldn't notice my predicament. But all I managed to do was brush my crotch against his and he froze at the contact. And then I saw it – the flare of arousal in his dark eyes. Even in my innocence, I knew it for what it was and as much as that terrified me, I wanted to cry out in relief too.

He wanted me.

His finger had stilled in its caressing of my bruised cheek and his eyes fell to my mouth. His whole hand drifted down to cup my jaw and I forced myself to hold completely still. Because I wasn't going to fuck this up. I wanted it too much.

Only there was one part of myself that I couldn't keep still. My mouth. Because before I knew it, I was whispering his name and his whole body drew up tight.

"Fuck," he suddenly snarled and then his mouth came crashing down on mine.

No amount of wishing for that exact moment prepared me for it in any way because once Ronan's mouth covered mine, I was completely lost. The kiss was brutal and rough and I didn't even get a chance to adjust to the feeling of Ronan's lips searing across mine before his tongue was pushing into my mouth. I gasped at the feel of it stroking over mine and a wave of heat washed through me with such force, that I was sure my knees would give out. I felt the hard edge of the counter digging into my ass as Ronan leaned into me.

I was completely overwhelmed by the sensations that bombarded me as Ronan consumed my mouth – and that's exactly what it was. I had no control, no comprehension of anything besides how good it felt. And no idea how to kiss him back. I had the fleeting thought that my inexperience would turn him off, but if he noticed, it didn't slow him down in any way and I was glad. Because I knew if he stopped, if he pushed me away and said I was too young or said he couldn't because I was Trace's little brother, I'd never recover. Hell, I'd likely never recover anyway because in my gut, I knew it was only this good because it was Ronan.

The hand that had been holding my face skimmed down my neck and along my side until it curved around my ass and drew me forward. The feel of Ronan's stiff length against mine had me gasping but Ronan stole that sound along with what little of my sanity was left. I gave myself over to him completely and didn't protest anything he did to me as his hands roamed all over me and his body rubbed against mine. At one point, I felt his blunt fingers pushing down the back of my jeans and I was sure I'd come in my pants as his pointer finger pressed into my crease. His sensual torture of my mouth didn't let up for even a second but my brain finally started to catch up, and I wrapped my arms around his neck as I tentatively speared my tongue into his mouth. He groaned and then he was suddenly pushing away from me.

I was certain the whole thing was over, but I didn't even have time to protest or question what was happening as I watched Ronan's eyes dart around the bathroom before settling on the bathrobe hanging on the back of the closet door. A quick flick of his wrist and he was pulling the belt free and then his mouth was back on mine. I forgot all about the strange pause and began urgently kissing him back as my hands settled on his hips. I felt him grab one of my hands in his and then he was folding my arm behind my back. The move pushed me even closer to him. When he did the same with my other hand, I was forced to lean against him as he tormented me with one drugging kiss after another. It was several long seconds before I even realized what he was doing behind my back and by the time I found my voice, my hands were already tied together.

"Ronan, what-"

Ronan stole my words with another kiss and then his hand was rubbing my erection through my jeans. I moaned at the rough contact and tried to ask for more by shoving my hips forward. The hand stroking me drifted up just enough to reach the waistband and then was pushing down into my pants while the other began working them loose. I cried out at the feel of Ronan fisting my cock but he stole that sound too with another mind-numbing kiss. I forgot all about my bound hands as Ronan tugged ruthlessly on my sensitive dick and then ran his thumb across the slit before dipping inside of it. I tore my mouth free of Ronan's and dropped my head against his shoulder and let out a long, heavy groan as he played with me. Cool air brushed over my hot skin as my pants were opened and shoved down along with my underwear.

Ronan's hands gently pushed me off of him as he dropped to his knees and I was forced to lean back against the counter to keep myself upright. The hard edge bit into my ass as I lifted my bound hands so they rested on the top of the counter. Even though I was watching Ronan and knew what he was going to do to me, I wasn't at all prepared for the moment he sucked me in deep. I shouted at the heat and wetness that engulfed me and I instinctively shoved my hips forward. Without preamble, Ronan began sucking me mercilessly as he bobbed up and down my length. One of his hands was cupping my ass while the other was rubbing back and forth over my taint before seeking out my balls.

"Ronan, please!" I begged as he dragged me closer and closer to an impending orgasm that was actually starting to frighten me. I'd jerked myself off plenty of times but I'd never felt this much, this fast, and the unknown scared the shit out of me. But Ronan's ministrations were expert and utterly ruthless. He showed me no mercy as he hollowed out his cheeks and began dragging up and down my length with almost brutal force. The fingers that had been rolling my balls around traveled over my taint and then pressed into my crack to search out my hole. And the second he pressed down on it, I lost it and began shooting into his mouth as my release took over every part of my body. I had no control as wave after wave of pleasure rocked through me and it was only Ronan's other arm around my hips that kept me upright.

I was struggling to catch my breath as Ronan rose to his feet and before I could even say anything, his mouth was on mine and I tasted the bitter, salty proof of my release. The kiss was wholly carnal and I loved every second of it despite the exhaustion settling into my heavy limbs. I had no idea if Ronan had found his own pleasure and was trying to figure out what I could to do give it to him, when he suddenly tore his mouth free of mine and spun me around and shoved me face down on the counter. I was still trying to get control of myself so I didn't realize what was happening until I felt Ronan's pelvis shove me forward. With my hands bound, I struggled to look up into the mirror so I could see him and my mouth went dry at the sight of him pulling a condom and a smaller packet of something from his wallet.

Surely he wasn't going to fuck me here? Like this?

"Ronan-"

I had no idea if Ronan heard the tremor of fear in my voice or not but he leaned over me and kissed me deeply before saying, "It's going to be hard and fast but I'll make sure you get off again."

I closed my eyes at the crude words that didn't mesh with the beautiful way he'd kissed me. God, was this how I wanted him? I knew if I told him that it was my first time, I'd likely lose my only chance with him. In my gut, I was sure he wouldn't hurt me but did I really want my first time with the man I'd been in love with for almost a decade, my first time with any man, to be just some down and dirty sex act that was more about getting off than anything else?

Fear began to niggle my brain as it warred with my need to be with this man in any way that I could and I automatically tried to pull free of the bindings on my wrists. Maybe it was just the lack of control that was freaking me out. If I could just get my hands loose…

My fear turned to full on panic when I realized Ronan had tied me up tight enough to keep me from getting loose on my own. In the back of my mind, I heard foil tearing along with a zipper being drawn down, but I couldn't focus on any of it because I was struggling to pull my hands free of the cotton belt that just seemed to get tighter the more I fought. Cold air drifted over my hole as Ronan opened me up and then something slick was pressing against my entrance. My throat seized up and I couldn't find my voice. I desperately yanked my hands apart in the hopes of loosening the belt, but then Ronan's hand closed over the spot where my wrists were tied.

I tried to tell Ronan that I needed him to slow down, but I knew I hadn't managed to get the words out because my throat was too clogged with fear. I felt his finger begin to massage me and humiliation went through me; I couldn't stem the tears that began to fall. And then Ronan was gone and the bathroom was gone.

It was just me and them and my father's broken voice as he begged and pleaded with my captors not to hurt me. I tried one last time to get my wrists free and then gave up and cried into my gag as I waited for the blade to slice through me again.

CHAPTER 3

RONAN

My fingers shook as I teased Seth's hole and I struggled to catch my breath as I willed my throbbing dick to settle down so I could make this good for the young man bent over in front of me, his beautiful body mine for the taking.

From the second I'd given in to my need and kissed Seth, I knew I wouldn't be able to take it slow and I knew I wouldn't be able to stop. I had no idea if the relentless pace I'd set was to keep me from realizing what I was doing and stopping it, or to prevent Seth from denying me what my body had finally decided belonged to it. There'd been a moment of hesitation as Seth's tentative and too innocent kisses had sent up red flags of warning in my brain, but then Seth had started mewling and whimpering in such desperation that I'd lost all semblance of control.

I shifted my hips so that my condom covered dick was pressed between Seth's spread legs and I rested more of my weight on his bound hands as I leaned over him to seek out his lips and to promise him again that I would make it perfect for him. But the second I saw the tears sliding down his face, I froze.

"Seth?" I whispered in confusion. When his only response was to squeeze his eyes closed even harder, I let out a hoarse shout and pulled him upright and spun him around.

"Seth, open your eyes," I commanded shakily.

What the hell had I done?

The reality of the situation slammed into me so hard that my knees actually buckled. "Seth, please," I whispered as I ran my thumbs over his wet cheeks. The move did nothing to stem his tears but he finally opened his eyes.

"My hands," he croaked. "Please..."

Fuck, fuck, fuck!

I carefully turned him around so he was facing the mirror and quickly worked the knot on the belt loose. As soon as his hands were free, he dropped them to the counter and hung his head. I ached to reach out and pull him into my arms but I couldn't move, couldn't think. I couldn't even find any words to tell him how sorry I was for what I'd done.

And then his gaze lifted to meet mine in the mirror and I sucked in a strangled breath. Fear, confusion...shame – they were all I saw.

I shook my head and tore my eyes from his. I barely managed to tuck my now flaccid dick back into my pants and close them as I rushed from the room, leaving him there exposed and vulnerable and...fuck...broken.

~

*H*e found me easily because unlike the last time Seth's touch had destroyed me, I hadn't run. Not because I didn't want to – I did. I wanted nothing more than to get away from this place that reminded me of what I'd lost...of what I'd become. But as much as I needed to escape, my gut was telling me that I couldn't leave just yet.

"Ronan, it's cold. Would you come inside please?" Seth asked as he came to a stop on the sand next to me. It had started drizzling within minutes of me fleeing the house but the moisture had felt good on my heated face. It had taken only a few minutes to make my way down the hill and I had no trouble finding the path that led to the beach. I'd ended up walking for a while before I'd forced myself to turn around and head back towards the house. But I couldn't make myself go back up to it so I'd sat down on an old, weathered log that had washed up onto the shore some time ago based on its distance from the water.

I didn't respond to Seth and when he sat down next to me, I saw that his wrists were still red from where he'd fought the bindings. Nausea rolled through me and I shifted away from him so no part of his body even stood a remote chance of touching mine.

"I'm sorry, Ronan," I heard him whisper.

I was certain I was going to throw up at his words and actually had to swallow back the bile that rose in my throat.

"What?" I managed to croak.

"I'm sorry," he repeated.

"Jesus, Seth," I groaned as I got to my feet and took a few steps forward. "You don't have a fucking thing to be sorry for," I said harshly. "God, I almost…"

I couldn't even finish the word because it was so disgusting and ugly.

"Ronan," Seth said and I felt him come up behind me. His hand closed over my arm and I immediately stepped out of his reach. He got the message and stepped around me but kept his distance. "Ronan, I wanted what happened between us. You must know that's all I've ever wanted," he admitted quietly.

I shook my head and turned away from him with the intention of making my way back down the beach but he blocked my path.

"I panicked because I couldn't get my hands free…"

Yeah, because I'd treated him like every cheap fuck I'd had in the years since Trace's death and I'd tainted him with the stain of my dark, twisted need.

"Seth, you don't have to explain. What I did to you was unforgiveable."

Seth seemed agitated as he studied me. Finally, he said, "Trace never told you, did he?"

"Told me what?"

"About what really happened that day."

I knew exactly what day he was referring to because there were only two days in Seth's life that he would refer to that way and Trace had only been alive for one of them. I'd been with Trace when he'd gotten the call that his family had been attacked during a brutal home invasion. At fourteen, Seth had been the only one who'd survived the nightmare and even then, it had been close because he'd been stabbed repeatedly. Trace and I had both been deployed in Afghanistan at the time and I hadn't been able to get leave to return with him to the States, since we'd needed to keep our relationship under wraps.

"What do you mean?" I asked as fear of what I would hear churned in my gut. Trace had been tight-lipped about the whole incident, but I'd always attributed his reluctance to discuss it as being due to the brutal way in which his parents had been killed.

"The men...they were convinced that my dad had a safe in the house. They didn't believe him when he said he didn't, so they used me and my mom to force him to talk."

I shook my head in disbelief as I began to understand what he was telling me.

"My mom...one of the guys, he took her upstairs. We could hear her screaming..." Seth managed to get out before he began sobbing. Even though I'd told myself I wouldn't touch him again, I dragged him into my arms and wrapped my arms around him as his tears soaked through my shirt. I dropped my lips to the top his head.

"My dad was begging them to stop. Then one of the guys grabbed me. My hands...my hands were tied behind my back..."

I closed my eyes as a fresh wave of guilt washed through me. "Jesus, Seth, I'm so fucking sorry."

"I tried to be brave. I thought if I screamed, it would be so much harder for my dad." Seth shook his head against my chest. "It hurt too much. They kept cutting me over and over. My stomach, my chest. My father was screaming and crying. Then they stabbed me before going after him. My mom...she'd finally stopped screaming at some point."

I held Seth as he continued to softly cry against me. Finally, he pulled back and I dropped my arms. "I just got scared, Ronan. But not of you...not of what you were doing."

I managed a nod even though his words did nothing to ease my guilt. No matter what the outcome, I never should have touched him. I remembered his inexperienced kisses and another layer of shame fell on my already heavy shoulders. "Seth, was that the first time someone touched you like that?" I asked.

His eyes dropped to the sand and I saw his pale cheeks flush with color.

Fuck.

"It won't happen again," I finally said. "It can't."

"But-"

"It can't," I repeated firmly, my eyes pinning him. The strands of his hair were starting to grow heavy with moisture and I noticed the way his skin glistened beneath the light drizzle. But when a shiver went through his body, I said, "Let's go back to the house."

He nodded but didn't move. I finally moved past him and hoped that he would follow.

He did.

~

After we'd reached the house, I'd urged Seth to take a shower and I'd used the time to retrieve my car which was parked about a half a mile from the house, on a small dirt road that provided access to the woods behind the Nichols estate. I had no trouble getting through the security gate at the end of the driveway since the code was exactly the same as it had been years ago when Trace had brought me here to meet his family. Back then, the house had been alive with warmth and happiness and I'd reveled in being so easily accepted into the fold. The concept of family was as foreign to me as my sexuality being accepted without question or contempt.

I'd met Trace Nichols at one of the most chaotic points in my life and I'd done everything in my power to discourage his pursuit of me. And that was exactly what it had been...a pursuit.

Eight years earlier

"Excuse me," I murmured without looking up at whomever I'd bumped into as they were getting off the elevator just as I was stepping on to it.

"No problem."

The husky voice caught my attention and I lifted my eyes from the chart I'd been reviewing and nearly stumbled at the sight of the young soldier watching me intently as he stood in the elevator opening, his body preventing the door from closing. I swallowed hard at how beautiful he was but common sense returned quickly and I dropped my eyes. I forced myself to keep my breathing slow and even as I tried to focus on the lab results I'd been studying, but my curiosity got the better of me when I didn't hear the elevator door slide shut and I shifted my eyes up for just a moment. The gorgeous man hadn't moved at all and his eyes were watching me with such open hunger, that I felt my dick responding instantly. I didn't need gaydar to know what his look meant and based on the way he was staring at me, his gaydar was working just fine...that or he didn't care whether it was or not.

There were no other people on the elevator or milling around the bank of elevators, but his open interest was making me uncomfortable, both physically and mentally, so I said, "Um, did you want to get off?"

He smiled widely at that and it hit me how the question must have sounded. To my dismay, he stepped back into the elevator and released the door which instantly slid shut, closing us off in the small space. I'd already pressed my floor and I watched in mute fascination as he began pressing every button between the floor we were on and the floor I was going to. And then he was moving to stand next to me, despite the ample amount of space available in the elevator car.

"I'm Trace," he said softly as his eyes traveled up and down the length of my body. I was insanely glad for the long white doctor's coat I was wearing because it hid my very obvious physical reaction to his perusal. "What's your name?"

The elevator stopped and I held my breath to see if anyone else was getting on. I wasn't sure if I wanted there to be someone on the other side of the door when it opened or not. There wasn't.

I let out a nervous chuckle and returned my attention to the chart. He didn't need to know that I was having trouble focusing on it.

I'd known I was gay for a very long time and while I hadn't ever tried to deny it, I'd kept it close to the vest just like I did all the other personal details of my life. It was something I'd learned to do early on when my father discovered me kissing my eighth grade lab partner in my room during a study session. What had happened afterwards hadn't been good for me.

I'd dated a few guys here and there in college and medical school but my busy schedule had often meant an early end to any potential long-term relationships. That had left random hooks-ups in bars and clubs that often left me feeling cheap and dirty as soon as the less than spectacular orgasm wore off. And since I regularly bottomed, I wasn't even always guaranteed said orgasm, at least not one that I couldn't have gotten on my own anyway.

"Dr. Grisham," Trace murmured and I looked down to see his fingers straightening the fabric of my jacket so he could read the name stitched on the pocket of my coat.

"Was there something you needed, Staff Sargent?" I asked as I scanned his insignia on his uniform. The rank surprised me considering he seemed to only be in his early twenties. His bright green eyes sparkled as he smiled at me and I realized I'd asked him yet another open ended question that I already suspected how he wanted to answer. "Forget I said that," I said with a smile of my own.

The elevator made another stop but I was strangely glad when no one got on.

"Yes and yes," Trace said as he shifted even closer to me.

I looked at him in confusion. "Yes to the first question, yes to the second," he drawled as his eyes fell to my mouth. "What's your name, Doc?"

If his voice had been more flirtatious, I would have been able to coolly dismiss him without a second thought. But the heavy thread of desire I heard had me wanting to do so much more than tell him something as simple as my name.

I was saved from doing anything when the elevator door opened and a couple of nurses got on. "Morning, Dr. Grisham," the younger of the two nurses said with a wide smile as she gave me a once over and then actually giggled as she turned her attention back on her colleague.

"Morning," I murmured in response. I couldn't remember her name despite the many times she'd sent me her not-so-subtle message that she was interested in me. I'd expected Trace to move away from me when the ladies joined us, but he didn't. To my dismay, he moved even closer and I barely stifled a moan when his fingers brushed mine. The sparks that flew were immediate and unlike anything I'd ever felt before, and the rush of having the other two occupants of the elevator car so close, yet so unaware, was heady. But Trace wasn't just content with the minimal contact because his arm actually stretched out onto the handrail at our backs. To anyone else, he would have looked like he was just bracing himself as he leaned against it but behind my back, his hand was busy as it skimmed over my lower back before dipping down to slide over the curve of my ass. Even through the fabric of my doctor's coat and pants, the shock of his touch reverberated through me.

I was barely aware of the elevator dinging as the door slid open or the nurses saying their goodbyes to me as they both stepped off the elevator. Before the door even finished closing, I turned on Trace with the intention of laying into him about his behavior but then his hand was snaking around the back of my neck and drawing me forward, and any argument I was about to make died in my throat as his tongue slipped between my lips. I'd been kissed plenty of times but what Trace was doing to me wasn't kissing. He was owning me, consuming me, changing me. In that instant, I didn't care that I had patients to see or rounds to finish or that there was even a fucking security camera in one corner of the elevator that was likely capturing everything Trace did to me. Somewhere in the back of my mind, I knew the elevator doors had to be opening and closing over and over again since Trace had pressed nearly every single button on the panel, but I didn't care about that either.

It was Trace who finally drew back from the heated kiss. "What's your name?" he asked breathlessly.

"Ronan," I responded without hesitation before I leaned forward to steal another kiss. He gave it to me before putting some space between our bodies.

"Have dinner with me tonight."

The request registered but I was still too off balance to answer. Luckily, my beeper went off. The sound was so jarring that I yanked myself away from him and silenced the damn thing and checked the number. It was a stat call to the OR.

"I have to go," I mumbled and it wasn't until Trace handed me the medical chart I'd been reading that I realized I'd dropped it when he'd kissed me.

"Dinner?" Trace asked again as he grabbed my arm before I could escape out the elevator door as it slid open.

"Can't, I'm working," I said, glad that my common sense was finally coming back to me. Random hook-ups and dead-end relationships were one thing but dinner with a guy who could fuck me up so completely with just one kiss...no way, not happening.

I tugged my arm free of Trace's hold and forced myself to not look back as I hurried for the stairwell. I blew out my breath at the close call and then let the chaos of the OR engulf me as I began the process of scrubbing in for emergency surgery.

It wasn't until a few hours later that I had the time to wonder if I'd blown a chance at something good...or at worst, a chance at some phenomenal sex. I had my answer as soon as I left the Surgery department intent on seeing the patient I hadn't gotten to before the emergency page.

Because sitting on the small bench near the bank of elevators, was Trace.

∾

"*R*onan?"

Seth's concerned voice knocked me from my thoughts and I looked up to see him walking down the stairs, his hair damp from his shower and wearing fresh clothes. I wasn't sure how long I'd been leaning against the inside of the front door for while I'd gotten lost in the past, but even the brief memory of Trace had my gut churning and my skin crawling.

"Are you okay?" Seth asked as he came to a stop in front of me. He settled his hand on my arm and I couldn't stop myself from yanking it away from him. I ignored his startled look and moved away from the door.

"I'm fine," I muttered. "Just need to get cleaned up," I said as I ran my hand through my wet hair. My clothes were soaked through but I felt hot all over, like I was burning up from the inside. It was a familiar feeling and I knew it would only get worse the longer I spent in Seth's presence.

"Um, sure. Use any room you want," Seth said quietly before finally turning away from me. It wasn't until he was out of sight that the tension inside of me began to ease and the heat dissipated. I didn't even realize my hands were clenched into fists until I reached for the handle to open the front door. I went back outside to my car to grab my bag and then made my way to the second floor where all the bedrooms were located. I bypassed the master bedroom which I knew had belonged to Seth and Trace's parents and ignored the next room as well, since it had been Trace's room…our room on the occasions he and I had visited his family together. That left only one room – a guest room that also happened to be right next to Seth's room.

The guest room was nearly as large as the other three bedrooms and was nicely furnished with an iron bed covered in thick, plush bedding, a flat-screen TV above the fireplace in the corner and a nice bay window overlooking the water. The attached bathroom wasn't as big as Seth's but had a nice shower and vanity. But just being in the room reminded me of what I'd done to Seth in his bathroom and I felt the shame crawl over me. I'd taken something that should have been special for Seth and turned it into something dark and ugly. And if I hadn't seen his tears, I would have fucked him without hesitation right there against his bathroom counter. Revulsion went through me even as my dick responded to the memory of seeing Seth bent over for me, his tight ass on full display.

God, I was one sick fuck.

I stripped off my wet jacket and removed my double shoulder holster with my twin 9mm Glocks and placed it in my bag. I searched out a change of clothes and stripped off the rest of what I was wearing and climbed into the shower. The hot water did little to soothe the raw lust that was tearing through me. I tried to bring up Trace's face as I began stroking my dick but all I could see was Seth, his head thrown back, his eyes closed as I took his thick shaft down my throat. He'd held nothing back as I'd wrenched his orgasm from him and then, just before I'd sent him over, he'd called out my name.

"Fuck!" I shouted as my balls drew up tight against my body and wave after wave of pleasure tore through me. I slapped my hand against the glass shower wall as jet after jet of come shot from my body. I fought to catch my breath and when I opened my eyes, I saw the proof of my release slowly sliding down the glass. An image of my come dripping out of Seth's ass flashed through my brain and I felt my half hard dick twitch in response. I let out a foul curse and reached up to angle the shower head to wash away the thick white streams and then finished cleaning up.

I took my time getting dressed. It was barely six o'clock but I seriously debated just calling it a night. Not because I was tired but because I wasn't sure I had the strength to face Seth again.

I actually laughed at the irony that my life had become. I'd spent nearly six years transforming myself into a man who would never again be crippled by fear. I could take down any opponent with any weapon I was given and I'd taken the lives of some of the most brutal of criminals with barely an afterthought. And yet, here I stood, afraid to confront an innocent, gentle young man because he held more power over me than any other living soul.

But I had good reason to fear Seth because I knew that all it would take was one touch…one perfect touch and I'd shatter into a million pieces. And there would be no coming back from that.

CHAPTER 4

SETH

I felt tears stinging the backs of my eyes as I began pulling things out of the refrigerator for dinner. I hadn't thought it possible that my day could get any worse after the mugging this afternoon but, oh, was I wrong. I'd been foolish to think that Ronan had shown up for any other reason than obligation, but my behavior in my bathroom had stolen the show because I'd actually believed for the briefest of moments that Ronan wanted me...not just anyone, not Trace...me. The fact that I wasn't even an adequate placeholder had become clear when Ronan couldn't get away from me fast enough in the front hallway. I'd thought he'd just been upset down by the beach when he'd pulled away from me after I'd touched him to get his attention, but when he'd done it again by the front door, I finally understood that I'd been utterly and completely wrong in thinking anything had changed since the day he'd walked out of my life three years ago.

I felt Bullet brush up against my leg and looked down to see his brown eyes watching me knowingly. My dog had a knack for sensing when my anxiety was starting to spike and had proven himself as more than just a pet over the years. I put down the knife I'd been using to chop vegetables and then slid down to sit on the floor, my back against the cabinet. Bullet instantly draped himself over my lap and tucked his head under my chin. I managed to stifle my tears but I didn't hesitate to bury my face in his soft fur as I tried to get a hold of myself. The irony that the very dog Ronan had gifted me with shortly after Trace's death was now my only source of comfort wasn't lost on me.

I still remembered the day Ronan had shown up with the squirming bundle of brown and black fur. It had been the first time I'd seen him since I'd received word of Trace's death two months earlier. The news had been devastating but even more so since I'd had to endure it by myself. My grandmother had come to live with me after my parents' deaths and Trace's return to the army, but within weeks of her arrival, I'd known that her mental health had started a rapid decline that took more and more of her from me each day. So when the Army Chaplain and representative had shown up to tell me Trace had died in a training exercise, my grandmother hadn't understood who the men were and why they were there. I'd ended up settling her in front of the television and turned on the sports channel which, for some inexplicable reason, was the only thing that kept her occupied for any length of time. And then I'd had to listen as the men made their speech about how valued Trace's service to our country had been. I hadn't cared about any of that, of course. All I'd cared about was trying to figure out how I'd gone from having a near perfect life with parents who'd loved me and a brother I'd idolized, to being an orphan at the age of fourteen.

And then Ronan had shown up. He'd never explained why he hadn't come sooner or why he hadn't been the one to tell me about Trace and I hadn't asked. I'd been too happy to see him to even care. He hadn't hated me back then because the first thing I'd done when I'd opened the door and had seen him standing there, was wrap my arms around him and cry for a good ten minutes. The puppy had been squashed between us and it had spent the whole time licking my face as Ronan had held me and told me everything was going to be okay.

And for a few years, everything *had* been okay. Because despite the challenges of trying to deal with all the things that had happened, as well as my grandmother's ailing health, I'd had the prospect of

Ronan's visits to look forward to. And although his visits weren't regular or often, just knowing he was there if I needed him was enough to keep me going.

Until he wasn't.

I still remembered the day I'd gambled everything…and lost.

I hadn't planned on kissing Ronan…yes, I'd dreamed of doing it, but I hadn't planned it. But when he'd wrapped his arms around me and said goodbye and that he'd be back soon, I'd felt his cheek brush mine as he began pulling away from me and a need unlike any I'd ever known had taken over me and I'd turned my head just enough to brush my lips over his. He'd frozen in place as I'd covered his entire mouth with mine and when I'd pulled back, I'd felt his fingers press into my back where he was holding me. I'd been sure it was a sign that he wanted me, had liked what I'd done, but then he'd slowly dropped his arms and stepped away from me. And the second I'd seen the look in his eyes, I'd known I'd fucked up.

He hadn't been angry, hadn't asked me why I'd done it or insisted it couldn't happen again. In fact, he hadn't said anything at all. He'd just looked at me like he didn't know me and then he'd turned and walked out the door and I'd never heard from him again.

Until today.

Bullet's wet tongue brought me back to the present and I shook my head as I gave him a pat. Footsteps in the hallway had me pushing the hundred-pound dog off me and I hurriedly climbed to my feet and went to the sink to wash my hands and run a towel over my face. I didn't look at Ronan as he entered the kitchen, but I could hear Bullet's nails clicking on the tile floor as he greeted the other man.

I focused on the tomato I'd been cutting up before Bullet had distracted me, but it took all my effort not to acknowledge Ronan as he came up behind me.

"Can I help?"

I swallowed hard because I wanted so badly to lean back against the big body I could sense behind me.

"Um, yeah. Do you want to finish making the salad?" I asked.

"Sure."

I was proud of myself for schooling my reaction as I turned to hand him the knife. Gone was the sharp looking suit and in its place was a pair of jeans that lovingly hugged his thick thighs, and a black T-shirt that stretched over his biceps and pectoral muscles. It had been years since I'd seen Ronan so casually dressed and I hadn't realized how much he'd bulked up since Trace's death. He'd always been fit but now he just looked…dangerous.

I gave Ronan the knife and thanked God it was a big kitchen because I needed to get as far away from him as I could before I did yet another stupid thing like touch him again. I went to the freezer and pulled out some chicken breasts and began the process of defrosting them.

"What are you making?" Ronan asked as he worked.

"Chicken Cacciatore."

"Hmmm. my favorite," Ronan murmured.

I stilled and then realized I'd started making the meal without any thought to that fact. It had been Trace's favorite too, but I knew that wasn't what had been in my subconscious as I'd begun gathering the ingredients. An insane, overwhelming need to escape rushed through me and I turned to look at Ronan.

I couldn't do this. I couldn't have him here and pretend everything was okay, that we were back to where we'd been before I'd kissed him three years ago. I was finally getting my life together but having Ronan around only to lose him again would destroy me. I knew it in my gut. Ronan's back was to me as he worked and I opened my mouth to tell him that he needed to leave but then I saw him reach up to get a strainer out of the cabinet above the sink. The fact that he knew that's where my mom kept it was telling, but even though it looked like Ronan belonged here, I knew better.

"Ronan…"

"Just a sec," he said as he stretched to reach the strainer, his T-shirt riding up.

And then I saw the gun tucked in the waistband of his pants.

"Yeah," Ronan said as he turned to face me.

I can't do this.

Four easy words that would free me from this man.

"Do you want something to drink?"

I kept calling myself a fool and a coward as I went to the fridge to get the soda Ronan asked for and then I began pulling the rest of the ingredients for dinner together. Ronan and I worked in silence and an hour later, we were sitting across the kitchen table from one another eating the same way. It wasn't until about half way through the meal that I finally found the courage to ask one of the many questions that had been bouncing around my head from the moment I'd suspected Ronan was watching me from the dense woods behind my house.

"He asked you to watch out for me, didn't he?" I murmured between bites, not daring to look up as I spoke. "Trace...he asked you to check on me before he died. That's why you've been watching me."

"Yes."

It was hard to swallow the piece of meat I'd been chewing when he responded. I'd figured obligation was his reason for coming to see me early on after Trace's death, but I'd hoped maybe things had changed.

I put down my fork and pushed my plate away. "Are you still practicing medicine?"

"No."

The one word answers were frustrating but at least he wasn't trying to evade my questions all together. I finally lifted my eyes and saw that Ronan had stopped eating and was staring at me. He had his arms braced on the table and his hands were pressed together. But he kept tapping the pads of his fingers together in a certain, rhythmic pattern.

"What do you do for work now?"

"Consulting," he answered.

"What kind of consultants carry a gun?"

"The kind who know how to use them," he quipped.

Irritation went through me and I reached for my plate and stood. I dumped the uneaten food into the garbage can and rinsed the plate before putting it in the dishwasher. I began cleaning up the rest of the dishes.

"Don't ask the question if you're not prepared to hear the answer," I heard from behind me.

Anger went through me as I turned around to see Ronan putting his plate on the island that separated us.

"That wasn't an answer and you fucking know it, Ronan," I snapped. He stiffened and then straightened his body. I couldn't help but wonder if he was trying to intimidate me. I realized I didn't care. "Here's a question," I said. "When did you become such a fucking coward?"

If not for the tension in his jaw and the darkness settling in his eyes, I would have thought him unaffected by the jab.

"You didn't want me three years ago," I bit out. "I get that. But not one word – not one fucking word to let me know that you were okay…to ask if I was okay?"

I snatched Ronan's plate off the island and dropped it into the sink, not caring that it broke. "Watching me from the woods like some stalker-"

I didn't get any further because Ronan grabbed me and spun me around and pushed me back against the counter. "You're a smart guy, Seth," he muttered even as his hands pinned mine next to my body. "You saw me in your bathroom," he said as he dropped his mouth close to mine. "You felt me," he nearly whispered against my lips. "Did it feel like I didn't want you?"

I cursed my body for responding to his nearness, but I cursed the fact that I was so desperate to believe him even more.

"You wouldn't let me touch you-"

"That's about me, not you," he interrupted. His mouth actually grazed the skin next to my lips as he spoke.

I wanted to ask what he meant, but I was too stunned to realize what he was admitting to. But my fledgling hope died a quick death as what he wasn't saying hit me. He wanted me but he didn't *want* to want me.

"I…I think you should go, Ronan," I managed to say despite the sudden tightness in my throat.

Ronan hung there for a moment and I wished like hell he'd ignore my request and seal his mouth over mine. But then his hands fell from mine and he stepped back.

"Not until I get some answers," he finally said.

I nodded because at that point, I was willing to do just about anything to get away from him for good.

CHAPTER 5

RONAN

To keep myself from reaching for Seth again, I went around the island and retrieved the few remaining dishes from the table. Seth had turned his back to me by the time I got back to the sink and I was glad, because I needed both the physical and mental distance. I'd already made myself more vulnerable than I wanted to admit by revealing my aversion to being touched to Seth. It would have been easier to let him believe I didn't want him but it was one lie I just couldn't stomach.

"You said you were attacked in your office building's garage – were you coming or going?" I asked.

"Going. I was on my lunch break."

"Is the garage secure?"

"What do you mean?"

"Are there security guards or parking attendants?" I clarified.

"Um, there's an attendant but I guess anyone on foot can technically get into the garage."

"You'll want to talk to your boss about adding extra security. If the owner of the building isn't willing to do it then your boss should foot the bill," I said. "The other companies in the building might be willing to go in on the cost together."

"Okay..." Seth responded non-committedly.

"Seth, if you want me to talk to someone for you-"

"No," he said. "I mean, that's not necessary. It's my building. I'll make the call tomorrow."

I was caught off guard by his admission. "Your building?"

"Yeah, well, it's the company's technically. My dad bought it just before...just before he died. The business was growing so fast that he wanted to make sure he had enough room to keep expanding."

I couldn't hide my surprise. "You took over your dad's shipping company?"

"I'm still learning but yeah, it's mine. My father's business partner is teaching me the ropes."

Seth's father had started a global shipping business several years before Trace was born and within a matter of years, it had become one of the top companies in the industry, netting millions in profit every year. At the time of their deaths, Trace and Seth's parents had amassed a personal fortune of nearly a hundred million dollars. Seth and Trace had inherited the bulk of the estate, but Trace had never shown any interest in running the company and Seth had been so young that I hadn't considered he might one day take it over. God knew he had enough money to do whatever he wanted with the rest of his life. Of course, then again, so did I since Trace had left his entire inheritance to me. At first, I'd been horrified by the prospect of profiting from Trace's death, but when I'd realized I could use the money to get justice for Trace and so many others like him, I'd been grateful for it.

"I didn't know that was something you were interested in," I said to Seth.

He cast me a look that didn't need words. I didn't know because I hadn't made an effort to find out. In the years that I'd been checking on Seth after Trace died, I'd been too lost in my own grief and hate to really focus on what was happening to Seth beyond making sure he had the basics covered. I hadn't even realized the extent of his grandmother's declining mental health until one of my last visits just before she died. Seth had only been sixteen at the time and I hadn't had any idea what to do for a guardian for him after he called me to tell me she'd passed, but by the time I'd arrived for the funeral, he'd taken care of the situation by getting himself emancipated.

"I'm sorry Seth, I should have done a better job of knowing what was going on after Trace-"

"Anything else?" Seth cut in, refusing to look at me. Beyond the hurt in his voice was anger.

"Who was the guy this afternoon?" I asked. The question had nothing to do with trying to figure out if Seth was in danger but the curiosity of what the man meant to Seth was driving me crazy.

"Barry?" Seth asked. "A friend."

"He said you were his patient."

Seth turned around, his hands clenched into fists. "Are you done?" he bit out. "Because I am. I want you to leave."

He walked past me but I grabbed his arm. I expected him to fight me but he didn't. He just stood there, completely still except for the slight tremor in his body but I couldn't tell if it was anger or something else.

"He wanted you," I said, hating the jealousy that took over me.

Seth looked at me and for once, his expression was unreadable. I didn't like that. I didn't like it one bit. Then he did something unexpected. Instead of pulling away from me, he stepped into me and his free hand came up to close over the fingers I had wrapped around his wrist. I automatically let go of him and stepped back until I hit the island behind me.

"At least someone does," Seth whispered and then he left the kitchen.

~

Seth was gone by the time I got up the next morning, so I pulled up the tracking app on my cell phone. I'd placed a tracking device on his car the day before, so I wasn't overly concerned about missing him leaving. The app showed that he was in downtown Seattle, presumably his office. Since it was barely seven o'clock, I figured he'd had to have gotten up pretty early to catch one of the first ferries from Whidbey Island to the mainland. I couldn't help but wonder if that was his normal routine or if he hadn't wanted to risk running into me this morning.

I hadn't slept well after my encounter with Seth the night before and for the first time since my arrival, I'd started to wonder if I was doing more harm than good. I'd known Seth would be angry with me for the way I'd cut him out of my life after he'd kissed me three years ago, but I was starting to realize that I'd started the process of cutting him out of it much sooner than that. I'd gone through the motions of being there for him but I hadn't really been what he'd needed.

After the death of their parents, I hadn't expected Trace to return to the military and I'd been fully prepared to ask for a transfer to a military hospital in Washington state so I could be with him and Seth. But when he'd shown back up on the base in Afghanistan less than two months after he'd left, I'd been stunned. We'd had our fair share of squabbles over the thirteen months we'd been together, but Trace's decision to choose the military over his own brother had caused a massive rift between us. And I hadn't even known at that point the full extent of Seth's trauma as a result of being used as a pawn to get information from his father.

From the moment I'd met Trace, I'd known that being in the military was in his blood. He'd thrived on every aspect of it, the comradery, the danger, the intense conditions. But it wasn't until he left Seth in the care of his grandmother that I'd realized it was something more...it was a need he couldn't give up...not wouldn't, *couldn't*. I'd argued over and over with him that Seth needed him more, but he'd assured me that their grandmother would look out for him and that Seth himself had told Trace it was okay for him to return to the front lines.

A surge of anger went through me at the realization that Trace hadn't just left Seth when he was vulnerable; he'd left him when Seth would have needed his big brother the most. There was no way in hell Seth would have been able to recover on his own from the brutal attack and knowing now what I knew about his grandmother's health, I had to wonder if he'd gotten any kind of help.

The realization hit me suddenly and I pulled out my phone and typed in *Barry Fields* into the search engine of the browser and hardened my jaw when I saw a picture of the young, smiling man next to a short bio saying he was a psychologist specializing in anxiety. I closed the browser and then hit a speed dial button.

"Hey boss."

I didn't bother telling the man on the other end not to call me that because he'd do it anyway.

"Mav, get me everything you can on a psychologist named Barry Fields," I said.

"Is he a mark?" Mav asked in confusion as I heard him typing in the background.

"No," I said but didn't offer any further explanation. Mav had been one of the first guys I'd hired when I'd started my pet project, and while he did his best work with a gun or knife in his hand, I'd relegated him to an information gathering role since I'd had to get rid of Benny, the analyst who'd been working for me for nearly just as long, but had sold me and all my men out for money to pay off years' worth of gambling debts. Benny had begged and pleaded with me to show him mercy, but I'd saved that for the young man whose life Benny had nearly taken when he'd accepted a contract to kill him and tried to use one of my own men to do it.

Luckily, Mace Calhoun had been smart enough to realize something was off with the assignment and hadn't taken Jonas Davenport's life, despite all the concrete evidence Benny had faked to prove the young artist had committed unspeakable crimes against several children. I'd taken care of Benny, as well as the men who'd put the contract out on Jonas, and then I'd spent weeks combing through all of Benny's information to see if Jonas and Mace were his first victims or if he'd used my group for his own financial gain before. I'd been more than relieved to find out it was the former because I doubted I would have been able to live with the guilt of knowing an innocent life had been taken because I'd trusted the wrong man.

"I'm on it," Mav said.

I was tempted to ask Mav to run Seth's name too, but didn't and not only because he would have figured out my connection to Seth and learned more about me, but because I didn't want to find out everything I'd missed – no, ignored – from a computer; I wanted Seth to be the one to tell me. Because I needed more than just what was on paper.

"Thanks," I said before hanging up on Mav. I grabbed my shoulder holster and dragged it on before tugging on my suit jacket. I gave Bullet, who was lying outside my bedroom door, a quick pat before I went downstairs and swallowed down a quick cup of coffee that I'd had to microwave since Seth hadn't left the machine on to keep the coffee that remained in the pot warm.

I ended up stuck in morning rush hour traffic, so it was late by the time I made it to the city. I searched out Seth's building and discovered that the parking garage where he'd been mugged was open to the public, which wouldn't help in terms of improving the security. I found Seth's car easily since it was in a reserved spot near the elevator and parked a few aisles over. It was only ten o'clock in the morning and since I didn't know what time he took lunch, I knew I could have a potentially long wait and that was assuming he even left the office for lunch today. But an hour later, I saw him step off the elevator. He hesitated as he cleared the bank of elevators and looked all around him. I was oddly proud of him when I saw him straighten himself, despite the look of abject fear in his gaze. He walked quickly to his car and kept scanning his surroundings but he remained calm. I kept my distance as I followed him out of the garage and east out of the city, but it wasn't until he began crossing the bridge over Lake Washington that I realized where he was going.

I didn't need GPS after that but I had to keep my distance as the traffic grew lighter as he made his way to a quiet community on the eastern side of the island. Just like the Whidbey Island house, the house Seth pulled into sat on lush acreage right up against the water. I'd only been to the Nichols's main residence a couple of times since the family had been vacationing at the Whidbey Island house the majority of the times I'd visited with Trace. Their vacation home was much larger and more remote, but that wasn't to say the Mercer Island house wasn't beautiful because it was; it just had a more sedate look to it and actually looked small and quaint compared to the mansions on either side of it. Which was why it seemed less likely that the men who'd burglarized the home had chosen it at random when there'd been much more secluded and well-off homes to choose from in the area.

I parked across the street from the house and watched Seth as he sat in his car in the roundabout driveway. I couldn't actually see him up close but I could see that he hadn't gotten out of the car. He sat there for a good twenty minutes before putting the car in gear and leaving the house again. I ducked down in my own car so he wouldn't see me but didn't follow him. Instead, I got out of the car and walked to a neighboring house across the street and a few doors down where I saw an older woman working on a garden bright with colorful flowers.

"Excuse me," I said.

She looked up and smiled, her floppy hat covering her brow from the glare of the warm Spring sun.

"Can I help you?" she asked.

"The house across the street," I said pointing to the Nichols house. "I heard it was for sale," I said, mustering a charming smile that I wasn't feeling.

"Oh no, I don't think so," she said. "I don't think that boy will ever sell it," she added.

"Boy?" I asked.

She shook her head and chuckled. "Well, I suppose he's not a boy anymore. Seth's all grown up now but I still remember him from when he used to mow my lawn and help me in my garden," she said as she motioned to the flowers in front of her.

"So this Seth, the house belongs to him?"

She nodded. "Inherited it after his parents passed. Poor thing," she added.

"Yeah, the realtor I was talking to mentioned there'd been a robbery and some people died," I said quietly, trying to keep as much emotion from my voice as possible.

She shook her head. "So sad. It could have been any one of us," she added and then looked around the neighborhood. She lowered her voice and said, "That boy and his mama weren't even supposed to be there that night. Bonita – that was their housekeeper at the time – she told me the next day that Seth and his mama were supposed to visit his grandmother up north but she hadn't been feeling well so they canceled their trip last minute."

I barely managed to keep my expression neutral as an idea began to rattle around in my head.

"So he still lives there?" I asked.

"Oh dear Lord, no," she said. "I haven't seen Seth in years. I keep expecting the house to go up on the market but it hasn't."

I nodded. "Well, thank you."

She gave me a smile and focused on her flowers as I made my way back to my car. The men who'd killed Seth's parents had never been found and it had been chalked up to a random event, but the idea that Seth's father was supposed to have been there by himself that night had me wondering things I probably shouldn't. I supposed I'd gotten too used to dealing with the worst of humanity to blindly accept that sometimes random events were just that – random.

The trip to Mercer Island caused more questions than answers, so I made my way back to the city but didn't go to Seth's office. The GPS showed he'd already gotten back there so I knew I had some time before he headed out for the day. I made my way to the southern side of the city and parked in front of a small, converted house that said *Harold Brighton, Esquire & Associates*.

I'd only met Harry Brighton once when I'd met with him to discuss the surprise inheritance Trace had left me. His office hadn't changed much over the years. The furniture and décor were outdated and worn and the reception area consisted of one small desk with the same old receptionist sitting behind it, her silver hair twisted around the top of her head in a sloppy bun with a couple of pencils shoved through it to hold it in place. She was looking over the top of her glasses at an ancient looking computer screen that took up about half her desk and there were papers strewn everywhere. There was no one in the waiting area but the TV in the corner of the room was tuned to a talk show of some kind.

"Can I help you?" the receptionist asked without looking up at me.

"Is Mr. Brighton available?"

"I'm afraid not," she said before finally straightening her glasses and looking up at me. "Mr. Grisham, how nice to see you again."

I couldn't help but be surprised that she remembered me, considering I'd only been there the one time nearly six years ago. Since I couldn't recall her name, I merely nodded.

"Dolores! I need the Conway file!" I heard a high pitched voice yell and then there was the click-click of heels. A woman rounded the corner from the back of the building where I knew the offices were and stopped when she saw me. Her frown disappeared and she straightened her elegant suit. She was quite attractive and put together and I couldn't help but notice that she didn't quite match the laid back atmosphere of the office.

"Tabby, this is Mr. Ronan Grisham," Dolores said with a wave of her hand. "He's a friend of the Nichols family."

The woman stiffened and then smoothed her jacket again before jutting out her hand. "Tabitha Brighton," she said formally, her high-pitched voice now low and clear and much less screechy.

"Tabby is Harry's daughter, Mr. Grisham," Dolores said as she began clicking away at her keyboard again.

"It's Tabitha," the woman said crisply, though I wasn't sure if she was telling me or Dolores that. "How can I help you, Mr. Grisham?"

"I was hoping to speak with your father."

Tabitha's face fell but she recovered quickly. "I'm afraid my father has retired. Are you looking for someone to assist you with your inheritance?"

The question caught me off guard and she must have sensed my surprise because she said, "I've taken over the majority of my father's clients. I remember seeing your file a few weeks ago as I was trying to familiarize myself with his cases. I noticed we didn't have an attorney listed for you..."

The not so subtle query irritated me, though I couldn't really explain why. Maybe because the woman seemed so much like the stereotypical attorney whereas I'd found her father to be much more relaxed and laid back when I'd worked with him so many years ago. "I'm just passing through town and I wanted to say hi to your father. Is he around?"

Tabitha's jaw hardened for a moment and then she forced a smile to her lips. "He's retired, Mr. Grisham," she repeated as if that was answer enough.

"Here," Dolores said as she handed me a piece of paper. "He's at Sunny Oaks – two streets over and down a few blocks. I'm sure he'd love the company," the old woman said as she shot Tabitha a stern look. Tabitha didn't look pleased and turned on her heel and stalked back in the direction she'd come from.

"Thanks," I said as I waved the paper at Dolores.

"He likes the fries from the diner down the street," Dolores said in response. "Mayonnaise, not ketchup," she added.

I chuckled at the subtle order. "Yes, ma'am."

It took about twenty minutes to get the fries from the diner and find the assisted living community. The receptionist pointed me in the direction of a common room where there were a few senior citizens milling around playing cards or watching TV. I recognized Harry almost instantly because of his hair. It was almost all white except for a thick patch of black hair above his forehead. I had no idea if he dyed it that way on purpose but it looked almost exactly like it had six years ago.

"Mr. Brighton," I said as I stopped next to the table where he was playing a game of Solitaire. His eyes lit on the white paper bag in my hand before lifting up. Like Dolores, he recognized me instantly.

"Mr. Grisham," he said with a nod. "I see you stopped by the office," he said with a nod towards the bag in my hand.

I laughed and handed him the bag and then took the seat across from him when he invited me to do so.

"How is Seth?" Harry asked the second I sat.

"I was going to ask you that," I admitted. "I've been away for a bit and just got back to the city yesterday," I hedged, not wanting to explain to this man the details of why I'd stayed away.

Harry began rifling around the bag for a fry and the small to-go container of mayonnaise I'd been given. "I'm sorry to say, I haven't been able to get up to see him as much as I'd like," he said. "Tabby doesn't have time to drive me up to Whidbey Island and cabs are terribly expensive."

"He doesn't come down to see you?" I asked.

"Oh no," Harry said as he began chewing on the fry. "Well, you know how tough it is for him to leave the house."

I wasn't sure what he meant by that so I said, "It is a long drive."

Harry stopped chewing for a moment and studied me. While his body might have aged, his brain certainly hadn't and I could see him putting the pieces together. His friendliness faded away and suspicion clouded his gaze as he pushed the bag away. "What can I do for you, Mr. Grisham?"

The man in front of me was the man I remembered. His less than neat office and too relaxed manner of dress had made me wonder about his abilities the first time I'd met him, but I'd known as soon as he'd started talking to me that he was much sharper than he appeared. And loyal. And not just to Seth's father who he'd gone to school with as kids, but to Seth as well if the current hard look he was giving me was anything to go by.

I knew it was going to be a challenge getting anything out of him at that point but I was desperate for answers that I doubted I'd be able to pull out of Seth anytime soon. "I fucked up, Mr. Brighton," I finally admitted. "I got caught up in my own grief and I wasn't there for him the way I should have been. I get that now."

Harry seemed to soften somewhat and the fact that he reached for the fries again was a good sign. "How can I help, Mr. Grisham?"

"It's Ronan," I said.

He nodded. "Ronan."

"Are you still his lawyer?" I asked.

He shook his head. "I retired about six months ago. Tabby handles some of the day to day stuff but I suspect her...personality might not be a good match for Seth."

"What do you mean?"

"I love my girl but she's got a lot of ambition and sometimes that can get her into trouble. Seth – he's a smart boy but my Tabby likes it when she's smarter."

"Is Seth looking to take his business elsewhere?"

Harry paused and then said, "I think he's holding off on making a decision out of respect for me, but a colleague who visits me once a month mentioned rumors that his father's business partner, Stan Sadorsky, is urging Seth to use the company's counsel for his personal affairs."

I could only imagine that with Seth's personal fortune, the financial loss would hit Harry's daughter pretty hard. But I didn't press Harry any further because I could see his loyalties were torn between Seth and his daughter.

"You mentioned it being tough for him to leave the house," I prodded.

"I didn't notice it myself at first when I went up to Whidbey Island to meet with him regarding his parents' estate. I thought he was just still grieving and he also had his grandmother to look after. He'd missed so much school that it made sense for him to have a tutor to help him catch up, but he ended up hiring the tutor to home school him so he wouldn't have to go back to school at all. About a year after the incident, my wife and I started inviting him down to the city to join us for dinner but he'd always say he was busy. After his grandmother passed, he asked me about his options when it came to a legal guardian."

"And you helped him become emancipated."

Harry nodded. "He was responsible, self-sufficient and he didn't have anyone..." Harry's eyes settled on me. "I asked him about you looking out for him but he said that wasn't an option."

I wasn't sure what to say to that so I remained silent.

"I thought with his grandmother gone, he'd start getting out more.

He got his GED just before he turned seventeen. The judge who'd granted Seth's request for emancipation assigned me as trustee of his inheritance until he turned eighteen, so I paid a lot of the bills. I was excited for him when he enrolled in college at the University of Washington in Seattle but he dropped out after a few weeks and enrolled in an online program. I'm not sure if he completed the program – he didn't talk much about himself when I'd go visit him."

"And his dad's company?"

"His father's business partner offered to buy Seth out of the controlling ownership of the business a couple of times but Seth always said no."

My mind was churning with all the new information but all it had done was make me feel even more guilty for how blind I'd been. I'd spent so much time lecturing Trace on how traumatized Seth must have been as a result of the attack that killed his parents and left him for dead, but when I'd had the chance to step up and make sure he was getting the help he needed, I'd said nothing. I hadn't even noticed. I'd just made assumptions that other people like his grandmother had helped him work through it. But from what Harry was telling me, Seth had suffered in silence for a long time.

"Thank you, Mr. Brighton," I said as I started to stand. "I'm going to do better by him. I'll try to bring him by for a visit real soon. Otherwise, I'd be happy to drive you up to see him."

Harry smiled and reached out his hand. "You're a good boy," he said with a smile. "I had my doubts about you, but Seth was right."

"What do you mean?" I asked in confusion.

"I wasn't so sure giving you half his inheritance was such a good idea, but he said you were family and he knew you'd do good with it."

I felt my stomach drop out. "*His* inheritance? You mean Trace's, right?"

"It was Trace's but it reverted to Seth when he died."

I could barely manage to get the words out of my mouth. "Trace didn't leave me the money?"

Harry finally seemed to catch on to my distress and he stood. "I thought you knew," he whispered. "I tried meeting with Trace about his half of the inheritance before he left the States after Seth got out of the hospital, but he kept putting me off. If he intended to leave the money to you, he never mentioned it. But Seth...Seth was adamant that the money should go to you."

I didn't think I even managed to say goodbye to Harry because I heard him call my name a couple times as I walked down the hallway towards the exit. I ended up sitting in my car trying to absorb the turn of events and when I finally got myself together long enough to pull out my phone, I saw it was almost two o'clock. I checked the app and saw that Seth was on the move and I realized from the location of his car that he was probably on his way home since he was nearing the ferry dock in Mukilteo.

Even with the early hour, traffic in downtown Seattle was starting to build so I focused on the road until I got out of the city and then let my mind start to wander. Somehow when it had been Trace's money I'd used to set up my organization, I'd felt like it was the universe's way of telling me I'd made the right choice to give up medicine and focus on bringing justice to men and women who had no qualms about taking innocent lives. But knowing that Seth had deliberately chosen to give me the money made me want to throw up.

He knew you'd do good with it.

Harry's words rang in my ears. I *had* done good with it but only in my eyes, not Seth's. What would Seth think if he found out I'd used the money to kill people or to set them up so they could be convicted of crimes the law couldn't otherwise prove they'd committed? What would he think if he learned that every bullet I'd fired into a man's brain was paid for by his money? Trace wouldn't have cared because he understood what the real world was like. He understood that doing what was right sometimes meant using methods most people deemed wrong...like Seth would. Because Seth was gentle and sweet and kind and utterly innocent. He hadn't seen the shit I'd seen. He hadn't felt it or touched it or tasted it...that evil that consumed every cell, every fiber of your being until you had no choice but to change to accommodate it, to accept it, to find a way to live with it.

Except that Seth had seen it. He'd seen and felt more than I'd realized and it had left its mark on him. I doubted it had changed the core of who he was but the reality was, it *had* changed him. And worse, the people who were supposed to bring him back to who he was, who he'd always been – Trace, me – we'd failed him and that had changed him too.

I'd come here to keep my promise to Trace to make sure Seth was safe, but I'd broken that promise every time I'd lied to Seth about his brother's death and about my role in it. Every time I'd asked Seth how he was doing but never really heard his answer, I may as well have been spitting on Trace's lifeless body. And when I'd walked away from Seth because of one innocent kiss, I'd flung my promise back in my dead lover's face. Because nothing I'd done had been about protecting Seth. It had been about assuaging my own guilt. It had been about protecting *me*.

By the time I reached the ferry dock, I knew I needed to make a choice. A very simple choice. I could try fixing what I'd broken or I could walk away for good this time. No watching Seth from afar, no tracking him, no using the endless resources at my disposal to make sure he was okay. A clean break. Or I had to find a way to be around Seth, to give him what he needed without taking what I wanted. Because now, more than ever, I knew he deserved better than me.

It wasn't until a car behind me honked that I realized the traffic in front of me had started moving onto the ferry. I needed to make a decision and I needed to make it fast.

CHAPTER 6

SETH

*R*onan was gone.

It was ridiculous to be so disappointed about losing something I'd wanted so badly, but I wasn't going to delude myself into believing a little piece of my heart hadn't broken off and disintegrated. Okay, a big piece.

I hadn't realized Ronan hadn't left last night until I'd stepped out of the house in the early morning darkness so I could catch the first ferry leaving the Clinton terminal. I'd been both relieved and upset to see his car sitting just behind mine in the driveway, and those same emotions had hounded me all day up until I'd pulled through the iron gate at the end of driveway and waited for the house to come into view. Then it had just been a stark feeling of disappointment as I'd stared at the empty spot where Ronan's car had been.

Work had been uneventful but only because I'd spent most of the day hiding out in my office so I wouldn't have to explain the bruises on my face. The only person I'd told about the mugging was my father's business partner - I still hadn't gotten used to calling him my business partner, though that was what he was now. Stan had been horrified and hadn't argued when I'd told him I would be hiring a security company to monitor the garage twenty-four hours a day. I'd left at lunch for my daily ritual of driving out to my old house and had been insanely proud of myself for having the courage to make the trip to my car by myself, despite Stan's offer to escort me back and forth. Stan was the only person besides Barry who knew how much I struggled with leaving my house. And while I liked how supportive Stan was, the first person I'd wanted to share the small success of being able to make it into work today despite what had happened yesterday was Ronan.

But Ronan was gone…because I'd asked him to go.

I tried to focus on the computer in front of me but couldn't make sense of the words I'd been staring at for several minutes now. I left the office early every day since I wasn't yet comfortable enough with my driving skills to be driving around downtown Seattle during the worst of rush hour, but I almost always continued work as soon as I got home. But it was clear that today was going to be another exception but, unlike yesterday when I'd had the excuse of the mugging and Ronan's untimely arrival to distract me, today it was just my own self-pity that kept me from making any progress on the contract I'd been studying. I turned off the computer monitor and started putting my papers back in the laptop bag I carried back and forth with me to work, but stilled when I heard the front door open. Bullet was outside but since I hadn't heard him barking like a maniac, I had to assume it was someone I knew.

I hated the silly little flicker of hope that flashed in my chest for just a brief moment before dying a sudden death when I heard Barry calling my name.

"In the study," I said loudly enough for Barry to hear me as I finished putting my stuff away.

Barry was becoming more and more of a problem for me, but I had no idea how to deal with it. When I'd first called him nearly six months ago to ask him to help me deal with my anxiety about leaving my house, I'd been grateful for his support and insight into the trauma I was dealing with. I hadn't told him all the details of the attack on my family, despite his incessant pressure to tell him everything. But he had offered me some tools to deal with the stress that came over me whenever I considered trying to walk out the front door. He'd even been the one to help me get my driver's license since I hadn't had an adult available to teach me to drive when I was sixteen.

I knew Barry was gay from early on because he'd told me he was when I'd admitted my sexuality during one of our early sessions. I wasn't sure why he'd told me – maybe he'd thought it would help me open up more, but since my parents had always been supportive of my sexuality, it wasn't something I was overly concerned with and I had mentioned it to him only when he'd asked if I had a girlfriend. I hadn't really ever thought of the relationship Barry and I had as being anything other than professional, but I'd started to realize a couple months ago that maybe things had changed for him. It had been subtle at first – touches here and there, a little bit of flirting that even I recognized. His questions about whether or not I had ever had a boyfriend, his jokes about me just wanting to get out of the house so I could date someone and his comments about how attractive I was, had all made me start dreading our sessions rather than anticipating them. But I knew from experience that I wasn't the best at reading people - my actions around Ronan three years earlier were proof of that - so I'd brushed all my discomfort off and focused on trying to find the courage I needed to get out of the house and finally start living. But when Barry had actually started to discourage me from testing myself with trips outside my comfort zone when he wasn't around, I'd known that I'd have to do something about our professional relationship sooner rather than later.

"There you are," Barry said as he entered the study. His skin was flushed like he'd been running, which didn't make sense since it was a short walk from the front door – the door that had been locked but which Barry clearly had no reservations about using the security code I'd given him for emergencies on. I'd asked him once to call ahead of time to let me know he was coming but he'd brushed me off with a little laugh. I supposed it would have been just as easy to change the code, but the non-confrontational part of me hadn't wanted to deal with explaining to Barry that his behavior was just too much.

"Hi, Barry," I said. "What are you doing here?"

"You never called me to reschedule our last session, so I thought I'd stop by and make sure you were okay," he said as he came right up to me despite the fact that I'd been hoping to use the desk to keep some distance between us. "Besides, I was worried about you. That... man," – his voice dripped with disgust – "was so rude yesterday."

I didn't bother to point out that Barry had been rude first by talking down to Ronan like he had.

"I'm doing okay," I murmured. "But I'm kind of tired so I just want to take Bullet for a quick walk and then settle in for the night."

Of course, Barry didn't take the hint because he stepped forward and ran his hands up and down my arms. "You know you can tell me anything, right Seth?" he said softly.

I had no idea what he meant by the question but I was too preoccupied with his touch to give it much thought. I should have enjoyed the contact. Barry was a good looking guy. He was smart, funny, successful. But all I wanted to do was pull away from him. His fingers didn't burn my skin with flashes of energy, his lips didn't look warm and inviting, his voice didn't rumble through me.

"I know," I managed to say.

"That man-"

"Ronan," I interjected because it annoyed me to hear Barry refer to Ronan that way...as if Ronan was somehow beneath him, beneath us.

"I didn't like how he looked at you," Barry murmured as he stepped even closer to me. I hadn't even realized he'd maneuvered me so that my back was to the desk until his hands came up to hold my face and I couldn't move any farther back.

"Barry..."

"Like he knew what you needed and I didn't..." Barry whispered.

Warning bells started going off in my head as Barry's eyes fell to my mouth.

"Barry-"

"You're so beautiful, Seth," Barry said as his finger trailed over my lower lip. If it had been Ronan, I would have been all over him. With Barry, I just wanted to get away. But when I brought my hands up to remove his from my face, he grabbed them. The move was something

I would have expected from Ronan, but I knew within seconds that wasn't quite true because whereas Ronan's hold on me hadn't hurt, Barry's did.

I tried saying Barry's name one last time, but the second I opened my mouth, Barry's lips slammed down on mine and his tongue shoved into my mouth. I was so caught off guard that I didn't react and he must have taken my stillness as acquiescence because he leaned against me hard, his slightly greater weight pressing me down onto the desk. My head was spinning from the shock of what was happening and I shoved at him as hard as I could. But he still had a hold of my wrists so I couldn't dislodge him. He pinned my hands to the desk and then he was thrusting his hips against me, his erection pressing into me. His sloppy, wet kiss was revolting and I was about to bite down on his tongue when his weight was ripped off of me. Barry let out a horrified shout as his body went flying and I managed to sit up just in time to see Ronan slam his fist into Barry's face. Blood spurted from his nose but it didn't slow down Ronan in the least as he punched Barry again. I managed to reach Ronan just as he pulled a gun out from his suit and put the barrel to Barry's forehead. Barry and I both froze.

"Ronan, don't," I managed to whisper, afraid if I spoke any louder, he'd fire the gun. As much as I wanted Barry to suffer for what he'd tried to do to me, I didn't want this.

I expected to see Ronan displaying some kind of anger or emotion but there was nothing. Everything about him was cool, calm and one hundred percent ice cold. That in itself was much more frightening than any rage he might have shown. Bullet had appeared by my side, but even the dog seemed to sense the tension because he didn't move towards either man.

"Please," I heard Barry croak.

I took a few steps forward and debated whether or not to touch Ronan. I said his name again but he didn't respond and now that I was closer, I could see a fine tremor in his arm so maybe he wasn't as emotionless as I'd thought. His finger was resting on the trigger just a little bit too comfortably. I held my breath as I finally reached out my hand to stroke over Ronan's upper arm, the one that was wrapped around Barry's throat, not the one holding the gun.

"Ronan," I said softly again. He didn't pull away from me like I expected, but he did finally draw the gun back just enough so it wasn't digging into Barry's forehead anymore.

"You come near him again, I will end you. Do you understand me?" Ronan asked, his voice low and even. But neither I nor Barry could mistake his tone for what it was – incredibly, undeniably dangerous.

With tears streaming down his face, Barry somehow managed to squeak out a "yes."

I continued to hold my breath until Ronan stepped back. Barry slowly got to his feet and Bullet chose that moment to start snarling. Between Ronan and the dog, Barry began backing out of the room and as soon as he reached the doorway, he turned and ran. Ronan followed but since he stuffed his gun back into the holster I had to assume was under his suit jacket, I relaxed marginally and then sucked in a deep breath. When Ronan walked back into the room a moment later, I was trying to use the sleeve of my shirt to wipe the taste of Barry from my mouth. A mix of humiliation and shame went through me at the way Ronan looked at me and the need to escape was overwhelming.

"Um, I need to take Bullet for a walk," I managed to say as I reached for the door that led to the patio. I fumbled with the lock as I felt Ronan come up behind me, but I managed to get it open before he touched me, though I wasn't sure if that had been his plan. How ironic that that was what I'd been wanting from the moment he'd stepped into the den yesterday, but now the idea of his hands on me made me want to curl up in shame. Because what I really wanted more than anything right then was for him to kiss me so I could get the taste and feel of Barry out of my head.

I pushed out the door and walked around the covered in-ground pool. Bullet darted past me and began running towards the beach. On any other day, I would have smiled at my dog's antics, but now I just envied his ability to get past the dangerous moment in the study so quickly.

"Seth," I heard Ronan say gently from somewhere behind me but I just shook my head. I didn't want kindness or pity or understanding.

"I just need a few minutes, okay, Ronan?" I managed to say once I realized Ronan was still behind me.

"Seth, just wait one second."

I swallowed hard and forced myself to stop and face him. He was almost directly behind me, but I couldn't make myself look at him. And when he tipped my face up, I actually closed my eyes. I waited for him to order me to open them but he didn't say anything. There was no order, no apology, no asking if I was okay, nothing. It felt like minutes had passed, though I knew it had only been seconds. I was just about to pull free of his warm, firm touch when I felt his lips brush tentatively over mine. He paused for a moment, maybe waiting for my reaction, before doing it again. Only this time, his tongue stroked over the seam of my lips and I instantly opened for him. I kept my hands fisted at my sides so my touch wouldn't send him running, but I couldn't stop the pent-up sigh that escaped me as his tongue stroked over mine. The kiss was so sweet and reverent and moving, that I felt relief sweep through my whole body. It was a kiss I could take with me for the next several minutes as I tried to process what had happened. Even if Ronan couldn't get Barry out of my head as easily as he'd gotten him out of my house, he sure as hell had managed to wipe away every last bitter taste of him.

Ronan finally released his hold on me and I opened my eyes. There was no pity or judgement. There was just understanding. The kiss had resolved nothing between us but he'd known I'd needed it.

"I'll be here when you get back," he said softly and then he was the one to turn away. I watched him walk back into the house and then I turned to follow Bullet down to the beach. I let my fingers press against my tingling lips as I cast a glance over my shoulder on the off chance that Ronan was watching me from the doorway.

He wasn't.

CHAPTER 7

RONAN

Six years earlier
"Dr. Grisham?"

"Don't call me that," I automatically said as I turned away from the man standing at the motel room door and continued to struggle with the cap on the prescription bottle. "Here," I said as I tossed my wallet at him. "Take whatever I owe you."

I didn't care when the man followed me into the room, although as I glanced at him again, I realized there could have been two men since my vision was fucked up. "How many of you do I see?" I asked stupidly as I searched for the bottle of vodka I'd put down somewhere when I'd gone to answer the door.

The man didn't respond and truthfully, I didn't give a shit because I'd finally gotten the cap off the pill bottle. But when I tried to dump the pain pills into my hand, none of them hit my skin and I stared in confusion at the array of white dots scattered around my feet.

"Here," the man said and he placed one of the pills in my hand. Somewhere in my muddled mind it occurred to me that the pill was round instead of oval and it looked blue instead of white but I didn't care.

"Need more than one," I muttered even as I shoved the pill into my mouth and swallowed since I hadn't managed to find the vodka.

"It will take me a few minutes to clean these up," he said. "Why don't you relax and I'll give you a couple more in a second?"

A voice in the back of my head said the motel manager was being a little too nice considering what an asshole he'd been all the previous times he'd pounded on my door demanding payment, but I realized I didn't give a fuck. Pretty oval white pills will do that for you. Hopefully round blue ones would too.

My eyes felt heavy as I watched the man kneel on the floor to collect the scattered pills and I put out my hand so he could give them to me. But as a calmness finally began to settle over my tired body, I dropped my head to the pillow and closed my eyes so I could enjoy it.

The next time I awoke, the uncomfortable bed beneath me was gone. My mouth felt like it was stuffed full of cotton and my head was hurting like a son of a bitch. It took me several long seconds to realize I wasn't in my motel room anymore and the lovely burn of the OxyContin I'd been swallowing like candy for the last few days since I'd been discharged from the hospital was gone. I had a vague recollection of the blue pill I'd swallowed without so much as a second thought and realized now it had likely been a sedative or sleeping pill.

I forced my eyes open and let them adjust. I was sitting in the front passenger seat of a car, but there was no one else in it and it was parked in the middle of a grassy field with nothing around as far as the eye could see. Well, not nothing. There was a small lake with a picnic bench about a hundred yards away and sitting on top of the table was a man, his back to me. I glanced at the ignition but saw no keys. I searched the car for a weapon but couldn't even find a scrap of paper to indicate who the car belonged to. My phone was gone, as was my wallet.

I was surprised to actually feel a tremor of fear go through me which was ridiculous since I hadn't given a shit whether I lived or died once I'd locked myself in the motel room and started chugging the pills that made me forget everything. My limbs felt sluggish as I opened the car door and got out. I kept my eyes on the man's back as I scanned my surroundings once again, but I didn't see any other cars, roads or any signs of life. There was a slight breeze that made the tall grass sway back and forth but otherwise it was obscenely quiet. I made my way towards the man, accepting whatever fate he decided to throw my way because I didn't care anymore. Trace was gone and the man I'd been had died with him. I'd watched our blood pool together between us in the dry, hot sand that had cradled our broken bodies and I'd felt my life end the second Trace's had. The stranger who'd brought me out here for whatever reason couldn't take anything else from me.

I hated that it took me so long to get to him, but while my body had healed enough for the doctors to discharge me from the military hospital in Bethesda, I wasn't fully healed enough to move much faster than a snail's crawl and without a very pronounced limp. As I got closer, I realized that while most of the land around us was flat, the picnic table the man was sitting on was on top of a small rise that led down to the water. So it wasn't until I was about fifteen feet away from the man that I realized we weren't alone and I came to a stop when I took in the sight before me.

A man was on his knees on the sand, his hands bound behind his back and a sack of some kind over his head. There were a few small blood stains on his blue button down shirt and he was wearing a pair of blue jeans that were covered in mud. His feet were bare, but it was the sheet of plastic beneath him that had me swallowing hard.

What the fuck?

My instinct was to check on the man but as I got closer to him, I took in the stranger from the motel, the stranger who'd brought me here, and noticed the gun he was holding in his hand. Panic went through me but I managed to remain absolutely still. I couldn't make out his face but I could see his profile and what stood out more than anything was the obvious burn scar that covered his right cheek, jaw and neck. The mottled flesh disappeared beneath his shirt collar and I perversely wondered if it continued down the rest of his body. And then a chill went through me as I took in the rest of his suddenly familiar profile. And then I knew the scar did indeed continue beneath his shirt.

"Brooke Army Medical Center," the stranger said. "2005."

"House...house fire," I managed to say. "I was an intern and you and your girlfriend-"

"Wife," the man interjected with little emotion.

"Wife," I whispered. "You and your wife came into the ER."

The case was one I would remember for the rest of my life and had been one of the reasons I'd decided to pursue surgery as a specialty. The ER had been overrun with cases that night due to a terrible car accident that had caused a chain reaction pile up. I'd jumped in to help where I could, but by the time the man and his wife had been brought in, the attending doctor and all the residents were performing lifesaving procedures on other patients. The man had been badly burned, but it was his wife who'd been the more critical case because in addition to being burned, she'd been stabbed multiple times and had been bleeding internally. With no other doctors available, I'd been forced to open her up to try and stop the internal bleeding while my attending told me what to do a few beds over as he tried to save a six-year-old kid's life. I'd managed to save the woman's life, but she'd died a few days later from the burns.

"Revay," I said softly. "That was her name, right?"

The man nodded.

"And you're Michael," I added.

"Hawke," the man corrected. "She was the only one who called me Michael."

"I'm sorry," I said gently. "I wish I could have done more."

"You gave me three days with her. Three days I wouldn't have had otherwise."

I glanced at the man kneeling on the sheet. I could hear him crying, but for the life of me, I couldn't figure out what the hell was happening. If this man was blaming me for his wife's death, who was the other guy?

"I can't give you three more days with Trace but I can give you this," Hawke said as he nodded at the man.

I was stunned to hear him refer to Trace. "How...how did you know about that?" I asked. The circumstances of Trace's death had been carefully covered up by the military and I'd been too out of it to even process what had happened to him...to us.

Hawke finally looked at me full on before nodding at the man on the plastic again. "Go on, take it off," he said.

I knew he meant the sack covering the guy's head. My fingers shook as I gave Hawke another glance and then I made my way down the slight incline. Stepping on the plastic freaked me out and I half expected to feel a bullet pierce my back as soon as I did, but there was only the man's muted crying so

I reached for the bag and pulled it off his head. His wide, terrified eyes met mine and he tried to say something around the fabric tied around his head, gagging his mouth. But I didn't care about that because all I saw were the piercing blue eyes...the ones that had been filled with bloodlust the last time I'd seen them.

I stepped back several steps as the memories washed over me and the man stopped trying to scream because he recognized me a moment later. Images of Trace's body jerking as the man before me brutalized him began playing on a loop in my head. I couldn't see his hands since they were tied behind his back, but I remembered their punishing strength because after he'd finished with Trace, he'd held me down while one of his buddies had done to me what he'd done to Trace. In my memory, the cruel lips that were pressed around the gag were open, and I could hear the heavy timbre of his voice as he kept asking Trace if he liked it.

I couldn't move, couldn't speak, couldn't do anything. I felt Hawke come up behind me but I couldn't take my eyes off the man in front of me who even now was begging me for mercy with his eyes. I had none. Not a speck. Just like he'd had none for me as I'd pleaded with him for Trace's life.

"How?" I managed to ask Hawke.

"Overheard him telling some of his buddies that he and his guys had fucked up a couple of faggots at Bagram two months ago. His words, not mine," Hawke added and I assumed he meant the slur. "A friend of mine was an MP at that base. He told me what they did to you and Trace and the cover-up that happened afterwards. When I found out you were one of the victims, I thought you might like to do the honors yourself," he said. "Or at least even the score a bit if you want to keep your hands clean."

Hawke held out the gun. "Your choice," he said. "You want him to walk, untie him and we're done here."

The man on the plastic began sobbing at Hawke's words, but the pity the doctor in me should have felt didn't exist. The hate and rage weren't there either. All I felt was an overwhelming warmth settle in my chest as I stared at the man. Maybe if the man and his friends had waited until Trace was dead before coming after me, I would have felt something different. Maybe I would have been able to call on some last shard of decency to spare his life.

But they hadn't. Just as I'd had to watch the man shove a metal pipe inside of Trace over and over while his friends held Trace down, he'd had to watch the same thing happen to me even as his body began to fail him. And I'd known that had been the hardest part for Trace – that was when he'd truly suffered. Because while I'd been the healer, he'd been the protector. And they'd stolen even that from him.

I wasn't interested in making the man suffer and I wasn't interested in prolonging the moment. And I didn't need my hands to be clean – they'd hadn't been clean since the first time I'd dreamed of this moment. I took the gun from Hawke and without hesitation or doubt, I strode up to the man, aimed it at his head and pulled the trigger. No final words, no wishing him to hell – I'd given him a much better death than he'd given Trace.

That was enough.

The second I closed the door leading to the patio behind me, I yanked out my phone and dialed even as I began walking through the house. I didn't bother to check the driveway to make sure that fucker Barry was gone because the fact that the guy had pissed himself as he was running to his car was reassurance enough that he wouldn't be coming near Seth anytime soon.

"Hey, I was just about to call you," Mav said when he picked up. "This Fields guy is a piece of work."

I managed to keep my cool as I said, "How so?" I'd reached the door I was looking for just before the kitchen and tore it open. I flipped on the light and started down the stairs into the dimly lit room as Mav spoke.

"I've found restraining orders in three different states. All from former patients who claimed their one-time psychologist, a one Dr. Barry Fields, was stalking them."

"Any violence?" I asked. For once, I was hoping the answer would be yes because it would be the excuse I needed to end the bastard.

"No. Lots of phone calls, harassing them at their place of business, that sort of thing…it seemed to have stopped each time the RO was issued and then he'd start on the next guy."

"Ruin him," I ordered as I reached the bottom of the stairs.

"What?" Mav asked in surprise.

"Take it all. His license, his money – all of it. Make sure he can't pick up in another state either."

I was glad when Mav didn't question me but he did say, "It will take some time."

"Make it your number one priority."

I knew it wasn't fair to dump the shit on Mav since he was just standing in until I found a new tech guy to replace Benny, but seeing Barry holding Seth down on that desk while he'd violated him had stolen away what little reason I had left.

"You got it," Mav responded quietly and then he hung up.

It didn't take me long to find what I was looking for in the chilly wine cellar and I sent a little prayer of thanks to Seth's father for keeping what was probably some very expensive whiskey in addition to the countless bottles of wine in the wine cellar. I also sent Trace a thank you for having the foresight to make me aware of the wine cellar's existence, by bringing me down here on more than one occasion when we'd needed some privacy for a hot and heavy make out session while we'd been visiting his family.

I grabbed the first bottle of whiskey I found and snatched one of several corkscrews from a drawer. I didn't bother going back upstairs for a glass – I just took several swallows, one right after the other, and let the burn roll through me. I had no doubt the alcohol had cost Seth's father a fortune, but I barely noticed the taste. But as much as I would have liked to get drunk in the hopes of obliterating the sight of Seth struggling beneath the weight of the other man, I knew he might need me to be at a hundred percent mentally, so I closed the bottle and put it away before going back upstairs.

In the six years since Michael "Hawke" Hawkins had helped me get justice for Trace, I'd taken more lives than I'd saved in all of my years of practicing medicine. No, they hadn't all died by my hand directly, but I'd given the order on every single one. But none of those deaths, no matter how vile the criminal, had ever brought me pleasure. Only watching every single one of Trace's killers die had ever done that for me. And I knew without a shadow of a doubt that taking Barry's life would have come a close second. That fact should have bothered me more than it did, but the only part that I was struggling with was the fact that Seth had seen the real me in that study.

For all the times I'd worried that Seth's hero worship of me would turn to something more when he'd been younger, I hadn't expected to now feel the loss of that last link between us so keenly. Maybe because I didn't want Seth to have to lose yet another thing from his past. More selfishly though, I wasn't sure what would happen when I lost that last link to myself.

Once I was back upstairs, I paced the kitchen restlessly as I waited for Seth to return. When I checked the time on my phone, I realized a mere fifteen minutes had passed since Seth had left so I kept myself busy by going up to my room and changing out of my pants and into a pair of jeans. I left my dress shirt on but got rid of the jacket and the shoulder holster. I tucked one of my Glocks into the back of my jeans and then went back downstairs. I glanced out the back door again but still saw no sign of Seth, so I busied myself with changing the security code on the front door. I'd have to do the security gate at the end of the driveway at some point too but since Seth's house had nothing protecting the perimeter from intruders, the gate wasn't much of a deterrent.

By the time I was done, Seth had been gone for less than a half an hour, but I was too restless to give him any more time or space so I went out the kitchen door and started walking towards the beach. But I stopped when I saw Bullet lying next to one of the lounge chairs on the far side of the pool. The chair was turned away from the pool and facing the dark blue waters of the Sound and the Olympic mountains beyond.

I didn't bother grabbing a chair as I moved to Seth's side and I was pleased that even though he didn't look up at my approach, he moved his legs out of the way when I sat down on the end of the lounger.

"I didn't see it," he whispered.

"What?"

"That thing that made him dangerous," he said. "I knew something was off the last few months but I thought I was overreacting. I didn't want to hurt his feelings if I was wrong. He...he helped me."

"He took advantage of you," I corrected.

Seth shook his head. "Why did you come back, Ronan?"

"I didn't leave, Seth," I said. "I ran some errands today," I hedged, not wanting to admit I'd been following him. "I left my stuff in the guest room."

A raw, ugly chuckle found its way out of Seth's throat. I could tell he was close to losing it.

"You go when I need you to stay and you stay when I tell you to go." Seth shifted and swung his legs over the side of the lounger but didn't get up. "You won't let me touch you but you won't stop touching me. You want answers but you won't give them."

Seth rose as he said, "I can't figure out what's more fucked up – wishing you'd stop seeing me as Trace's little brother or being terrified that you already have."

I let Seth go because how could I tell him that the only thing fucked up about this whole thing was me?

CHAPTER 8

SETH

After leaving Ronan on the patio, I'd hidden myself away in my room like a child. Between Barry's assault and Ronan's reappearance, I was mentally and physically drained. I hadn't bothered telling Ronan to leave again because it was clear to me now that Ronan was going to do whatever Ronan wanted to do. Just like I wasn't strong enough to fend off Barry, I wasn't strong enough to force Ronan out of my life.

For what was likely the hundredth time since I'd crawled between the cool, crisp sheets of my bed, I glanced at the clock on the nightstand. It was almost two in the morning but I had yet to find any momentary peace through sleep. My only consolation was that tomorrow was Saturday so I didn't have to deal with the stress of having to endure the endless hordes of people and cars as I made my way to the office. Not that I really had to deal with those things on a daily basis – they just seemed that way to me after years of self-imposed isolation.

I hadn't really even realized how bad my fear of the outside world had gotten until after my grandmother died and I'd decided to enroll in college to pursue a degree in business so I would be well equipped to take over my father's company. After I'd gotten out of the hospital following the home invasion, it hadn't made much sense to return to my high school since there were only a few months left in the school year. So I'd gotten home schooled instead and ended up sticking with it when I realized the added benefits.

The ability to set the pace at which I learned ended up being the perfect distraction, especially after I learned of Trace's death. Every hour I wasn't caring for my grandmother or sleeping, I spent studying. I'd ended up getting my GED early and began taking college courses online just to challenge myself. But it wasn't until I'd lost the connection with Ronan that my loneliness had started to consume me. Attending college had been the logical choice and I'd been excited about the prospect of finally interacting with kids my own age. I'd even envisioned meeting someone who might finally take away some of the sting of losing Ronan.

My first day had been utter hell. The noise, the crowds…I hadn't been prepared for any of it. And it wasn't until I'd managed to make my way back to the Whidbey Island house that night that I'd realized how little I'd left the house in the years since I'd lost my parents. My grandmother had set up regular grocery deliveries shortly after her arrival and I'd never thought to change them even after she died. I bought all the things I needed like clothes and books online. The only time I ventured out was for doctor appointments and even those had been few and far between. But I'd attributed the anxiety I'd experienced to my overall fear of doctors after my lengthy hospital stay and not the fact that I had to leave the safety of the house to go to the doctor's office.

I tried going back to school the next day, but I'd only made it as far as the parking lot and then I'd had the chauffeur I'd hired to shuttle me back and forth take me back home. By day three, I'd been convinced it was all in my head and I just needed to work through the newness of it all. But all it had taken was for a big guy bumping into me as he passed me in the hallway of the building where my first class was held, and I'd had a full-blown panic attack. I'd managed to avoid a trip to the hospital after I told the paramedics that had been called that I was declining treatment and that was it. I didn't venture out of the house again for almost three years.

Another glance at the clock showed that less than five minutes had passed and I debated whether or not I should head down to the kitchen to search out some food since I'd skipped dinner so I wouldn't have to deal with Ronan. I almost laughed because I'd actually managed to make myself even more of a prisoner in my own house than I'd already been.

I decided against the snack run and flipped myself over so that I could stare out the glass doors that led out to my balcony. But within a couple seconds, I felt Bullet pressing his nose against my back. I turned over and patted the bed in invitation, but instead of jumping up, Bullet sat down and dropped his head on the edge of the bed. I let my fingers trail over the soft fur on his head but then he jerked away, his ears snapping up as something caught his attention. A shot of terror went through me as I was instantly transported to the night I'd been woken up by a stranger's gloved hand pressing down on my mouth, but I managed to recover when Bullet merely whined and then looked back at me expectantly. If there'd been any danger, Bullet would have taken off towards it.

As Bullet cocked his head, I sat up and listened for whatever the dog was hearing. And then I heard it. Moaning.

Coming next door from Ronan's room.

I waited quietly to see if the moaning would stop but it grew louder and I finally swung my legs over the bed and left the room. Ronan's door was slightly open so I could hear that in addition to moaning, he was talking.

"Ronan," I called as I pushed the door open.

Bullet brushed past me and trotted up to Ronan's bed.

"Trace," Ronan whispered. "Please stay with me, Trace."

I swallowed hard at the sound of my brother's name, but Ronan's broken voice kept me moving forward. I carefully turned on the light next to Ronan's bed, but didn't touch him despite wanting to. I'd learned my lesson long ago when I'd tried waking Trace from a nightmare when he'd been home between deployments. I'd been lucky that all he'd done was punch me in the chest but my parents had had to take me to the hospital to make sure he hadn't broken anything. Trace had been wracked with guilt and had warned me over and over again not to touch a soldier while he was having a nightmare, since the reaction could be lethal.

Ronan's brow was dotted with sweat and the blanket was bunched around the lower part of his body. His fists were clenched and I could see that his face was drawn up in agony. But what really had my attention were the dozens of jagged scars that covered his chest. I knew instantly what they were because they looked like mine. But they weren't like the penetrating stab wounds along my chest and side. No, they were shallower, longer – designed to inflict pain, not death.

The knowledge that Ronan had been tortured in the same way I'd been distracted me and it was actually Bullet who woke Ronan up by putting his paws on the bed and licking Ronan's face. Fortunately, Ronan didn't strike out at the dog but he did jerk upright. His panicked eyes settled on me and then slowly cleared as he looked around the room.

"You were having a nightmare," I managed to say, though my eyes were still on his chest.

"Sorry," he muttered before dropping his legs over the side of the bed and resting his head in his hands, the blanket draped over his lower body.

"Ronan, your chest-"

"Go back to bed, Seth."

I knew it was the wrong thing to do before I did it but some sick, twisted part of me ignored the mental warning and I reached out to run my fingers over one of the scars. Ronan grabbed me long before my skin connected with his and his eyes lifted to meet mine, but I couldn't get a read on what he was thinking. Not that it mattered because the iron-hard grip he had on me was answer enough. And at that point, I knew I was done. I had nothing left to give this man. He'd broken me.

I tugged my hand free and he released it instantly.

My chest hurt as I took a step back. If I hadn't known better, it had been me who'd woken him up and he'd struck out at me just like Trace had years earlier. I was glad that I didn't feel any tears tugging at my eyes, though I wasn't sure why since the pain I was feeling was a thousand times worse than the agony I'd felt as the blade had cut through me over and over again that terrible night so long ago.

I turned to go but sucked in a breath when I once again felt Ronan's fingers close around my wrist.

"I lied." Ronan's whisper was barely even that, but I didn't dare turn back in case I broke whatever spell had caused him to stop me from leaving.

"About what?" I managed to ask, my voice sounding loud compared to his.

"You asked if Trace asked me to keep an eye on you…"

"You said he did," I said as I carefully turned back to face him. His head was hanging but he still had a hold of my wrist.

"He did. But I could have done that from anywhere. I could have paid someone to do it. That isn't why I keep coming back here…why I keep watching you from the woods…"

The admission was so much and still not enough, but I didn't know what to say so I remained silent.

"God forgive me, but I stopped seeing you as Trace's brother a long time ago," he said hoarsely. His eyes finally lifted and where they were expressionless before, they were filled with turmoil now. My insides knotted up when I felt his finger brushing back and forth over the inside of my wrist.

"Seth," Ronan whispered. I realized my eyes had dropped to the spot where our bodies were joined and I forced my eyes back up. "I'm not that man anymore."

I knew which man he was talking about. The one I'd only seen through a child's eyes. The one who'd never really existed – at least, not on his own. I'd seen only parts of Ronan, but it wasn't something I'd understood as a naïve boy of thirteen. I'd never really known the whole man.

Ronan finally released my hand and I felt the loss immediately. And as I stood there, I knew we were both at a crossroads. Our relationship would change tonight one way or another. But looking at Ronan, his head once again hung and his hands resting on the edge of the bed, I knew I would have to be the one to make the next move.

CHAPTER 9

RONAN

I didn't manage to take a deep breath until Seth finally moved away from me. I'd known it would be a mistake to grab him a second time, but I'd been terrified that I'd lose him forever if I'd let him leave with only the memory of me holding him back from touching me. I'd seen it in the way he looked at me. And the reality was, my admission about watching him all these years had likely come too late anyway.

My body ached and the scars on my chest tingled, but I knew the psychosomatic pain was a result of my nightmare and that it would fade within a few minutes. It was the first time I would actually miss the phantom pain, though, because the agony of letting Seth go was so much worse. I began making plans in my head for which of my men I could trust to make sure there was no threat to Seth – that the mugging in the garage had been just that…a random act and nothing else. I knew the answer before I could even complete the thought, because there was only one man who knew what Seth meant to me.

I reached for the light on my nightstand but stopped when I sensed movement in the room. I looked up to see that Seth hadn't left yet. He was standing near the chair by the door – the chair I'd draped my pants, jacket and shoulder holster over when I'd changed earlier. One of my Glocks was on the nightstand next to my wallet, but I hadn't thought to grab the other one. I saw Seth reach for the holster and I was about to tell him not to touch the gun when I realized he was just moving it out of the way. He shifted so I couldn't see what he was doing, but a second later I had my answer because when he turned back to face me, he was holding my belt in his hand.

I cursed the heat that flooded my system at the sight of the smooth leather resting in the palm of his hand. I watched with bated breath as he came towards me but for the life of me, I couldn't take my eyes off the sight of the belt in his grip. In the back of my mind, I knew what was happening but I couldn't really believe it.

Seth handed me the belt and as soon as I took it, he held his arms out in front of him, the insides of his wrists pressed together. I shook my head at the offering but I couldn't find any words.

I couldn't do this.

I shouldn't.

It would just fuck everything up even more.

I lifted my gaze to tell Seth no but then I saw it. The thing I'd feared I'd lost. It wasn't hero worship or the wayward emotions of an innocent child. And it wasn't some distorted reflection of a man who no longer existed. All I saw was me...the way he saw me.

And in that moment, he wasn't Trace's little brother and I wasn't the broken man who couldn't bear to be touched.

We were just us.

Instead of reaching for his wrists, I stretched out my arm and settled my hand on his lower back to pull him forward. He was wearing a pair of sweats and a gray T-shirt, so I had to maneuver my hand until I could touch bare skin. I heard his breathing tick up as I caressed him but his hands never moved. And they stayed exactly where they were even as I drew him forward until he was straddling my lap. I studied him for a long time, just taking in every bit of him that I could. The bruises on his face had darkened considerably but they took nothing away from his raw beauty. I let my fingers trail over his slightly parted lips before I pulled him down for a long, slow kiss. I felt his fisted hands press against my chest, but he didn't actually caress me. But he did kiss me back without any hesitation or fear.

I let my hands settle on his thighs as we kissed and I could tell when he felt my erection press up against him because he gasped against my mouth. I stroked up and down his thighs a few times before I reached for the hem of his shirt and pulled it off of him, forcing him to release the position he'd been holding his hands in. But instead of reaching for me as soon as the shirt was off, he put his wrists back together.

As much as I wanted to take the belt and throw it across the room, I knew I wouldn't be able to because I could feel the fear building inside me as Seth returned every one of my kisses. When I reached for the belt, Seth didn't stiffen or change his posture in any way and I saw nothing but trust in his gaze as he looked down at me. I settled my arm around his lower back to support him as I stood and shifted our positions so that I could lay him flat on the bed. I straddled his hips and didn't miss his startled gasp as he realized I was naked. His eyes shifted to my cock which was already heavy with need and he actually licked his lips. I bit back a moan and forced my attention on wrapping the belt around his wrists. The move got his focus back on my face but he was watching me with anticipation.

I did one loop around his joined wrists with the belt before lifting his arms above his head and putting the end of the belt through the iron rungs of the headboard. The belt was long enough that I could wrap it once more around Seth's wrists before securing the end into the buckle. I made sure the belt was tight enough to hold him but not tight enough to hurt him in any way. Knowing he was at my complete and total mercy had my cock tightening to epic proportions, but I managed to control myself as I dropped myself down on him and sealed my mouth over his. We were both breathless by the time I finally released his lips.

"You can stop this any time with one word, no matter what," I said firmly.

"I know," he said and then he smiled and I felt my heart constrict painfully. A surge of doubt went through me but then he kissed me, his tongue tentatively searching mine out and I knew I was too much of a bastard to not take what he was offering.

I broke the kiss and skimmed my lips along his jaw before trailing them down his throat. He was panting with anticipation long before I even reached his chest and when I bit gently down on one of his nipples, I heard a whoosh of air leave his lips. There was a slight shift in the headboard as I turned my focus on his other nipple, but when I looked up to check on Seth, all I saw was him watching me with rapt attention. I couldn't resist stealing another lusty kiss from his lips before sitting up so I could examine his body the way I'd always longed to…with my fingers, my eyes, my mouth.

I hadn't missed the scars on his body, but I kept my exploration of the old wounds brief since I didn't want to make him self-conscious. There were multiple scars on his chest and sides that I knew were from when his attackers had stabbed him and left him for dead – that much Trace had shared with me when he'd told me about the attack on Seth and his parents. But as hard as those scars were to look at, it was the long, narrow scars running across the length of his abdomen that almost bothered me more because I knew what each drag of the knife would have felt like for Seth as he was tortured to try and force his father to talk. The wounds wouldn't have been deep, but the terror Seth must have been feeling would have left far deeper scars on his psyche…scars like mine.

"I'm okay," Seth whispered and I lifted my eyes to see him watching me with quiet strength. It was then that I realized I'd failed in my intent not to give the stretches of raised flesh too much attention. At some point, I'd even started fingering one of the scars on his stomach. I nodded and then took my time removing his sweats so I could drink my fill of the rest of him, including his weeping cock that lay nestled thick and full in a thatch of wiry, blond hair.

I leaned over Seth and settled my weight back down on him as I kissed him again. It took just minutes to get him squirming and bucking beneath me and then I focused on bringing him the pleasure I so desperately needed to give him. But as much as I wanted to sink into his warm, welcoming body, I knew this would be my only chance to consume every part of Seth that I could, so I took my time with my sensual torture. He kept repeating my name over and over as I licked and nipped my way down his body, but he changed over to flat out begging as soon as I bypassed his weeping cock in favor of worshiping the rest of him. To my surprise, his feet turned out to be an erogenous zone that I had no problem exploiting to keep him near the edge.

"Ronan, please…it's too much."

The desperation in his tone had me releasing the leg I'd draped over my shoulder. I trailed my fingers back up his body until I reached his pulsing dick, but instead of playing with it like he clearly wanted me to, I pressed my fingers against the sensitive skin behind his balls. He jerked hard at the contact and the headboard rattled as he struggled against his restraints. The sight and sound had my own cock filling even more and I willed myself to remain in control.

"Open your eyes," I ordered, more harshly than I'd intended. As soon as he did, I removed my fingers from his taint and stuck one in my mouth. I made sure he saw my saliva sticking to my digit as I moved it back down to his body. He stiffened when I pushed my finger between the globes of his ass and he actually held his breath as I pressed the pad against his hole. But before he could think too long and too hard about what I was doing, I leaned over and sucked his cock into my mouth.

"Fuck!" he shouted as he shoved his hips up. I used his distraction to press my finger into his body and as soon as he froze at the contact, I hollowed out my cheeks and sucked hard. The sensual onslaught did exactly what it was supposed to and Seth began desperately thrusting into my mouth. Every time he pulled out, he impaled himself on my finger, and soon I couldn't tell if he was more desperate to get more of himself inside of me or more of me inside of him. But in the end, it didn't matter because one press of my finger on his prostate and he began shooting down my throat. I barely managed to keep from coming myself as his salty flavor coated my tongue and I heard the sound of my name falling over and over again from his lips. When he finally stilled and I'd consumed every last drop of him, I gently pulled my finger free and crawled up his body and sealed my mouth over his. I'd purposefully kept from swallowing all of his come and I nearly smiled at his gasp of surprise when I shared his essence with him.

"So sweet, Seth," I murmured against his mouth. "So fucking sweet."

CHAPTER 10

SETH

I could only lay there as Ronan kissed me, because much like the day before when he'd gotten me off in the bathroom, I felt completely boneless. My arms ached from the strain of being braced above my head, but I didn't care if it meant I could get more of Ronan kissing me like this…like I was more than just a convenient body. I had no idea if that was what I was or not, but I'd reached the conclusion that I would take whatever I could get as soon as I'd known that walking away from Ronan tonight meant it would be over for good.

But the promise I'd made to myself to not let the aftermath of being with Ronan destroy me disintegrated when Ronan whispered my name as he kissed me. Because part of me really had believed he wasn't really seeing me as he touched and kissed me. I'd had this sick fear that he'd say my brother's name as he made love to me but to hear my name fall from his lips…it was a thousand times better than the mind blowing orgasm he'd just given me.

Ronan kissed me for what seemed like an endless amount of time and by the time he sat up again and reached for something on the nightstand, I felt the excitement and nervousness returning to my body. I watched him fish a condom and a packet of lube out of his wallet and I swallowed hard as he opened the lube before moving farther down my body. Even though his long, thick finger had just given me so much pleasure, I still couldn't help but worry about what would come next. I'd been too far gone too really notice any pain as his finger had entered me but now that the orgasm had started to wane, I could feel my body drawing up tight and I was worried he wouldn't consider that as he got me ready. But I kept my mouth shut as I watched him put some lube on his fingers.

He was kneeling between my spread legs and I figured he would just open me up and started pushing into me but he surprised me again by dropping his weight back down on my body and kissing me. I was lost in the sensation of his tongue dancing with mine so I barely noticed the cool lube being spread over my hole. It wasn't until his finger began probing me that I realized he was distracting me with the pleasure his mouth was bringing me. And it was at that exact moment that I realized the childhood love I'd had for this man had never disappeared and it never would. It had morphed into something deeper and scarier and that conclusion was more terrifying than the change my body was about to go through. Because Ronan wasn't about to just take my virginity; he was going to take everything else too.

My body was still loose from Ronan's initial intrusion but when he added a second finger, I felt my whole body lock up. But instead of forcing himself farther inside of me, Ronan just went right on kissing me and when he released my lips, it was only so he could settle his mouth next to my ear.

"I've dreamed of this moment," he said, his rumbly voice barely a whisper. "It's kept me awake at night…wondering what it would feel like to be buried inside of you. Wondering if I'd survive it."

"Survive what?" I managed to ask even as I felt his fingers sink deeper into me. I let out a loud groan when they brushed my gland but the contact was all too brief.

"Knowing your body was made for mine and mine for yours…a perfect fit."

I didn't get a chance to respond because he was kissing me again and his fingers started massaging my inner walls. The burning sensation began to ease as he started finger fucking me and I found myself trying to push down on his digits to get more of their thick length inside of me because suddenly, I felt too empty.

Ronan released me so that he could sit up and search out the discarded condom. I missed the feel of his fingers as he pulled them free so he could work the condom on, but just seeing how big his engorged cock was compared to his fingers had me squirming both with nerves and excitement. He spread the remaining lube from the packet over his sheathed cock and then got into position between my legs. He reached past my head and grabbed a pillow and then worked it beneath my hips. The new position made me feel on display but even more so when Ronan used his hands to spread me open for his perusal and then trailed his hungry gaze over my entire body. I held my breath as he studied me. A bout of anxiety overcame me as I wondered if he liked what he was seeing. While I'd never really given my looks much thought as I'd gotten older, I couldn't help but compare myself to the man who'd been lucky enough to have every part of Ronan…Trace…the man who would always be a part of us no matter what the future brought.

"Seth," Ronan said gently and I looked up, not even realizing I'd dropped my gaze.

"You're fucking perfect," Ronan said, the words sounding more like an order than a compliment. And I knew he'd realized the train of my thoughts.

I managed a nod but that didn't seem to satisfy Ronan so I said, "I know you see *me*, Ronan. I know it."

To my relief, Ronan leaned over and kissed me hard. "Tell me you want this."

"I do," I said. "More than anything." I realized they were dangerous words to say, but luckily Ronan didn't seem to dwell on their double meaning and he leaned back and shifted his lower body until I felt the head of his cock brush up against my hole.

"Bear down on me," was all Ronan said as he finally began to breach me. I did as he said but nothing prepared me for the intense pressure and discomfort I felt as his crown pushed inside of me. I tried holding my breath but that seemed to make it worse so I just focused on watching Ronan's face. The extreme concentration and determination in his gaze as he focused on where our bodies were joined had me holding my tongue when the pain started to increase. But then something in my body gave way and Ronan sank inside of me. The relief was instantaneous because the pain dissipated and all I felt was the slight burn and pressure that I already knew from when Ronan had used his fingers on me, would turn into something better.

"Okay?" Ronan managed to ask through gritted teeth. I could see the sweat dotting his brow and I knew he was struggling just as much as I was. But while I was trying to accommodate the newness of what was happening to me, he was struggling to make sure all I felt was perfection.

He shifted just as I was about to answer and the move had him sliding deeper inside of me. Right after the burning sensation was a flash of something so raw and pleasurable that I actually tried to drive my hips forward onto him just so I could feel it again. "Please, Ronan, more," I begged, barely recognizing the keening tone coming from my lips.

As I jammed my hips up again, Ronan let out a loud curse and then he pushed forward until he bottomed out inside me. I swallowed hard at the rush of near pain that came over me but just knowing that I was finally joined with Ronan in this way was enough for me to ignore the sting that was firing through my ass. I expected Ronan to start moving at that point but he surprised me by leaning over and crushing his lips down on mine. As he kissed me, I felt his cock pulsing and throbbing inside of me and I cursed the latex barrier that was keeping every part of him from me.

Ronan was still kissing me when he began pulling out before gently sliding back in and I gasped against his mouth as a delicious sensation swept through me. Another thrust had me giving up on trying to kiss Ronan back and I guessed he could tell because his lips settled against my cheek as he increased the pace. The pleasure began to spike with every roll of his hips against mine and for the first time, I began to fear that I wouldn't be able to keep back the words my heart wanted me to call out as Ronan loved me. His abdomen was pressed against my now rock hard cock and every time he slid forward, I tried to press up against him to increase the sensation. Ronan must have sensed my need because I felt his hand slip between our bodies a second later and then he was jerking me off as his body began to ram into mine. I struggled against my bonds because I wanted nothing more in that moment than to wrap myself around him completely, but there was no give whatsoever so the only thing I could do was wrap my legs around him in a vain effort to keep him as close to me as possible. And then my mouth was searching out his because I knew the only way I could make him understand what I was feeling was through the few ways I was permitted to touch him.

Ronan kissed me back but the kisses were short and jerky because we were both panting too hard to do any different. I felt my balls drawing up tight against my body but I couldn't find the oxygen I needed to tell him how close I was. But it didn't matter because his hand on my dick increased its pace and his cock was slinging in and out of me without reservation. Our sweat-slickened bodies rocked against each other over and over and when I was certain I couldn't take any more, my body gave in to its need and fire shot up my spine and radiated out to all of my limbs. I cried out against Ronan's mouth and closed my eyes as the climax threatened to steal my consciousness away. Ronan's hoarse shout followed a moment later and then I felt his free hand grab onto the belt where it was looped around my wrists. His grip on the restraints bordered on painful as he humped into me over and over but then to my surprise, he released his hold on the belt and closed his fingers over one of my hands. It was the most natural thing for me to separate my fingers just slightly but I couldn't contain the emotion that flooded through me when his fingers linked with mine.

The tears came without warning but I was powerless to stop them.

But Ronan said nothing and he didn't pull away in disgust. He simply held my hand and then he began kissing the tears away one by one.

~

Waking up alone wasn't a surprise since I'd felt Ronan get out of bed within minutes of him untying me. I hadn't been disappointed at first because he'd returned within a minute with a warm washcloth and he'd gently cleaned the come off my stomach and the residual lube that had clung to me. But instead of climbing into bed next to me after he'd drawn the covers over me, he'd left and I'd lain there hoping against hope that he was just going to get something to drink or to check to make sure the house was locked up for the night. As the minutes passed though, the same feeling of abandonment I'd felt after he'd walked out on me three years earlier came over me and the tears that had started to fall had nothing to do with the joy of finally being made love to by the man who'd been my entire world for so long.

I managed to lift my head long enough to check the time on the nightstand clock and was shocked to see it was well after eleven a.m. I wasn't particularly hungry but my tired body had other needs so I forced myself to sit up. The slight sting in my ass was both good and bad. I'd finally had the night I'd always dreamed of and even though I hadn't been able to touch Ronan the way I wanted to, the way he'd loved me had felt real. It was something I hadn't had in a really long time. But I was going to pay for it because I'd had a taste of perfection but it was just that…a taste.

My legs felt shaky as I got out of bed and I took my time making my way to my own room. As I was leaving the room, my heart stopped when I noticed that the chair Ronan had been using as a luggage holder was empty. Not only were his clothes gone but his bag was too. I forced myself to go to the closet but couldn't bring myself to actually open it so I left the room. I just needed a few more minutes of pretending. I needed to remember last night for what it was, not for what it wasn't.

As I neared the kitchen, Bullet trotted out of it to greet me but just as promptly turned around and ran back into it, his tail wagging happily. A ridiculous surge of hope speared through my chest and I quickened my pace.

But the man sitting at the kitchen table wasn't Ronan.

CHAPTER 11

RONAN

"What the hell do you mean, he locked you out?" I snarled at Hawke who was casually leaning against the side of his car.

"It means he locked all the doors-"

"Fuck off," I snapped, cutting an amused Hawke off. He was checking something on his phone and I wanted more than anything to rip it out of his hand and throw it across the driveway but I knew better. As relaxed and laid back as Hawke looked, I knew it was just an illusion because in reality, he was brutally lethal and pissing him off for any reason was something only a man with a death wish would do.

I forced myself to step away from him and began pacing the small portion of the driveway on the outside of the heavy iron gate that hadn't opened when I'd punched the code into the keypad. Bullet was sitting on the other side, his big tail thumping heavily against the ground as he whined. I put my hand through the bars to give him a pat and then he dropped to the ground and watched me in solemn silence. Like he was wondering how I'd ended up on the wrong side of the fence.

"What happened?" I finally managed to ask in a steady voice.

Hawke glanced up at me and then stopped fiddling with his phone and tucked it into his pocket before crossing his arms. Michael Hawkins wasn't a huge guy but something about the way he carried himself always made him seem bigger than he was. He stood an inch or two shorter than me but there was nothing average about him. Despite the cool weather, he was wearing a black T-shirt that stretched across his broad chest and did nothing to hide his bulging biceps, both of which were covered in tattoos. Even though he'd long ago left the army, he kept his hair in the traditional buzz cut the military favored. His flinty blue eyes watched me as I tried to use constant movement to work out my growing frustration – it was a behavior I'd long ago managed to curb but had struggled with more and more in the past few weeks. Of all the men in my employ, Hawke was the only one I would ever allow to see me like this…because he'd seen me even worse.

"He came downstairs a few hours after you left. I told him you asked me to keep an eye on things for a bit."

"What did he say?" I interrupted. God, I sounded like a high school girl pumping her best friend for information.

"Not much. He made himself a cup of coffee, refilled mine and then asked me to leave when I was finished. I told him that that wasn't an option."

"Did you tell him I texted him about why I had to leave?"

Hawke tilted his head at me. "Yeah. That went over real well, by the way. A fucking text, Ronan? Jesus, what are you, twelve?"

I ground my teeth together in frustration because I didn't have a reasonable comeback for the jab. I'd taken the coward's way out from the moment I'd released Seth from the restraints. I'd barely managed to do the right thing by cleaning him up and getting him settled under the comforter before the desperate need to run had overtaken me.

I'd made a terrible mistake in fucking Seth. Shit, that word didn't even fit what we'd done. We'd made love, pure and simple. I'd been selfish in taking what he should have given to someone more deserving. Because I had no doubt that Seth could have his pick of strong, giving, loving men as soon as he started putting himself out there…as soon as he realized the truth about what I'd become and let me go.

But worse than being selfish, I'd been foolish too. Foolish in thinking that in tying Seth up with my belt, that he wouldn't be able to touch me. Because everything Seth did touched me. Every look, every smile, every emotion filled kiss he'd given me, the way his body had cradled mine. That was why I'd run. Being with Seth had been the fuck up of fuck ups and I knew it would happen again the second he looked at me with that longing gaze that had me wishing I could be what he needed.

I'd left three days ago and I hadn't been man enough to even call Seth once. I'd taken his virginity – an act that had been incredibly emotional for him if his tears had been anything to go by – and I'd disappeared just like I had three years earlier.

"You followed him, right?" I asked as I turned to face Hawke.

He nodded. "He stayed in his room Saturday and Sunday. Yesterday and today he went to work, the house on Mercer Island, and home – that's it."

I turned back to stare at the gate. Seth's message couldn't be any clearer. Even in the three years after I'd walked away from him after he'd kissed me, he'd never changed the codes on the gate or the doors.

Because he'd hoped I would come back…because he would have accepted me back.

"You take care of things on your end?" Hawke asked.

"What?" I asked in confusion as I glanced over my shoulder at him.

"The girl…" he said.

"Daisy," I supplied. "Yeah, she's onboard."

When I'd called Hawke in the early morning hours after I'd made love to Seth, I'd told him I needed him to watch Seth so I could fly to Ohio to recruit a potential new tech guy…well, girl in this case. Daisy Washburne was a twenty-year-old hacker who'd spent the last several years trying to track down the men who'd raped and murdered her mother. And while she'd managed to find the men and use her extensive talents to ruin them financially and personally, they'd sought their own form of vengeance. I'd been lucky enough to come across the notes Benny had collected regarding the chatter between the two men as they'd searched for someone to find Daisy and take her out. I'd managed to stop the hit in time while Hawke had taken care of the men who'd killed Daisy's mother.

I hadn't considered offering Daisy a position in the organization because I'd learned my lesson with Mace Calhoun. As wounded and damaged as Daisy was, I didn't want to exploit her talents for my own gain; not if it meant deepening her wounds instead of healing them. But somehow she'd found me, though I still had no idea how she'd done it and she refused to say. I could only assume she'd found something in the men's emails that led to the Deep Web where they'd recruited the hit man and subsequently been tagged by Benny's algorithm.

In any case, I'd gotten an email a few weeks later asking to meet. I'd agreed but more out of curiosity than anything else. But the meeting had quickly turned into a pitch of sorts – as in, she was pitching herself to me. I'd resisted but it wasn't her surprisingly vast knowledge of me and the group I'd set up to protect people like her that had me relenting. It was the unfettered desperation in her voice, the frantic need for something more than just the closure the deaths of her mother's murderers had brought her. It was a look I knew all too well. I'd finally told her I'd think about it. I'd spent the last two days researching what Daisy's life had become after the loss of her mother and her quest for vengeance and when I'd realized I could give her the piece that was missing from her life, I'd gone back to Ohio to offer her the job. I hadn't held anything back when I'd told her in detail what she was signing up for and I'd watched her carefully for any sign of hesitation. All I'd seen was a fierce determination along with a look of hope so strong, that I'd had no reservations about giving her instructions on how to meet up with Mav so he could show her the ropes.

And not once in all that time had I reached out to Seth. And unlike the last time I'd left him, Seth didn't contact me.

"I really fucked this up," I whispered more to myself than to Hawke.

"Yeah," I heard Hawke say from somewhere behind me.

I hadn't told Hawke I'd slept with Seth but from the inflection in his voice, I suspected he had already figured it out. "How'd you know?"

"The look on his face when he walked into the kitchen and saw me sitting there instead of you. Revay used to get that look when she found out I was only home for a day or two between missions."

"He's never been very good at hiding what he's feeling," I mused, my eyes still on the heavy iron gate in front me.

"Maybe," Hawke said quietly. "Or maybe you've just gotten too good at it."

I glanced over my shoulder at the man behind me. It was on the tip of my tongue to remind Hawke that I'd had a good teacher but I kept silent. He wasn't saying anything that wasn't true and just because I felt the need to physically lash out at someone didn't mean I should. And least of all a man I knew wouldn't hesitate to knock me on my ass...and was also the closest thing I had to a friend these days.

While I'd undergone basic training as part of joining the army, it was Hawke who'd shown me what fighting for my life really meant. Before Hawke, I could manage to fire a weapon at a target and perform a few self-defense moves, but it wasn't until after he'd spent the better part of a year showing me the many ways I could take a man's life, whether it be with a gun, a knife or just my hands, that I'd actually felt some of the power and control that had been stolen me from the night of Trace's death come back to me. In reality, they were things I'd never really had and now I couldn't imagine a life without them. Even if I somehow found the courage to pick up a scalpel again, I'd be more inclined to think about how to take a life with it rather than save one.

My thoughts drifted back to Seth and I could actually see his expression as he walked into his kitchen, his body sore but sated. He would have been nervous to see me but he would have been excited too. Even not knowing where we stood, he wouldn't have been able to keep the emotion out of his gaze as he watched me with hopeful eyes...hopeful that I'd draw him into my arms and tell him how fucking amazing the night before had been. Hopeful that I would have closed my mouth over his and shown him that everything had changed between us.

Everything *had* changed. Just not in the way Seth wanted. Not in the way I wanted, either.

"You mind checking the perimeter?" I asked as I gave Hawke a quick glance.

He studied me for a long moment but didn't say anything. He merely brushed past me and reached up to pull himself over the short wall that bordered the front of the property. Bullet took off after Hawke as he began walking towards the side of the house so he could check out the back of the property. I left my car where it was and followed Hawke over the wall. Bullet came running back to give me a cursory greeting and then he was chasing after Hawke again.

I didn't bother going to the front door when I reached the house since I doubted Seth would answer it. As I walked around the back of the house, I saw Hawke and Bullet disappearing into the tree line to the right of the house.

Once I reached the patio, I passed by the study door but stopped when I saw Seth sitting at his father's desk. I rapped my knuckles on the door and felt instantly bad when I saw Seth jump in his chair. His eyes fell almost immediately when he recovered but I didn't miss the message when he turned his attention back to his computer.

"Seth," I said loudly enough so I was sure he'd hear me. "I'll break it down."

I saw Seth's jaw harden and I hated to admit how it turned me on. As much as I loved when Seth was willing and pliant in my arms, I loved this side of him too. It was a reminder that he wasn't some innocent, naïve kid. My Seth had a gentle soul but a backbone made of steel.

Fuck. *My* Seth? He wasn't my anything.

To my surprise, and my traitorous body's excitement, Seth ignored me. I didn't bother with another warning because I was too keyed up as it was. I needed to get us back to where we'd been before I'd made the mistake of touching him. Reaching under my jacket, I pulled one of my Glocks free from the shoulder holster and prepared to knock out the glass panel closest to the deadbolt when the sound of a gunshot ripped through the air. It was off in the distance but close enough to have come from Seth's property. Concern rushed through me and I grabbed my phone and hit the speed dial for Hawke.

"What was that?" Seth asked as he tore the door open. "Was that a gunshot?"

"Go back inside," I ordered as Hawke's voicemail picked up.

"Ronan-"

"Seth, go back inside!" I demanded. "Lock the door and don't come out until I come back."

I didn't wait to see if Seth did as I said because I was already striding across the back yard. Within seconds, I heard footsteps behind me and I was about to turn and order Seth to go back when I saw movement by the tree line. A second later, Hawke cleared the vegetation and as relived as I was to see that he appeared to be unharmed, my stomach fell when I saw what he had in his arms.

"Bullet?" Seth whispered from behind me. "No-" he suddenly cried out and then he was running past me. It was easy to catch up to him before he reached Hawke but I didn't grab Seth's arm to pull him away from his dog because I saw Bullet move his head slightly.

"What happened?" I asked Hawke.

Hawke shook his head. "I didn't see the shooter. The dog heard something and took off. Then he started barking and a second later came the shot. He's bleeding pretty bad, Ronan," Hawke said quietly, though with Seth right there, he had to have heard it.

"Give him to me," I said as I took the dog from him. "Can you move my car from in front of the gate?"

Hawke nodded after giving Seth a quick glance. "I'll stay here and check things out," Hawke murmured. "Keys?"

"In it," I said, though my eyes were on Seth who'd gone deathly quiet and seemed frozen in place. All the color had drained from his face as he stared at his dog who was dead weight in my arms.

"Seth," I said gently as I tried to get his attention but with my hands full of dog, I couldn't get him to focus on me. I could feel blood seeping into my shirt so I gave up on niceties and yelled, "Seth!"

Seth jerked at the sound of my voice but he finally looked up at me.

"I need you to go get your keys and start your car, okay? And call your vet to make sure they know we're coming." Seth managed to nod but he didn't move otherwise and his water-filled eyes were back on Bullet. "Baby," I whispered in the desperate hope of snapping him out of it. The endearment seemed to work because Seth finally seemed to come back to himself.

"Please, Ronan, I can't lose him too," Seth managed to croak out as tears slipped down his cheeks.

"You won't," I promised, though it was a promise I had no right to make. I could feel Bullet's labored, shallow breaths against my body and I willed the dog to hang on because like it or not, he really was all Seth had left.

Because I could no longer deny that Seth *had* lost me. Only it hadn't been the day I'd walked away from him – it had happened the same night Trace had died. Because I'd died that night too.

CHAPTER 12

SETH

Even though I was numb inside, I couldn't stem the tears that slipped down my cheeks and kept dripping onto my folded hands. Every once in a while I managed to dab at my face with the wadded up tissue that had been placed between my fingers by someone, but the effort was pointless since the tissue was nearly soaked through. I felt like my brain had already processed that I was going to lose the only important thing I had left in my life, the only living soul that I knew, unlike Ronan, would never choose to leave me. But for whatever reason, my body couldn't rid itself of the mantle of denial that had settled over it.

It had taken me a long time to find the car keys after Ronan had ordered me to get my car started and by the time I'd found them, Ronan was already rounding the house, a deathly quiet Bullet in his arms. I hadn't had the courage to ask Ronan if Bullet was still alive but he'd told me anyway with a gentle, "He's hanging on, Seth."

Although Bullet had been quiet, he hadn't been unconscious and he'd spent the entire car ride to the vet's office licking my arm as I'd cradled his head in my lap. I'd used my other arm to keep Bullet's body from sliding off the back seat of the car as Ronan took every turn nearly as fast as the straightaways. It wasn't until Bullet licked me that first time that I'd nearly lost it all together. Because even with all the pain my loyal friend had to have been feeling, he'd still sought to comfort me in the same way he always had.

The vet had been waiting for us when we'd arrived and Bullet had been rushed into surgery. I hadn't been able to see the actual wound, just the large swath of blood covering his side. My hands had been covered in blood by the time we'd gotten to the clinic but now they were clean again and I had no clue how that had happened. Ronan probably. But for once, I couldn't bring myself to care or to wonder what it meant. I didn't even care that he was there. I just wanted my dog to be okay.

"Drink this," Ronan said as he handed me a small paper cup full of water. I did as I was told because I didn't have the energy to argue. I felt the tissue in my hand replaced with a dry one but when Ronan settled his hand on my lower arm, I pulled it away. I nearly laughed at the irony – suddenly I was the one who couldn't stand to be touched.

Ronan didn't move away from where he was sitting next to me but he didn't try to touch me after that. Minutes could have been hours for all I knew before the vet came out. I'd known Dr. Anna White for many years, ever since Ronan had given Bullet to me. She'd been one of the few vets who'd been willing to make house calls to give Bullet his yearly exam and shots. I'd explained to Dr. White that Bullet was too afraid of the car to make the trip each year, but I suspected she knew even before I did that it wasn't Bullet who'd been afraid.

"He's going to be okay," Dr. White said even before she'd closed the door to the back room behind her. Ronan and I were the only ones in the office since it was after hours.

I sucked in a breath and felt my body sway in relief. I didn't even remember standing up. Ronan's fingers closed around my elbow but I was too unsure of my ability to stay upright to shake him off the way I wanted.

"The bullet damaged his spleen so I had to remove it but he'll make a full recovery."

I couldn't stop the hoarse cry that erupted from my throat and if Dr. White was surprised by the hug I gave her, she was kind enough not to show it.

"Thank you," I whispered against her shoulder.

"You're welcome," she said with a small, gentle pat to my back and then she was pushing me back so that I could focus on her. "I need to keep him here overnight but you can take him home tomorrow. He'll need to take it easy for a while…"

I nodded. "I…I'm supposed to fly to New York in a couple of weeks. I was going to take him with me. It's a chartered jet so he wouldn't be in a crate or anything. But I can cancel…"

The vet shook her head. "That should be fine," she said. "He's a strong dog, Seth. He'll be back to his old self in no time."

I swallowed hard. "Thank you, Dr. White."

She nodded and gave me a pat on the arm. "You can come see him in a few minutes."

As the vet turned to go, Ronan said, "Doctor, were you able to extract the bullet?"

Dr. White gave Ronan a strange look and then glanced at me but I had no idea why Ronan had asked the question.

"Um, no, the wound was a through and through," the vet said.

"Can you tell what kind of weapon it might have been? The caliber?"

She shook her head. "No, I'm sorry. I don't really know much about that kind of thing."

Ronan nodded. "Thank you."

The vet gave him another confused look and then disappeared through the door leading to the back of the building.

"Why did you ask that?" I asked.

"Just hoping to get a better idea of who hurt Bullet," Ronan responded as he returned to his seat.

"It was probably a hunter," I said. "They show up once in a while. My parents posted *No Trespassing* signs but they ignore them."

Ronan only nodded and I was too exhausted to pursue the subject.

Dr. White returned about a half an hour later and I got to spend several minutes with Bullet who was still heavily sedated.

Ronan drove home and I was too tired to argue with him when he followed me into the house. I assumed Hawke had been the one to pull Ronan's car into the driveway, but he wasn't around when we entered the house and I hadn't seen his car at all.

I hadn't made any effort to get to know Hawke the morning I found him sitting in my kitchen because I'd been too raw and hurt from discovering that Ronan had walked out on me yet again. I hadn't cared why Hawke was there or what his relationship with Ronan was. I'd simply asked him to leave and had gone to hide out in my room for the rest of the weekend. It wasn't until Sunday night as I'd forced myself out of bed so I could ready myself for work the next day that I'd finally conceded that my love for Ronan was slowly destroying me. I knew changing the codes on the door and the gate wouldn't keep Ronan out but I'd hoped it would send a message.

Clearly, it hadn't.

"I'm going to go get cleaned up," I heard Ronan say behind me as he closed the front door and locked it. The sound of the lock engaging pissed me off and I turned to face him. I hesitated at the sight of Bullet's dried blood on the front of Ronan's shirt but I shoved my emotions back down where they belonged.

"Do it someplace else," I said quietly. "You're no longer welcome here."

I turned and headed towards the kitchen and wasn't surprised when I heard heavy footsteps directly behind me.

"Seth," Ronan said gently as he followed me to the fridge. I was in the process of opening the refrigerator door when he grabbed me and I felt all my fear and anger come rushing over me. I spun around and slammed my hands against Ronan's chest and was actually glad to see him stumble back.

"Get the fuck out!" I snapped. "I don't want you here."

Ronan's gaze clouded over with a look of shame but then he stiffened. "Once I know you're safe-"

"Safe?" I yelled. "From what? I was mugged, Ronan. It happens every day. Bullet got shot by a hunter! There's no conspiracy here; no one's out to get me!" I sucked in a couple of deep breaths as I tried to get control of myself.

"The only one I need protection from is you," I finally said tiredly. "I would take this," – I pointed to the bruises on my face – "every day for the rest of my life over what you did to me three days ago."

Ronan paled but I was beyond caring. "Just go, Ronan. If there's any part of you that cares about me even a little bit, please go...and don't come back this time."

I turned back to the refrigerator and opened it. My hand was shaking badly but I covered it up by gripping the edge of the door as tightly as I could.

"So that's it?" Ronan said from behind me. I didn't dare turn around to check if he was as close to me as it felt like he was. I was terrified that if I took even the slightest step back, I'd feel his big, warm body pressed against mine and I'd beg him to forget everything I'd just said.

"That's it," I whispered. "I'm done...we're done."

I was right about Ronan being right behind me because he grabbed me a split second later and dragged me back a step before slamming the refrigerator door shut and shoving me up against it so I was facing him.

"No!" was all he said and his voice was so rough and chalky, it sounded like a snarl. And then his mouth was on mine, his hands holding my wrists in place against the stainless steel at my back.

I'd like to say I fought Ronan's kiss but I didn't. Not even a little. My brain may not have wanted Ronan but my body welcomed him like it always did. But this time around, I wasn't content to just take what Ronan was giving me. I battled for control of the kiss and when I finally won, I managed to pry my hands free of Ronan's hold. I let my tongue search out every recess of his mouth as I maneuvered us so it was his back pressed up against the refrigerator. I had my hands on his waist but, to my surprise, he didn't move away from my touch or try to stop me from pressing my fingers into his sides. But I could also feel the tension running through his frame so I knew I only had precious seconds to maintain what little power over him that I had for the moment.

As I continued to make love to his mouth, I let one of my hands slide down to stroke over his erection. Ronan gasped against my mouth and then he took over the kiss. But he didn't stop me from exploring his length where it bulged impressively against his pants. There was enough give in his waistband to allow me to sink my hand inside so I could grip his cock. I shouldn't have been surprised by the softness of his skin stretched over the hardness of his flesh since I'd touched myself like this more times than I could count, but nothing about it was the same.

Ronan finally stopped kissing me once I began exploring his cock but his lips hovered over mine, his hot breath fanning my mouth as he tried to get control of himself. But I didn't want him to be in control and I began stroking him in earnest, hoping that I was using enough pressure to bring him pleasure. I could only assume as he began thrusting into my hand that I was doing a reasonably adequate job. But it was over too soon because Ronan let out a muffled curse before grabbing both my arms and forcing me back against the island counter behind me. I'd definitely succeeded in snapping his control because all his movements after that lacked finesse.

He spun me around and shoved me down over the butcher block countertop. His weight pressed against me as he began rubbing his crotch all over my ass and a second later, I felt his fingers working my pants open. We'd been in this exact position before but this time there was no fear and not because my hands weren't tied. No, I wanted this. I didn't want to want it but I couldn't deny the need to feel Ronan inside of me again.

I shoved my ass back against Ronan and groaned when I felt his erection push against me. Ronan separated from me only long enough to shove my pants and underwear down and then he was back and I gasped at the feel of his bare cock nudging my cheeks. I had no idea how he'd managed to get his pants open too but as his hot flesh speared through the globes of my ass, I didn't care. Ronan's lips sought out the nape of my neck and he kissed, sucked and nipped at my skin as I squirmed desperately beneath him. My hands were flat on the wood beneath me but I couldn't stop myself from reaching behind me to seek Ronan's warm skin out. My fingertips brushed over the hair on his thighs and I relished the feel of it as I ran my palms up and down his hot flesh.

I'd been too distracted to notice Ronan getting the lube, presumably from his wallet, but I couldn't help but shiver from the coldness of it as his finger breached me without warning. But unlike the night he'd made love to me, Ronan didn't take his time letting me adjust. There was no pain as he sank his finger inside of me but I groaned at the feel of a second finger splitting me open just a few seconds later. It was then that I knew I was going to be fucked hard and fast just like the way Ronan had promised that day in the bathroom before he'd realized my distress. But there was no fear this time. I wanted it…badly.

Ronan's weight pressed down on my back once again, his hips shoving me forward. I was forced to use my hands to brace myself but I couldn't dwell on missing out on touching Ronan because I felt his cock nudging at my hole a second later. And while he didn't just shove into me, he also gave no quarter as inch after inch of hot, rigid flesh speared into me. The burn bordered on painful but then the heat began to flare out to my limbs and I pressed back to try and take more of him into me. His flesh felt so hot inside of me that it took me several long seconds to realize why.

Ronan wasn't wearing a condom.

I didn't get a chance to say anything because Ronan bottomed out inside of me at that exact moment and I let out a hoarse groan and buried my mouth against my arm to stifle the sound. Ronan stilled and then pressed his mouth against my ear.

"I've been tested. I'm negative," he whispered. "Tell me it's okay."

I knew it wasn't the responsible answer, nor was it the answer that would keep me from losing more of myself to this man but I didn't even hesitate for a second. "Yes."

The one word was like a starter gun for Ronan because he pulled almost all the way out of me before shoving in hard and deep. A throaty moan erupted from deep inside of him as he said my name and then he slammed into me again.

CHAPTER 13

RONAN

Taking Seth without a condom was the second stupidest thing I could have done, the first being putting my hands on him yet again. And I didn't even have the justification that I was too caught up in the moment to worry about protecting Seth the way I should have. Because I'd done it deliberately. I'd seen the condom in my wallet when I'd gotten the packet of lube and I'd made the decision that I needed all of Seth before he made me walk away from him.

Worse, I needed him to have a part of me that no one else had ever had, not even Trace.

Beyond the vise-like grip Seth's ass had on my cock, his heat burned me and the feel of his smooth walls sliding over my ultra-sensitive flesh had me struggling to keep my orgasm at bay. The only man I hadn't ever used condoms with had been Trace and since he'd steadfastly refused to bottom for me, I'd had no idea what to expect when I slid into Seth without the latex barrier separating us. And anything I could have come up with would have been utterly lacking. Because being inside of Seth this way, having him bent over in total submission, his tight body cloaking me in a veil of perfection I was afraid I would never escape from, was beyond anything I could have imagined. But what was worse, and what I suspected had little to do with being bare inside of Seth, was the feeling of completeness that came over me as Seth's body cradled mine.

As physically close as we were, it didn't seem like enough so I wrapped my arm around Seth's chest and drew him up until he was flush against my body. He groaned as the position forced even more of my length inside of him and I couldn't resist taking his mouth with mine as I continued to hammer into him. With my arms wrapped around him like they were, Seth couldn't move his arms but he used his kiss to touch me instead. As badly as I'd hurt him and as angry as he was with me, he didn't hold anything back as his tongue mated with mine and his inner muscles tightened on my aching shaft as if trying to keep me inside of him.

I could feel the end drawing near as electricity began firing up my spine and I began pumping into Seth with shallow, jerky thrusts that I had no control over. Seth whimpered as his own body stiffened against me and I reached my right hand down to close around his leaking cock. The second I lowered my arm, his hands came up to grab a hold of the forearm I had wrapped around his chest. His nails dug into my skin as he shouted against my lips and his ass clamped down on my dick with so much pressure that I could barely breathe. My orgasm ripped through me as I felt Seth's hips jerk against my hand and then his come was dripping over my fingers. I yanked my mouth from Seth's as wave after wave of pleasure rocketed through me and I bit down on his shoulder, grateful that his shirt separated my teeth from his skin. I held him that way as I rutted into him over and over as each ripple of his internal muscles pulled my come from my body. The heat from my climax bathed us both and when I finally released my hold on Seth's shoulder, he slumped forward and I followed him down and let all my weight pin him to the countertop. Aftershocks kept making my body jerk and Seth would let out a little moan each time as his body twitched in response.

If I'd been a smarter man, I would have left things where they were at and just pulled free of Seth's body. But Seth's last words to me kept playing on a loop in my head and I couldn't stop myself from leaning down, putting my mouth next to his ear and saying, "We'll never be done."

Seth's whole body tightened beneath mine and I knew it wasn't because he was still enjoying the aftermath of our simultaneous orgasms. But he didn't say anything or try to push me off. He just lay there, his eyes going blank and his features loosening to the point that I saw no emotion whatsoever. I was tempted to kiss him to see if I could bring him back to me, but I was too afraid I'd find out what kissing Seth and having him not kiss me back would feel like so I didn't do it. Instead, I carefully lifted myself off of him. My cock slipped free of his body and I nearly swallowed my tongue when I watched a line of my semen drip out of him a second later. I wanted so badly to lean down and clean him up with my tongue just so I could share the proof of what he'd done to me with him, but I knew he wanted nothing more to do with me at that point. It was written in the way he held himself.

He may have wanted what had happened between us but that didn't mean he wasn't regretting it too. I hadn't really believed making love to him would change anything, but a tiny part of me had hoped he'd hear the words I couldn't say.

I tucked myself back into my pants and then reached for Seth to pull him upright but he pulled away from me the second I made contact with him. "Don't," was all he said. He ignored the semen running down his inner thigh and bent to yanks his pants up. He turned to face me but didn't look up. "You proved your point," he muttered before lifting his eyes. "But it doesn't change anything. We're done."

And with that, Seth was the one to walk away this time.

CHAPTER 14

SETH

*B*ullet tugging on the leash I was holding was what made me realize I was no longer alone. I glanced over my shoulder and cursed the shadow of disappointment that went through me at the sight of Hawke walking towards me.

In the week since I'd asked Ronan to leave, I'd spent a lot of time in this same spot – the old, weathered log on the beach at the base of the bluff my house sat on. I'd made the excuse that Bullet needed the fresh air as he recovered from his injury, but it was just another lie among many that I'd told myself. Like that I didn't miss Ronan. Or that I didn't have dreams about how right it felt to have him inside of me and that I didn't ache to feel his warm body pressed against mine. And that I didn't wonder if it was him I sensed watching me throughout the day.

I'd been surprised when Ronan actually left but also relieved. I'd always believed I'd take any piece of Ronan I could get but now that I'd had just that, it wasn't enough. It would never be enough.

Bullet began jumping up and down on his hind legs as Hawke approached and I quickly put my hand on his back to settle him down. The big dog was struggling with not being able to run loose like he wanted, but the vet had said he just needed a few more days of limited activity to give his body more time to heal. She'd also pointed out that if we'd gotten Bullet to her any later, he wouldn't have made it. I had Ronan to thank for the fact that I still had my best friend with me.

And the man standing next to me.

Hawke wasn't quite as big as Ronan but there was something about his presence that had me on edge. Like the relaxed, easy demeanor was an illusion and he could strike out at any moment. I'd suspected the man had still been watching me at Ronan's request but I hadn't actually seen him until now.

"How's he doing?" Hawke asked as he sat down next to me and ran his hands along Bullet's face. Somehow my big, powerful dog had become mush in the man's presence.

Just like with Ronan.

"He's good. He's got a couple more days of down time and then he should be good to go. Thank you for what you did for him."

Hawke merely nodded. His silence unnerved me as he stared across the dark blue waters of the Sound. My parents had built our vacation home on the top of a bluff along the southwestern part of the island and they'd bought enough of the surrounding land and waterfront so that there weren't any neighbors for miles. I'd used the remote location to my advantage in the years after they'd died, but having had Ronan here even for a few days made me realize how truly isolated my life had become.

I expected Hawke to start talking at some point but ten minutes passed, then fifteen and nothing. Bullet had dropped down to lay between us, his big head resting on Hawke's black boot.

"Is he gone?" I finally asked, since I was too worn out to try to figure out what Hawke's presence meant.

Hawke shook his head.

"I haven't seen him," I said.

"Wasn't that the idea?" Hawke asked, though his eyes remained on the water.

I didn't know how to answer that…or maybe I didn't have the courage to answer it. "Why are you still here?"

Hawke was quiet for so long that I didn't think he'd answer but then he finally looked at me. "If you could have a few more minutes with your parents, your brother, even knowing you were still going to lose them, would you want them...the minutes, I mean?"

I nodded.

"Ronan gave me that," Hawke said before shifting his gaze up and down the beach and then checking over his shoulder.

"How?" I asked.

"My wife. Ronan was working the night my wife and I came into the ER."

I saw Hawke finger the obvious burn scar on his jaw and I wondered if he even realized he was doing it.

"She would have died then and there if he hadn't done what he did. He gave me three days to say goodbye to her, to feel the warmth of her hand in mine, to hear her tell me she loved me one last time. To feel the softness of her lips before she had to be intubated. To tell her all the moments in my life that were perfect were only that way because she'd been a part of them."

The heartbreaking words caught me off guard. "I'm sorry," I whispered, my throat feeling tight as I remembered my own loss and how I would have given anything to be able to tell my parents and my brother how much I loved them one more time. "So you owe him?" I finally ventured.

Hawke shook his head. "No, not anymore."

I didn't know what to make of the cryptic statement. Bullet sat up and pressed his nose against my hand and I realized he'd sensed my building stress. "I'll never be enough for him," I whispered as I let my gaze fall to the black and brown fur on the top of Bullet's head. It was ridiculous to admit my fear to a virtual stranger, but the need to understand Ronan's behavior was overriding my common sense. I'd been so sure after the night that Ronan had made love to me for the first time that he saw me as something more...as someone apart from Trace's brother. And last week he'd told me we wouldn't ever be done even though he was the one who'd walked away from me the morning after our first night together.

I felt the thickness in my throat growing as Hawke didn't respond, but just as I was about to get up to escape the humiliation, he spoke. "Seth, there's going to come a day when you learn the truth about what happened to your brother."

My hand stilled on Bullet's head and I snapped my eyes up to Hawke who was watching me intently. I opened my mouth to ask the obvious question but he cut me off with a shake of his head. "As hard as it's going to be to hear about what was done to him, just remember that Ronan is the one who needs you now."

I shook my head as Hawke rose and dropped a hand on my shoulder before stepping over the log and walking away. I didn't bother chasing after him because I was too caught up in what he'd said. I felt my stomach roll violently.

"Hawke!" I called, but I didn't look at him to see if he stopped. "Where is he?"

"The Water's Edge Motel. Room 127."

I may have nodded in response; I wasn't really sure. I wanted to go running to that motel and demand Ronan tell me what Hawke was talking about but Hawke's words kept repeating themselves in my head.

Ronan is the one who needs you now.

Had the military lied to me? They'd said Trace had been killed by friendly fire during a training exercise. I'd never even thought to question them – why the hell would I? But if they had lied, why hadn't Ronan told me the truth?

Another sick feeling went through me.

He wouldn't have told me if the truth was something he didn't think I could handle. Which meant it was really bad.

Bullet began nudging me in earnest and I realized I'd gotten so worked up that I was nearing a panic attack. I sucked in several deep breaths and focused on one of the mountain peaks across the water. I carefully worked my eyes to the right, counting each peak in turn until I felt my fear subside.

Ronan is the one who needs you now.

I didn't know what that meant but I knew Hawke was telling the truth. And I finally realized that the Ronan I'd known hadn't been lost to me simply because Trace had been taken from him...it was how he'd been taken that had changed everything.

But if I wanted answers, it meant I had to do what I promised myself I wouldn't. I had to see Ronan again.

∽

It took several long seconds for me to get up the nerve to rap my knuckles on the motel room door. When Ronan opened it, I couldn't say what surprised me more – his appearance or the gun he was holding loosely against his leg.

I'd never seen Ronan in anything other than a suit and on the rare occasion, jeans, so to see him in a pair of sweats and a simple white T-shirt caught me off guard. But it was the smudges under his eyes and the bleakness in his gaze that had me wishing more than ever that I had the right to touch him.

"Can I come in?" I asked, not liking how shaky my voice sounded.

Ronan studied me for a long moment and then finally opened the door wider. The room was dark because the curtains were drawn despite it being early afternoon. My conversation with Hawke the day before had left me too rattled to go see Ronan last night and I'd ended up sleeping in this morning after tossing and turning all night. I'd told work I wouldn't be in today and I hadn't even bothered trying to work from home because I was too distracted.

From the condition of the motel room, it seemed like Ronan hadn't been faring much better than me. I supposed it wasn't unusual for the bed to be unmade but the half empty bottle of scotch sitting on the nightstand definitely wasn't the norm. In all the time I'd known Ronan, I'd seen him drink on only the rarest of occasions and always in moderation. I glanced over my shoulder as Ronan closed the door, drenching the room in darkness. I was glad when he flicked on the floor lamp near the door because it gave me a chance to study him. He had yet to say anything and he hadn't put the gun down. That bothered me...a lot. Not because I believed him to be a danger to me, but because I couldn't figure out why he had it out in the first place.

Ronan's eyes held mine for a moment but his expression was unreadable and after what seemed an unnaturally long time, he finally went to the chair by the table and tucked the gun into the shoulder holster that was draped over the back of it. Once the gun was put away, I was surprised to see the hand he'd been holding it with start to flex and release several times before the pad of each finger began tapping rhythmically against the thumb.

The nervous gesture hit me hard and I actually had to sit down on the end of the bed as Hawke's words went through me again. My intent when I'd come here had been to demand answers about what had really happened to Trace but seeing Ronan so broken had me hesitating. I nearly shook my head when things finally clicked into place for me. I'd wanted to prove to Ronan that I could be the man he needed instead of the boy he remembered. But maybe what he needed – what he'd always needed since the day he'd lost Trace – was the same thing I'd needed after my parents had died…someone to trust, someone to hold on to when the pain became too much.

I'd never really realized that I'd spent these last few years making it all about me and what I'd needed. I'd wanted to lean on him after the loss of Trace but I'd never considered that he might need someone too. I'd wanted to draw from his strength but I'd never offered mine. I'd wanted to be the man he desired instead of considering the fact that he might need something else…a friend. And in that moment I knew I wouldn't be demanding answers. I wouldn't be demanding anything anymore. If Ronan needed to protect me from an evil I wasn't so sure existed, so be it. If he needed to slake his physical need on me, I'd offer myself willingly and find a way to live with the ramifications. If it meant I would never be able to touch him the way I wanted to, I'd find other ways to show him I was there.

I glanced at Ronan and saw that at some point, he'd sat down in the chair his shoulder holster was draped over. As usual, I couldn't tell what he was thinking and his continued silence meant whatever happened next would fall on me. I dropped my eyes to my clenched fingers and realized I had the same strange, anxious ticks that Ronan did.

"I want you to come home," I finally said.

Ronan took a long time to respond so I just sat there and waited. He finally said, "You said-"

"You were right. We'll never really be done," I interrupted. "I don't want us to be. I want us to be what we should have been after we lost Trace." I looked up at him. "Friends," I whispered. "I want us to be friends."

I held Ronan's gaze until the tightness in my belly became too much and then I lowered my eyes again. "If you think there might be a threat against me then keep me safe. Do it for Trace, for me…I don't care. Just come home."

"Why?" Ronan asked, his voice sounding uneven.

I swallowed hard. "Because I don't want the only one who cares whether I come home each night to be my dog," I whispered. The admission sucked at my insides but I managed to keep the tears at bay. But when I heard Ronan shift in his chair and a moment later heavy fingers sifted through my hair, I feared I wouldn't be able to keep it together.

I expected Ronan to tell me he cared about me but he surprised me when he leaned down and pressed his lips against the top of my head. "Me too…except I don't even have a dog."

I let out a chuckle and then felt my whole body relax as Ronan pulled me to my feet and wrapped his arms around me. My hands were pressed against his chest but as badly as I wanted to slide them up to wrap around his neck, I managed to keep them where they were.

Friends with Ronan…just friends. Fuck, how the hell was I going to pull this off?

CHAPTER 15

RONAN

"Wow, you are a really terrible driver," I said as I studied the tight grip Seth had on the steering wheel he was hunched over.

"What? No I'm not," Seth responded in irritation as he checked his rearview mirror for what had to be the twentieth time in the last minute.

"You're going five miles under the speed limit and I'm waiting for the hunchback to appear on your back any second now. And if you hold on to that steering wheel any tighter, they may need the jaws of life to pry it from your fingers."

Seth snorted but he did straighten somewhat and eased up on his stranglehold on the wheel. I'd been surprised when Seth agreed to let me go with him to work and to my amazement, he hadn't asked me why. He'd done a lot of things that had surprised me since he'd shown up at the motel the day before. That in itself had been a shock I still couldn't get over.

I'd finally forced myself to walk away from Seth after I'd made love to him in his kitchen a week earlier but I hadn't been able to walk away completely. It would have been easier to bring out another guy to work with Hawke to provide round the clock security for Seth without him knowing it, but just the idea of actually leaving Seth all together had made my chest hurt in a way that I couldn't explain. So I'd resorted to my old habit of watching him from afar and I'd spent my days following him using the tracker I'd planted on his car. And I'd spent my nights tossing and turning as I remembered the feel of Seth beneath me, surrounding me in a way that I was coming to fear that only he could. On the few occasions I'd actually managed to fall asleep, I kept hearing Seth's broken voice telling me not to come back.

That's when I'd gone in search of the alcohol. It was the only thing that gave me any measure of peace but it never lasted long. Maybe if I'd been willing to give up my monitoring of Seth all together, I could have drowned myself completely with the mind-numbing liquid, but I'd been too afraid that something would happen to Seth and I wouldn't be there to protect him.

Like I hadn't been able to protect Trace.

I'd felt only shame yesterday when Seth had spied the alcohol on my nightstand, even though I had no reason to since Seth didn't know anything about my history with it. The only other time I'd relied on alcohol to numb me was in the weeks following Trace's death and I'd gone a step further and made it part of a lethal combination with the painkillers the doctors had prescribed after I was discharged. Hawke was the only one who'd seen me in that time and I suspected he'd noticed my downward spiral in the last several days as he and I met up to switch shifts watching Seth. He'd finally told me to go back to the motel a couple days ago to get some rest when I'd been too out of it to do Seth any good if something were to happen. I had no doubt that Hawke was well aware that my lack of sleep wasn't the only thing that had me bleary eyed and confused. I'd managed to sober up somewhat before Seth's arrival, but only because I'd just woken up a half an hour earlier and hadn't had the chance to lose myself in my bottle again.

My negative relationship with alcohol had been something I'd struggled with my entire life, though I hadn't been the one with the problem. While I'd always hesitated to label my father an alcoholic, there was no doubt that's what he'd been. Of course, there hadn't been anyone around to ask if he'd always been that way since my mother had died giving birth to me and the aunt who'd raised me for the first few years of my life had been killed in a car accident just before I'd turned five. I'd been too young to understand the dynamics of my family but I'd learned very quickly the penalty for referring to the woman who'd raised me as "Mommy."

It was the first of many times that my father took his fury at my perceived role in my own mother's death out on me. But as the years passed, his rage turned into something else…something that often had me missing the beatings. Because those bruises had healed…the ones he'd inflicted on my soul hadn't.

"You okay?"

Seth's question knocked me out of the past. "Yeah, why?" I asked as I glanced at him. His eyes fell to my hands and I realized I'd reverted to my habit of tapping my fingers together. I had no idea at what age I'd started doing it but to this day, it was a vice I just couldn't shake, mostly because I never even realized I was doing it. It had driven my father crazy but no amount of slaps or punches had broken me of the habit.

"Yeah," I said as I separated my hands and rested one of my arms on the armrest between me and Seth. "Just wishing I'd had time to grab some coffee," I said lamely, hoping the excuse would satisfy him.

"I told you we had to leave at five sharp to make it to the terminal in time," Seth murmured. "They have coffee on the ferry," he added, his voice sounding lighter than it had since I'd shown up over a week ago.

The idea of being friends with Seth was such a foreign and seemingly absurd concept to me considering everything that had happened between us, but in the twelve hours since I'd moved back into the guest room, I'd seen a different side of Seth. Sure, there was the initial awkwardness between us when I'd joined him for dinner, but then he'd starting talking to me about inconsequential things and I'd felt myself relaxing once I realized he wasn't asking me about anything more personal than what types of movies I liked and if I'd read the latest book in a detective series that his favorite author had written. When I'd said I hadn't, he'd gone on and on about the speculation over what had happened to the main character who'd been stuffed in the trunk of a car that went over a cliff at the end of the most recent book. He'd become so animated in telling me all about Detective Nick Archer and his troubles, that I'd ignored what remained of my dinner and just sat back in my chair to watch his excited hand gestures as he spoke.

The awkwardness had returned after dinner was finished and there'd been a point while we were cleaning up the dishes that I'd caught Seth looking at the kitchen island almost longingly, as if remembering what we'd done against it just one short week ago, but the moment had passed quickly when he'd realized I was watching him. He'd made an excuse about needing to catch up on some work and I'd gone up to my room to take a shower and call Mav to see how Daisy was settling in. Just before ten o'clock, Seth had knocked on my door. His pale skin had flushed with color when he spied my belt draped over the same chair he'd taken it from the night we'd made love for the first time and it had taken everything in me not to drag him to me at that point. With a mumbled explanation that he was heading to bed, he'd handed me the book he'd been holding and told me I should check it out if I was interested and then he was gone. The book was the first one in the series he'd talked so excitedly about at dinner and I'd ended up cracking it open a few minutes later and finally forced myself to put it down just before two in the morning when I could no longer keep my eyes open. My grumpiness as I'd stumbled into the kitchen a couple hours later was met with a wide, knowing smile and a declaration that there was no time for coffee and Seth didn't have any travel mugs.

"Hey," Seth said again and then he briefly nudged my arm where it was resting on the armrest with his elbow. "First cup is on me." I felt my heart constrict painfully in my chest at the sight of his smile but I managed a nod. Seth was taking this friends thing to heart but all I wanted to do was to tell him to turn the car around and take us home so I could get him beneath me again.

"You told the vet you were going to New York," I managed to say in a desperate effort to distract myself from my thoughts.

"Um, yeah. Stan...that's my dad's business partner, well, my business partner now – he set up a meeting with another shipping firm that's interested in buying our company."

"You're selling?" I asked in surprise. "I thought you wanted to run the business."

Seth shrugged his shoulders. "I do but Stan convinced me to hear them out – he says they're offering a lot and Dad's company has been struggling since he..."

I waited quietly as Seth pulled himself together. As much as I would have liked to take his hand in mine, it wasn't an option.

"This company is the industry leader and Stan says they'll make sure no one loses their jobs. That was always real important to my dad...he thought of the people who worked for him as family, you know?"

Seth glanced at me and I nodded. I'd never met more kind-hearted people than Fred and Corrine Nichols. They'd welcomed me with open arms from the second Trace and I had walked in the door and I'd been overwhelmed that not only would I not be judged for my sexual orientation despite their own son being gay, but that they weren't looking down on me for being from humbler roots than Trace. Yes, I had achieved a certain level of success in my career but I was a blue collar guy through and through, despite my attempts to appear otherwise.

"Yeah, I know," I said reassuringly. "You'll do what's best for the company, Seth. Everyone knows that."

The words seemed to soothe Seth because he visibly relaxed before continuing. "I'm thinking about seeing if they might be interested in a partnership instead. They have a really strong presence in Europe and the Middle East but our company has had more success with the Asian and South American markets."

I listened as Seth explained the intricacies of the business and I couldn't help but admire how much he knew for his young age and limited hands-on experience. I'd known Seth was smart but I was realizing it was another thing I'd underestimated about him. And he'd clearly inherited his father's passion and work ethic, something Trace had never managed to pick up. From the time he was a kid, all Trace had ever wanted was to join the military. And while he'd been intensely devoted to it and, more often than not, it had been his sole focus, he'd consistently struggled to commit himself to anything beyond the life he'd built for himself. It was the reason he'd left Seth in the care of their grandmother rather than leave the military to take care of Seth himself – because he couldn't see himself in any other role...not wouldn't, couldn't. I'd struggled with Trace's selfish choice but as I'd thought back to my own father, I'd realized that in some strange way, maybe Trace's decision had been the right one. I'd figured maybe it had been better that Seth hadn't had to suffer his brother's resentment.

That was before I knew the truth about how much Seth had suffered during the home invasion that killed his parents. Or that he'd been left in the care of a woman on a spiraling mental decline.

By the time we arrived at the ferry terminal, there was already a line but Seth had timed it perfectly and the line of cars began moving onto the ferry minutes later. True to his word, Seth bought me a cup of coffee and we stood at the railing near the front of the slow moving ferry and watched the mainland come into sight as the sun began its morning ascent. We didn't speak, but I couldn't help but notice how right it felt to be standing there next to Seth. It would have been so natural to move just a little bit closer to him so our bodies were touching but I managed to stay where I was.

Friends.

Something I desperately needed but wasn't anywhere near what I wanted to be with this man. But it was all I could give him. And it was all I could take from him.

Seth's driving was even worse once we got off the ferry and into heavier traffic but I held my tongue. As mentally mature as Seth was and as grown up (and hot) as he looked in his crisp navy business suit, there were a lot of areas of life that he'd been deprived of any kind of normalcy and driving was one of them. And it had to be made a hundred times worse by the anxiety he felt about leaving the safety of his home. It wasn't until he'd pulled his car into his space in the parking garage of his building that he relaxed, but only marginally. It was tough to see Seth struggle with tasks that everyone else, myself included, took for granted and part of me felt a shimmer of anger at Trace for him choosing his own needs over his brother's. As much as I'd loved Trace, I'd struggled to accept his inability to see beyond his own needs. Since I'd been more than happy to not have to share too much about my own past, Trace's lack of sensitivity hadn't bothered me overly much, but knowing the pain his choices had caused his younger brother was hard to stomach.

As we rode the elevator to the office, I glanced at Seth and noticed a slight tremor in his frame. But as soon as the door opened, he pasted a slightly too big smile on his mouth and began greeting people as he made his way through a set of glass doors. The receptionist greeted him and it was strange to hear her referring to him as Mr. Nichols.

It took less than a minute to reach Seth's office but once he'd closed the door behind us, his whole body seemed to sag in relief. A pang of guilt went through me at my part in this – if I hadn't been blinded by my own grief and hatred, I would have been able to stop Seth from suffering such an extreme level of anxiety brought on just by merely being in the presence of less than a handful of people. Since it was still relatively early in the morning and he was the boss, I presumed his day would only get harder as he had to deal with more and more people.

"Um, you can work over there if you want," Seth said as he motioned to a small round table in the corner of the spacious office. "I'll get you the password for the wireless network," he said uneasily as he moved past me. I wondered if his nervousness had to do with the remnants of his agitation or if it was because we were once again enclosed in a small space together. Not that Seth's office was all that small, but somehow it seemed like no room we were ever in together was big enough to lessen the heat that simmered between us. Even as electric as my chemistry with Trace had been, it was never as all-consuming as this. Guilt went through me at the thought. I'd loved

Trace with everything I was but I couldn't deny my almost crippling need for Seth.

Comparing the two men was wreaking havoc on my already worn out mind so I went to the table and dug my laptop out of the small leather bag Trace had given to me years earlier on my birthday – my first birthday with him and the first gift I'd gotten in a long time. Until I'd spent Christmas with Trace's family...then the gifts had flowed like water. A then thirteen-year-old Seth had given me a beautiful ball point pen that he'd had engraved with my name. He'd been embarrassed by the low cost, low quality item as compared to the expensive watch Trace had given me but I'd been touched by the gesture. I'd asked Trace to return the watch since I rarely wore one. I still had the pen Seth had given me.

"Here you go," Seth said as he came up to me and put a sticky note down on the table with the wireless password on it. "Um, I have a meeting at nine – it'll take a couple of hours. Then I was going to go to lunch. Did you...did you want to come with me for that? For lunch, I mean?"

"Yeah, I would, if that's okay."

Seth hesitated and then nodded. "You should know that I don't actually go to lunch-"

"Seth," I interrupted. "I know where you go."

"What?" Seth said in confusion.

I'd debated about telling Seth the truth about the extent of my surveillance of him but decided I'd have to risk his anger. He deserved much more than that for the olive branch he'd extended yesterday.

"Have you been following me?" he asked.

I nodded. He stepped back and I grabbed his wrist in case he was considering moving away from me. "Sit, please," I said as I pushed the chair next to mine back from the table with my foot. He paused and then finally sat and I felt a wave of relief wash through my body.

"Seth, I can't explain this feeling I have that something's not right. I hope to God I'm wrong, I really do. But I can't risk it if I'm not. And you were so angry with me for coming back into your life so suddenly...for knowing I'd been watching you all this time..." I shook my head. "I'm not sorry I did it but I am sorry that I didn't tell you sooner."

Seth swallowed hard a couple of times and then said, "I never saw you."

"I put a tracking device on your car."

Wariness crept into Seth's gaze but then he nodded. "Is that all?"

Fuck.

"No. I also went to see your old attorney."

I hadn't realized I was still holding on to Seth until he actually pulled free of my hold. "Ronan-"

"I needed answers that I knew you wouldn't give me. I also had someone look into Barry before he attacked you. I...I didn't like the way he looked at you...touched you."

Seth was quiet for a long time. "No more lies, okay, Ronan?" he finally said. "We can't do this if you're going to lie to me."

I nodded in understanding. There were things I could never tell him, not even if it meant losing him but I could give him most of the truth.

"I know about the inheritance," I admitted. "Your lawyer let it slip by accident."

Seth began chewing on his upper lip nervously.

"Seth, I can't get it all back to you right away but I've got a good chunk of it available – I just need to talk to my bank about moving it to your account."

I was startled when Seth suddenly leaned forward and placed his hand over mine where it was resting on the table. His skin felt warm against mine and sparks shot up my arm. I waited for the tingling to change into something far less pleasant, but to my surprise, the electricity kept building and I wanted to moan as my cock reacted to the pleasurable sensation. But just as quickly as he'd touched me, Seth seemed to remember himself and he jerked his hand back. I was still struggling with my own reaction so I barely heard his whispered "sorry."

Seth tucked his hand in his lap and said, "Trace told me he was going to propose to you. It was a couple days before he left to go back to Afghanistan. I'd been discharged from the hospital a few weeks earlier and my grandmother was in the process of moving down from Bellingham to come live with me." Seth lifted his eyes from where he'd been studying his hands. "That money is yours Ronan. Just because Trace didn't tell Mr. Brighton that himself doesn't mean he didn't want you to have the money...you know how he was about stuff like that."

I did know. Trace was the kind of guy who'd felt like he was untouchable. Even the prospect of his own mortality hadn't changed that.

"He wanted to spend the rest of his life with you, Ronan. I'm so sorry that you didn't get to have that but he would have wanted you to be taken care of."

I managed a nod but inside I was struggling. And not just at Seth's reminder of what I'd lost but at the realization of what I still had. Even with all that had been taken from him at the tender age of fourteen, Seth had been looking out for me...*he'd* been worried about *me*. And even after admitting I'd been trailing him and asking questions about him behind his back, Seth was still looking out for me by making sure I knew how much Trace had wanted to be with me.

I was reaching for Seth before I could think better of it but the sound of Seth's office door opening stopped me. I barely remembered not to reach for my gun.

"Oh, I'm sorry, Seth. I didn't know you were in a meeting," the older man said as he put up a hand to straighten his already straight tie.

"It's okay, Stan. Come on in," Seth said as he stood. "I'm not sure you two ever met but I'm sure my dad mentioned him to you. This is Ronan Grisham, Trace's fiancé."

Hearing Seth call me that was strange but I was saved from having to examine the unexpected feelings that came with his words because Stan was striding across the room, his tall, thin body suddenly relaxing. He reached out his hand and shook mine fervently. "We were all so terribly saddened to hear about Trace," he said solemnly. "My condolences for your loss."

"Thank you," I responded. Since the members of Trace's family were the only ones who'd known about my relationship with Trace, it felt odd for a virtual stranger to be extending what I knew was a common courtesy.

"I understand you're a surgeon," Stan suddenly said. "Where are you practicing?"

"Stan," Seth interrupted before I could even try to consider how to answer. "Was there something you needed?"

I stopped listening as Stan and Seth began speaking about some sales figures for their meeting and went back to the small table and got my computer going. The shitty, off-balance feeling was back and for once, I was actually looking forward to going through the notes Daisy and Mav had sent me about potential marks. It was a sad commentary of what my life had become that I'd rather immerse myself in the business of death rather than face the difficulties of trying to accept who I'd been.

"Sorry about that," Seth said as he returned to the chair next to me a few minutes later.

"It's no problem," I muttered. I knew I was being an ungrateful asshole considering what Seth had said to me before Stan's untimely arrival, but I'd come too close to saying something to Seth that would have done more harm than good. He wanted to be friends. I needed to remember that.

But Seth must have sensed something was off because he began shifting nervously as he waited for me to say something else – probably to finish the conversation we'd been having. He finally stood, his jaw tight and began moving away from me but I grabbed his wrist to stop him. "Thank you," I managed to say, though I didn't look up from my computer.

Seth didn't say anything and he didn't linger. But as I opened my hand to release his wrist, I felt his fingers stroke over my palm briefly just before he walked away.

CHAPTER 16

SETH

I ended up letting Ronan drive to my old house on Mercer Island since I was still on edge from the rough morning I'd had. Somehow the information that I was meeting with our biggest competitor in New York to discuss a possible buyout had gotten out, and I'd spent the morning fielding phone calls from worried employees and one very angry union president. To make matters worse, Stan had gone home sick so I'd been on my own. I'd debated whether I should even take the time to make my daily run to the house that played a starring role in my darkest of nightmares, but I'd decided the sooner I could come to terms with the events that had unfolded there, the sooner I could be rid of one of the last links to one of the worst days of my life.

"You did really great this morning," Ronan said and I glanced over at him. His eyes kept shifting to me as he drove. Ronan had been in my office when the news had broken but after the first couple of phone calls, I'd actually forgotten about him.

"Thanks," I murmured. "I'm not sure they believed me," I said.

"Your employees?"

I nodded. "So many of them worked for my dad…I could hear it in their voices, you know?"

"Hear what?"

"The disappointment...like I was letting them down." I turned to look out the window. "Like I was letting *him* down."

I felt Ronan's hand close over mine where it was laying on the middle arm rest. "He'd be proud, Seth. The way you handled yourself...they'd all be proud."

I felt tears stinging the backs of my eyes but I managed to keep them at bay. I'd always hoped that wherever my parents and Trace were, they'd approve of the life I was leading and the choices I'd made. But somehow hearing the confirmation from Ronan was more comforting than just hoping for it on my own.

I'd had an idyllic childhood and I'd been smart enough to know it. While my parents had been more than just "well off," they hadn't let our family's upper class status and wealth go to Trace's and my heads. We'd had chores just like any other kids our age and when Trace wanted his own car when he turned sixteen, he'd had to pay for it and the insurance himself. And that was after he'd had to produce a stellar report card. I hadn't been old enough to worry about a car, but I'd spent nearly all the money I'd saved from chores and doing odd jobs for the neighbors on books.

Trace and I had been polar opposites from the get go but somehow that and our ten-year age difference didn't affect the bond we'd shared. Trace was the classic high-energy extrovert who excelled at athletics and earned every popularity title known to man. I'd only been eight when he'd come out to our parents at the age of eighteen, so I hadn't understood the struggle he'd been going through from the time he'd turned fourteen and figured out he was gay. And while he hadn't been around much as I'd struggled with my own sexuality, I had no doubt that the risk he'd taken in telling our parents had paved the way for me, because my mother had actually hugged me when I mustered enough courage to tell my parents the truth one night over dinner when I was twelve. My father had given me a hearty slap on the back, said it was about time and asked me to pass the peas.

My brother had also been my protector from the time my parents brought me home from the hospital and told him he needed to look out for his little brother. Trace had taken their words to heart and had spent the next six months sleeping on the floor next to my crib so that he would be there if I needed him. And while we'd had our tussles as we'd grown older, I'd known Trace would always be there for me. But there was one love I couldn't compete with and it wasn't Ronan. Trace's love for the military held no equal and I'd finally understood that when I'd gone with my parents to Trace's graduation from basic training. I'd never seen my brother more alive and in his element and I'd been strangely envious because I'd feared I'd never be a part of something like that.

Like Trace, I'd excelled in school but unlike him, I'd struggled to find my place in the various social circles that ran rampant in the private school I'd attended. I'd ended up escaping into my books more often than not and could count on one hand how many friends I had managed to scrape together. But where Trace was always on the go, I'd relished staying home and spending time with both my parents. My mother had been a music teacher so I'd spent many hours learning various instruments, though it never became a true passion for me like it had been for her. My father had often worked long hours but weekends were our thing and he'd often taken me boating on all the different lakes the region had to offer. As I'd gotten older, I'd started asking him questions about his work and that had turned into dreams of one day standing side by side with him running the company. I'd even spent the summer before they'd died working at my father's office. I hadn't done much more than get coffee and perform basic administrative tasks like sorting the mail and filing, but it had given me a chance to see my father in action. I'd idolized him in every sense of the word.

And now I was him...or I was trying to be anyway. But as much as I'd hoped to feel that thing that Trace had felt when he'd joined the military, it hadn't happened yet. My teachers and Stan said I had a head for business but I still felt like I was playing a role...like I was trying to fill shoes that maybe weren't meant to be filled.

I glanced at Ronan whose hand was still covering mine. "How did you know you wanted to be a doctor?"

Ronan's grip on me tightened before he released me and I instantly regretted the question. As much as I wanted us to be friends, I needed to remember that we weren't those kinds of friends. We were friends with boundaries…a lot of boundaries, if the tight look on Ronan's face was anything to go by.

"Sorry," I mumbled before turning my attention back out the window.

"I didn't know," Ronan said quietly. I risked looking at him as he spoke. "Not at first. I enrolled in medical school for someone else."

I knew next to nothing about Ronan's past and I could tell from the hard set of his jaw that he likely would prefer it that way. But I wanted desperately to know more so I said, "Who?"

Ronan swallowed hard. "My father."

I would have liked to explore that revelation more but I sensed it was a topic that was off limits. "But you fell in love with it?"

The tension eased from Ronan and he nodded. Finally, safer ground.

"Where did you go to school?"

"Stanford."

We were back to the one word answers but I didn't care. He was still talking. "Wow, I had no idea you were a geek," I said with a smile.

Ronan glanced at me in surprise. "What?"

"Stanford…that's like Ivy League shit, right?"

I felt my body go all warm when Ronan chuckled. "Actually, no."

"Well, it should be."

Ronan didn't respond but I didn't miss the small smile that graced his lips and actually stayed there. "So did you do anything bad while you were in school?"

"What do you mean?"

I shifted in my seat so I could see his reactions better. "Pranks, practical jokes, that sort of thing."

Ronan didn't say anything but I laughed when I saw his jaw tick. "You did!"

An even wider smile spread across his mouth and I wanted to lean in and kiss him. "Tell me."

He glanced at me and then finally said, "One of my classmates and I rigged a cadaver to move. Scared the shit out of the guy who was about to cut into it."

"No," I whispered in horror. "What else?"

"Nothing. That one act of rebellion almost got me expelled so I walked the straight and narrow after that."

"So what, you were a goody two-shoes?" I asked in surprise.

"Does anyone even say that anymore?" Ronan teased. I was so caught off guard by the jab and the grin on his face that I didn't realize the car had stopped moving until he turned to face me. "We're here," he said gently and then motioned behind me. I turned and sure enough, we were sitting in the driveway of my old house. The anxiety was instantaneous and I was glad when Ronan covered my hand with his again.

The home where my parents had chosen to live during the week was a sedate colonial that looked like countless other homes in middle class neighborhoods, but it sat on a large lot that had a great view of the water and beautifully landscaped gardens that my mother had spent years getting just right. At nearly ten thousand square feet, the gothic Tudor style house on Whidbey Island dwarfed this house and no expense had been spared in designing it. But as much as I'd always liked our vacation home, it was the relatively small, four-bedroom house with the black shutters and simple window boxes that had always felt like home to me...until it hadn't.

"Do you want to go?" Ronan asked.

Yes.

I shook my head. "No. I just need a minute."

Ronan fell silent but he didn't release my hand which I was grateful for since I wasn't sure if I'd be able to actually let him go at that moment. I wasn't sure how long we sat there for but when I heard someone shouting from across the street, I nearly jumped out of my skin.

"It's just some guys working on the roof across the street," Ronan said gently.

I nodded but I couldn't stop the panic that started to overtake me.

"Seth, look at me," Ronan ordered and then his hands were on my face. "Take a breath and hold it," he ordered.

I did as he said but couldn't manage to hold it. "Try again," Ronan urged.

I swallowed hard and then sucked in a breath. It seemed like forever before Ronan told me to release it and then he was telling me to do it again. I did it at least a dozen times before Ronan told me to stop and I was surprised to find it easier to breathe again.

"How long have you been coming here?" Ronan asked.

"Not long," I admitted. "I started going into the office about a month ago. The choice to come out here was an impulse…I hadn't seen it since that night."

"Have you gone inside?"

I shook my head. "I haven't been able to get out of the car."

Ronan nodded in understanding. "Are you hoping to move back here someday?"

"No," I said adamantly. "Never."

"Then why not just sell it?"

I'd asked myself that same question a thousand times. Even Barry, who I'd expected would have encouraged me to slay my demons before getting rid of the house, had said it would be a mistake to come back here.

"I…I need to let it go first, you know? If I don't…"

"You're afraid you'll only remember it the way it was that night."

I nodded. "So many good things happened in this house. But it's hard to remember them."

"There's no rush, Seth. It'll happen when you're ready."

I dropped my eyes. "It's been six years, Ronan. I need it to be over."

I could feel Ronan's eyes on me for a long time and then he released my hand. But instead of starting up the car, he got out and walked around to my side and opened the door. He took my hand and linked our fingers together. "Then let's do this."

CHAPTER 17

RONAN

Seth's hand was clammy and cold in mine and part of me wanted to turn around and lead him back to the car so he wouldn't have to do this. But the desperation in his voice and knowing how long the home he'd once loved had tormented him for had me steeling myself to face whatever struggle Seth would have to go through so he could end this. Although I was in front of Seth, I made sure not to force him forward and when we finally reached the front door, I handed him the car keys. I waited patiently as he sucked in a deep breath and took the keys and then searched through them until he found the house key. It took him a few seconds to get the key into the lock but then he froze. His whole body was stiff with tension and he was shaking violently.

I put my hand on the back of his neck and leaned down to put my face next to his. "I'm right here," I whispered. "You can do this." I held myself there until Seth closed his eyes and nodded. He took a deep breath and turned the key and I released him as he pushed the door open. We were greeted with a dank, stale smell and the house was completely dark since all the curtains were drawn. Seth's hand sought out mine again and I gladly took it and followed him inside. I found a light switch near the front door and flipped it on and was relieved to see the power was on because light flooded the darkness. We were standing in the front foyer and the first thing I noticed was a small stack of mail sitting on a side table. Next to the mail was a set of keys and a handful of change. It looked suspiciously like someone had emptied his or her pockets as they were coming in the door. Seth's father probably.

I had only been to the Mercer Island house a couple of times but I remembered enough of the layout to determine that the stairs in front of us led to the second floor where all the bedrooms were. The living room and dining room were off to the left and the kitchen was to the right. The rooms on the lower floor were connected in a way that they formed a complete circle when you added in the front parlor. I wasn't sure where the attack had happened so I didn't know what to expect when Seth led me to the left. But within seconds, I had my answer because the living room was a disaster. Debris littered the floor and there was black powder covering many of the surfaces – it took me a moment to realize it was the powder crime scene investigation units used to look for fingerprints. The couch and chair were upright but the cushions were slashed. The glass in the coffee table had been shattered and lay all over the expensive oriental rug beneath it. All of the artwork and pictures that I remembered as having covered the walls were lying strewn on the floor and I realized the intruders had likely pulled them off in search of the supposed safe they thought Seth's father had.

Seth had frozen next to me as we entered the living room but his eyes were focused on one spot. At first I thought he might be looking at the couch but when I moved to the right just a little bit to get a better view, I saw what looked like gauze lying on the floor. I tightened my hold on Seth's hand and gently pulled him forward so I could get a better look. As soon as I walked past the couch, I realized why Seth had gotten stuck where he'd stood.

I'd been right that the white stuff was gauze. But there were a lot of other items too and most of them were covered in blood. Discarded bandaging, latex gloves and what looked like a blood soaked shirt littered the floor. A pool of dried blood that was nearly black stained the carpet and there was an even bigger one a couple feet away. I swallowed hard as I realized I was looking at the spot Seth had been tortured and stabbed and where the paramedics had fought to save his life. Which meant the bigger stain of blood had belonged to Seth's father.

"They cut his throat," I heard Seth whisper next to me.

I closed my eyes to try to hold back the tears that threatened to fall. I'd seen my fair share of horrible things but knowing the suffering Seth and his parents had endured made me want to throw up. I instantly felt like I was back in the darkened alley between the two storage buildings at the base Trace and I had been stationed at. An image of Trace's blood stained-face assailed me but I forced it away and turned my attention on Seth.

He was deathly pale and his breathing was rapidly increasing. I used my free hand to check the pulse on his hand that was still gripping mine and felt it thrumming rapidly. Seth's gaze was stuck on the horrific scene in front of us so I stepped in front of him to block his view and gently grabbed his face and forced his attention on me. "Seth, tell me something good that happened here."

"What?" Seth asked in confusion.

"Tell me a good memory you have of this room."

Seth hesitated and then nodded slightly. "Um…Christmas. We'd always put the tree over there," he said as he motioned to one corner of the room.

"Was there one that stood out?" I asked as I stroked his skin with my thumbs.

A deep breath rattled through Seth's lungs and I felt him relax marginally. "When I was eight. We always opened presents on Christmas eve. My parents gave me this really elaborate racetrack with all these loops and stuff but they said it was too complicated to set up that night and I could play with it the next day. I was so excited that I couldn't sleep, so I got up and came down here to try and put it together myself but I didn't know how. Trace came down because he heard me messing around. He…he helped me set it up and we played on it for the rest of the night." Seth managed a smile. "It was one of the best nights of my life."

I smiled. "He was a good big brother, wasn't he?"

Seth nodded.

And I realized it was true. Even though I hadn't agreed with the choices Trace had made after his parents were killed and I hadn't liked how he'd teased Seth over his crush on me when he was a kid, he'd loved Seth and he'd looked out for him.

"What else?" I asked as I gently turned Seth away from the couch.

"The piano," Seth said with a nod at the baby grand piano near the window.

"Is that where your Mom taught you to play?"

Another nod. "But I liked listening to her play more than anything else."

"I remember," I said. "She was amazing. But you know what I remember about this room?"

"What?" Seth asked shakily.

"You at that piano with your mom. You did a duet…it was incredible."

Seth nodded with a smile. "Handel's Passacaglia. I kept messing up."

"I couldn't tell," I said as I led Seth from the room. But as much as I would have liked to take him right out the front door, I knew he wasn't done doing what he needed to do. We ended up in the kitchen which wasn't as torn up.

"What about in here?"

"Mom cooking," he said. "She was terrible at it," he added.

I laughed. "I thought I was the only one who noticed."

Seth shook his head. "None of us could bear to tell her because she always tried so hard. Dad actually bribed Bonita – that was our housekeeper – to cook some dishes in secret for us so we could hide them in the freezer and pop them into the microwave after Mom went to bed."

"She never found out?" I said. We were nearing the dining room so I knew we'd be in view of the living room again.

"No. We had a close call once. Dad and I were standing over the sink eating some chicken casserole Bonita had made and when we heard Mom coming, he threw the food out the window. He had to get up early the next morning to clean it up because it landed on her rose bushes."

I chuckled as we reached the dining room and was pleased when Seth started speaking on his own. "The night I told them I thought I was gay," Seth said with a nod at the table. "I thought they'd try to convince me that I was confused because Trace was gay and I was just trying to be like him but they didn't. They were amazing."

I'd kept Seth moving as he spoke and was glad when he only spared the bloody mess on the floor a passing glance. We reached the front parlor and began going up the stairs. Seth kept up the stories on his own as we made our way to the second floor. The bedrooms were all a mess but he seemed to ignore all of them, his own included, and continued to talk about the various memories from his childhood. It wasn't until we reached his parents' room that he shut down again and I knew why as soon as I saw the blood-stained bed. It was the room his mother had been raped in…the rape he and his father had been forced to listen to.

I didn't bother asking Seth to try to remember a memory from the room because I could tell he was drained.

"Did Trace ever tell you that your mom threatened me?"

That got Seth's attention. "What? When?"

I led Seth back down the stairs. "I think it was the fourth time Trace and I came to visit…Christmas. She told me she thought I was a nice boy but if I hurt her son, I'd be sorry."

"No she didn't," Seth scoffed.

"She did," I said with a laugh. "Then she gave me a hug and asked me if I wanted pie."

"Oh God, not her apple pie."

I nodded. "Yep. I had to eat it right in front of her. I only got out of a second piece because you asked me to help you finish decorating the tree."

"I remember that," Seth said. "I thought you were just *really* excited about decorating the tree."

We both had a good laugh and by the time we reached the front door, Seth was considerably more relaxed than he'd been when we entered. He looked around the parlor and then reached over to the side table and grabbed a picture off of it. The picture had been turned over when we'd come in so I hadn't seen what it was of but when Seth flipped it over, I was surprised to see it was a family picture and I was in it. My heart seized up at the relaxed, happy expression on my face. Seth handed the picture to me.

"There's another one just like it at the other house," he explained.

I nodded as I studied the photo. Trace had his arm around me and Seth was standing slightly in front of me, his smile wide. "Thank you," I said, my heart suddenly in my throat. Seth's fingers drifted over my cheek as he lifted my face so he could look me in the eye. He kept the contact brief.

"Thank you," he whispered. And then he leaned up to brush his lips over mine. The kiss was quick and chaste but it rocked me to my core. Seth went out the front door and waited for me to catch up and then locked it behind us. He seemed physically worn out as we reached the car and truthfully, I was feeling the same way.

"How about we call it a day?" I said as I went around to the driver's side.

Seth nodded but didn't say anything. But the relief on his face told me that even if we hadn't exorcised all of his demons, we'd made a pretty good start.

CHAPTER 18

SETH

"Seth, wake up."

I didn't want to open my eyes but only because I was afraid if I did, I'd find out everything had been a dream. And the feel of Ronan's fingers on my skin would be a figment of my imagination.

"Okay, buddy, have at it," I heard Ronan say and I thought he was talking to me until Bullet's wet tongue swiped over my face. He managed to get in a few more licks before I escaped his reach and luckily Ronan kept him from jumping on the bed. I wiped at my face with the edge of the blanket before opening my eyes and then felt my heart stop when I saw Ronan sitting on the side of the bed, his backside pressed against my hip and his arm braced on the other side of my body so he was hovering over me.

"What time is it?" I managed to ask, though my voice sounded way too high.

"Six 'o clock," Ronan said.

Hell, I'd been asleep for more than four hours. And that didn't even include the time I'd been passed out in the car after we'd left the Mercer Island house. The only time I'd woken up on the ride home was when the car had rolled onto the ferry, but I hadn't managed to keep my eyes open for very long. I had a faint memory of turning my head to face Ronan as he sat behind the wheel and him reaching his hand out to stroke my face, but I couldn't be sure if it was real or just my desperate imagination.

"You should come eat," Ronan said. Where my voice was high and pitchy, Ronan's was deep and husky and in that moment I didn't give a shit about food. I sat up and felt an almost giddy rush of joy when Ronan didn't move. My position put our bodies only a few inches apart and it would be so easy to lean in and take his mouth. When Ronan's gaze shifted to my lips, I knew he was thinking the same thing.

The kiss back at the Mercer Island house had been an impulse I couldn't contain, but I'd managed to keep it brief so that Ronan knew it was my way of thanking him for the gift he'd given me. No, the visit to the house hadn't fixed everything, but I hadn't expected it to. But what I'd gotten out of the encounter was exactly what I'd hoped for… a chance to revisit the life I'd had and start putting the rest behind me.

I'd been sure the second I'd stepped up to the front door that I wouldn't be able to go through with it, but Ronan's voice in my ear, his hand warming my ice cold skin, had made it easier to turn the key in the lock. And it had all been my choice. I could have turned around and gone back to the car and Ronan wouldn't have thought any less of me. I knew that without a shadow of a doubt. And on the occasions where I had needed that nudge forward, Ronan had given it to me.

I wished desperately that I could do the same for him. Because for every layer Ronan seemed to strip from me, his own past became more and more of a blur. I'd had tiny glimpses today when he'd told me about medical school, but what he'd shared had been like a pebble being thrown into a lake…look away for even a second and you miss the ripples.

Trace had never told me anything about Ronan's childhood and at thirteen, I hadn't given it much thought. But two words today and the way he'd said them had me realizing there was so much to Ronan that I didn't know and it likely wasn't good.

My father.

"Come on, get up," Ronan murmured before he pushed himself up. "I don't make my famous spaghetti and meatballs for just anyone."

Ronan avoided my gaze as he left the room and I didn't manage to take a deep breath until he was out the door. I reached for my cell phone on the nightstand as I got out of bed and grimaced at the sight of several missed calls and texts from work. A glance at the switch on the side showed it had been turned to silent mode. I sent Ronan a telepathic *thank you* because I definitely would have gotten sucked back into work stuff if I'd heard the phone going off. And even though I was still feeling emotionally drained, physically I felt a little better.

I'd managed to change into a pair of sweats and a T-shirt before collapsing on my bed after we'd gotten home and Ronan had urged me to lie down. Under normal circumstances, I would have been happy to leave the comfortable clothes on but wearing the too-loose sweats around Ronan just wasn't a good idea so I swapped the sweats for a pair of jeans.

The smell of garlic reached me long before I entered the kitchen and I briefly wondered if I would have to play the same game with Ronan that we'd had to play with my mother regarding her cooking. But one look at Ronan in my mother's apron as he tasted what I assumed was spaghetti sauce and the thought fled my mind completely. The apron had been a gag gift from my father but my mother had gotten a kick out of seeing the shocked expression on his face every time she wore it so it had quickly replaced the pretty, flowery one she'd bought for herself years earlier.

"Come taste," Ronan said as he glanced at me and held up the wooden spoon expectantly. "What?" he asked when he took in what I assumed was my stunned expression.

"Nothing," I said quickly, though I couldn't take my eyes off the curvy woman's bikini clad body covering the apron. "Nice," I said as seriously as I could as I looked Ronan up and down.

"Fuck off," Ronan said, though there was no actual anger in his voice. "I just did laundry."

I laughed at that which earned me an irritated look. I quickly grabbed the spoon and took a taste of the sauce. "Wow, that's good," I said.

Ronan nodded knowingly. "Can you get the garlic bread out of the oven?"

And so it went. It was dinner, plain and simple. I had no idea if we were friends, lovers, family…and in that moment, I didn't care. Whatever we were, we just enjoyed each other's company. I still did most of the talking but it was a role I was happy to take on for as long as Ronan was willing to listen.

I did the dishes as Ronan cleared the table. Once everything was done, I tried to garner the courage to ask him to sit with me and watch a movie but I didn't want to press my luck. "I think I'll go read," I said quietly. "Thanks for dinner."

But Ronan grabbed my arm just as I turned away and my whole body drew up tight with excited anticipation. Shockwaves went up my arm and filtered out to all my limbs but it was my cock that reacted the most violently to his touch. God, I needed him again. I didn't care what it would cost me in the long run. I just wanted to feel his body pinning mine down, his flesh buried deep inside of me.

"I thought maybe we could hang out a bit," Ronan said as he released me. I couldn't help but notice that he didn't seem to be as strongly affected as I was. Shit, did that mean his attraction to me had already started to wane? Had my weakness today turned him off?

"Um, sure, we could watch a movie," I said awkwardly. Suddenly I just wanted to get away from him as my self-doubt increased.

"I have something else in mind," he said and I had no choice but to follow him. We ended up in the TV room but I didn't realize what Ronan was doing until he picked up the remote for the video game machine and turned it and the big screen TV on.

"This is your favorite, right?" Ronan asked as he motioned to the game that was booting up. I only managed a nod because I hadn't actually played any video games after my parents and Trace had died, because it was another link to them that I couldn't bear to deal with.

I dropped down onto the couch next to Ronan as the game started up. It was a racing game that Trace and I had spent countless hours playing whenever he was home and on a few occasions, Ronan and I had played as well, though being in Ronan's presence had always made me too nervous to really focus on the game.

I was beyond rusty but luckily, so was Ronan. And while I was still nervous around him, I still managed to kick his ass on the first game. He returned the favor on the second and by the third, we were in an all-out death race to the finish line. We played for more than an hour before switching to Tetris, another one of my favorites.

"Trace loved this game," Ronan suddenly announced as we started up a new round. It was so strange to have Ronan initiate a conversation about Trace that I actually held my breath in hopes that he would continue. He didn't.

"He used to let me win," I ventured.

"Yeah, early on. But then you got good." Ronan glanced at me and smiled. "He used to practice as much as he could on his downtime so he could beat you. It drove him crazy that his kid brother kept kicking his ass."

I chuckled. "He did like to win at everything."

"He did," Ronan mused.

"What about you?" I asked.

"What? Did I like to win?" Ronan asked.

I nodded.

Ronan thought about it for a moment. "I liked being the best at things like school and work. But I liked not having to worry about it with him. He liked to win but he knew how to have fun doing it. I needed that in my life."

I knew we were treading on dangerous ground so I considered my next words carefully. "You didn't get enough of that growing up? Fun, I mean?"

I saw Ronan's thumb start rubbing the edge of the game controller and I couldn't help but wonder if he weren't holding it, would he be tapping his fingers together instead? As his silence went on, I didn't expect him to answer me and I reached for the button that would start the next game.

"I didn't have what you guys had, Seth," Ronan murmured as his eyes fell to the controller in his hand. "I didn't even know what I was missing until I met him...till he brought me home to meet you guys."

I forced back the lump of emotion in my throat. "What did you have?"

Another lengthy silence, then, "Hate, anger, guilt."

I wanted desperately to touch him but I remained perfectly still. "Your parents?"

"My father."

I swallowed hard at hearing the same two words he'd said to me earlier. "What about your mother?"

"She died giving birth to me," Ronan said. "The way he talked about her...I knew they were happy. He used to tell me stories about how they met in high school and he asked her to marry him when they were both fifteen. He gave her a promise ring and they got married the day after they graduated."

The story should have been a happy one but I could tell from his tone that it hadn't been told that way to him. But I held my tongue.

"He used to say it should have been me instead of her...he said the doctors should have let him decide which one of us to save."

Anger surged through me but I managed to keep quiet. But I instinctively moved closer to him before I realized what I was doing, but Ronan was too lost in himself to notice. "She wanted to be a doctor," Ronan whispered.

I stilled. "Your mom?" I asked gently.

He nodded. "She'd been accepted to medical school when she found out she was pregnant. I was born a few weeks before she was supposed to start. She and my dad had it all planned out...how they were going to take care of me but still make it so she could go."

I ached to touch Ronan, but I settled for carefully removing the controller from his grip because his hold on it had turned brutal. The move allowed me to get closer to him but he didn't seem to notice because he began tapping his fingers together. His eyes were on the paused game on the screen but I could tell he wasn't seeing it anymore.

"I...I actually thought he'd forgive me if I followed in her footsteps."

"By becoming a doctor, you mean?"

A curt nod. "It didn't matter. None of it mattered."

"Is your dad still alive?"

"No. He had a stroke. I was still in my first year of med school. He was still alive when I got to the hospital." Ronan's voice cracked as he said, "I told him I'd take care of him. He...he told me to go to hell." Ronan sucked in a deep breath as if trying to get control of himself. "His brain started swelling the next day. There wasn't anything anyone could do for him."

"I'm sorry, Ronan," I whispered, and I took the risk and placed my hand on his arm. He immediately flinched and pulled away. The move hurt but I didn't recoil in on myself the way I wanted.

"Sorry," Ronan murmured as he realized what he'd done.

"It's okay," I said. "I'm glad you got to be a part of our family, Ronan. Even if my crazy mom did threaten you and force feed you pie."

I was thrilled when Ronan smiled a little bit. "That really was a bad pie," he finally said.

"You have no idea," I said as I grabbed the controller and handed it back to him. I hit the start button on the game and then leaned back against the couch cushions and began telling him all about how bad a cook my mother had truly been.

CHAPTER 19

RONAN

I couldn't focus on the email on the screen in front of me as I listened to yet another person chew Seth out over the phone. I couldn't make out the actual words from where I was sitting at the table in the corner of Seth's office, but the raised voice was obvious even coming through the handset that Seth was holding to his ear. It had been two days since the employees had found out about Seth's meeting in New York the following week and the anger and resentment hadn't let up in the least. I suspected if I hadn't been sitting in Seth's office, many of the employees who'd barged in would have been even more disrespectful than they already were. But as rude as some of the clearly anxious workers had been, Seth had handled himself well and he'd never lost his patience or raised his voice in anger despite some of the barbs comparing him to his father and finding him lacking.

I'd struggled with the turn of events that had happened the night Seth and I had played video games. I'd ended up revealing much more than I had intended and in fact, it was more than I'd ever told Trace about my tumultuous relationship with my father. Maybe it was because of everything Seth had so openly shared with me, I wasn't sure. Maybe, like Seth, I needed to lance the wounds that had been festering inside of me for so long. And while I hadn't expected to miraculously feel better, I also hadn't felt the need to escape Seth's presence either. But I hadn't been able to accept his touch. I had no doubt that my actions had hurt him but he'd let me off the hook without question. There'd been a few brief awkward moments as we both tried to get our bearings but they'd passed quickly and we'd ended up playing video games for another three hours before Seth had actually dosed off and fallen asleep on my shoulder. If he hadn't had to work the next day, I would have been content to enjoy the feel of his body pressed against mine all night.

Because he wasn't dangerous to me when he was asleep.

While Seth worked, I focused on the updates I'd gotten from Mav and Daisy. I was pleased to discover that Mav had made a lot of progress in destroying Barry Fields's life. Not only had the multiple restraining orders issued against the piece of shit therapist been leaked online via the man's own social media accounts and website, Mav had emptied his bank accounts, fucked up his credit and made every accrediting and licensing agency in the country aware of a criminal history that didn't actually exist.

Since Seth had no longer felt the need to make the daily run to the Mercer Island house, he'd ordered us a couple of sandwiches at lunchtime. Afterwards, I'd started looking through the bids a few security firms had submitted for taking over security of both the garage and the office building.

Seth hadn't balked at the surveillance system I'd suggested despite the high price tag and when Stan had called the measures extreme, Seth had simply reminded him that as majority partner, it was his call to make. It turned out that despite Stan's position as Chief Executive Officer, he had very little legal control over the company. His share of Nichols Shipping came out to less than fifteen percent, a high enough number to make him a wealthy man but nowhere near what Seth was making from the company. I had my reservations about the older man because he had a tendency to talk down to Seth, but Seth was clearly grateful for the insight Stan provided so I held my tongue.

I heard Seth hang up the phone and I glanced over my shoulder to see him hanging his head and running his fingers through his hair. I was about to ask him how he was doing when the office door flew open so hard that it slammed into the wall. A red faced, portly guy surged through it, a folder in his hand.

"I've left you three messages, Nichols!" the man bellowed. He threw the folder at Seth. "If you even think of trying to pull a fast one on us, we'll hit you with everything we've got. Our lawyers will have your ass wrapped up so tight, you won't be able to shit for weeks!"

"Mr. Abernathy-"

The man, who I now realized was the union president for some of the men and women who worked for Seth, slapped his hands on the desk and got in Seth's face as he grabbed him by the shirt. "Listen here, you little shit-"

I didn't even listen to the rest of what the fucker had to say as I got up and strode across the office. I grabbed him by the back of his collar and yanked him upright. "I think you're the one who needs to listen, you fat little fuck," I bit out as I used my free hand to propel the guy backwards until he hit the wall next to the office door. I ignored the startled look Seth's assistant gave me from her desk just outside the office.

"Ronan-" I heard Seth call, but I ignored him.

"If you ever speak to him that way again or lay even one fucking finger on him, I will kick your fat ass until you're the one who can't take a shit without crying. Get the fuck out!" I snarled before shoving the guy so hard that he stumbled to his knees outside the office door. I grabbed the door and slammed it shut, then flipped the lock. I turned to find Seth just feet behind me, his face drawn up tight with anger.

"Damn it, Ronan, I was handling it."

"That fucker-"

"Is an important part of this company," Seth interrupted. "Like it or not, I need to be able to work with him! You can't just-"

"I can and I will," I nearly yelled. My anger was still simmering as I closed the distance between us. "No one touches you like that. No one!"

The rage at seeing the man put his hands on Seth was still pouring through me and I knew I needed to get control of myself, but my whole body was aching to go back and find the guy and beat on him just because I could. I was seriously thinking of doing just that when Seth suddenly reached up and grabbed me by the back of the neck. His hold was firm and strong. I expected him to argue with me some more but instead, he yanked me forward and then his mouth was closing over mine.

He used my shock against me and stole into my mouth in one swift move. But my recovery was quick and I dragged him forward as my hands searched out his ass and my tongue dove into his mouth. I showed him no mercy as I consumed his mouth, but I couldn't stop him from jerking backwards when someone knocked loudly on the office door.

"Seth!" I heard Stan call. "Are you all right in there?"

Seth was breathing hard and we were staring hungrily at each other. "I'm fine, Stan," Seth called but he didn't move otherwise. I could see the indecision in his gaze as he looked me up and down and then his eyes settled on my dick and I nearly groaned out loud.

"Seth, open this door, please! Mr. Abernathy said he was assaulted."

I didn't give a shit about that but Seth straightened and then moved past me. He ran his fingers through his hair and then straightened his tie before unlocking and opening the door.

"Tell Mr. Abernathy that I will call him later once he calms down," Seth said firmly. "Also tell him that if he ever lays a hand on me again, his pride won't be the only thing that'll be hurting."

I saw Stan's stunned expression at Seth's words but the man kept sucking in air without actually saying anything.

"Nancy, I don't want to be disturbed for the rest of the afternoon," Seth ordered and then he was slamming the door and locking it. My cock twitched hungrily as he turned to face me. I had no idea where the hell we stood, but I was painfully aroused and I wanted nothing more than to finish what we started, friendship be damned.

Seth reached his fingers up to loosen his tie. But he did more than just loosen it. He took it off all together and then he was striding towards me with singular determination. I held my breath as he stopped in front of me and handed me the tie. Then he was grabbing my hand and leading me to the bathroom at the far end of the office. As soon as he closed the door behind us, he was on me, his mouth searching mine out. My lust exploded as my brain finally caught up and I wrapped my hands around Seth's neck to hold him in place as I kissed him. If I expected any shyness on Seth's part, I was completely mistaken because as I was desperately sucking on his tongue, his hand was snaking into my pants and closing around my dick. I groaned against his lips as he stroked up and down my length. His hold wasn't tight enough so I quickly reached down to undo my pants. I closed my hand around his and showed him how much pressure to exert. The friction of his palm against my flesh was exquisite, but my need was so intense that I couldn't just stand there and enjoy it, so I ripped my shirt off before working on the buttons of his.

Once the shirt was gone, I got his pants open and began playing with the crown of his dick which was peeking out from just under the waistband of his underwear. Seth moaned and I nearly came when he squeezed my cock hard. I saw Seth's eyes fix on my aching dick and I realized why when I looked down at myself. A bead of pre-come had formed at my slit. It began to drip down over the head when Seth suddenly slid his hand up and collected it with his finger. I held my breath as I watched him carry his finger to his lips and then he was sucking it inside.

"Christ," I muttered as my blood began to simmer beneath my skin. I ignored the look of wonder on Seth's face as he processed my taste and knelt so I could get Seth's shoes off. I basically ripped his pants and underwear off of him and then I was searching out the discarded tie which had fallen to the floor during our tussle. Seth already had his hands together in front of him by the time I rose and I wanted to kiss him all over again for his unquestioning understanding of what I needed. I wrapped the tie around his wrists and knotted it and then turned Seth and pressed his back against the door. I lifted his tied hands above his head and pressed the coat hook on the back of the door between the folds of the knot. I was glad it was long enough that it would hold Seth in place if he started squirming. Because between the last few days of being around Seth and not being able to touch him and this moment, I was way too vulnerable and needy to handle it if he did unwittingly touch me. Worse, I was coming to fear that I actually wanted his touch…no matter the consequences.

Seth's eyes were glazed over with lust as he watched me pull the lube from my wallet. I could already feel my orgasm threatening to overtake me so I quickly reached between Seth's legs and slathered some lube over his quivering hole. I covered my dick with the rest, making sure to use an extra generous amount since I knew I couldn't last long enough to prep Seth as thoroughly as I should. I used my arms to lift Seth's legs and he quickly caught on and wrapped them around my waist. I spread my hand under his ass to support his weight and used my other hand to guide my cock to his opening. My whole body was shaking with excitement and I could feel that Seth wasn't faring much better.

"God, I can't fucking slow down," I muttered as I began to press inside of him.

"Don't," Seth urged and I lifted my eyes to meet his. The emotion I saw staring back at me actually caused me to freeze in place and a combination of fear and joy went through me.

God, I couldn't really be seeing what I thought I was seeing, could I?

I didn't get to think on it too long because Seth closed his eyes and began to bear down on me. I bit back a curse and pushed against him until I felt his outer muscles give way. Seth was panting as he adjusted to my entry and I forced myself to stop long enough to give him the time he needed. When his legs tightened around me again and he closed one hand over the coat hook to support his weight as he lifted up just a little bit, I knew he was good and I surged up to meet him as he lowered himself onto me.

"Shit, fuck," Seth growled as he did the move again, drawing more of me inside of him. By the time I bottomed out, he was calling my name desperately. I sealed my mouth over his as I began plunging into him. Seth tried to kiss me back but he couldn't stop groaning every time I slammed into him, so I gave up and just let my lips rest against his neck as the lube began to make my gliding motion smoother. Seth was rocking himself back and forth over me as best he could, considering he had little leverage to work with and I could only hope his frantic movements didn't put too much strain on the restraints or the coat hook that was helping support his weight.

My own control snapped when Seth clamped down on my dick with his inner muscles and I let out a muffled curse as I slammed him back against the door as I drove into him. The door rattled in the frame as I pounded into him over and over and I once again sought out his mouth as I felt my orgasm start to crest. It occurred to me that I needed to release my hold on Seth's ass so I could get one hand between us, but he suddenly screamed my name against my mouth and then he bucked wildly against me. Hot liquid hit my chest and stomach as Seth's cock jerked against my skin. Knowing I'd fucked him so well that he didn't even need my touch to find his release had me coming an instant later and I felt Seth's dick twitch against me some more as my come filled him. I knew my fingers were going to leave marks on Seth's ass as I held him in place while I rammed into him over and over, riding out my orgasm, but I doubted Seth even noticed because he was still trying to jerk and twist his hips to take me in deeper as aftershocks quivered through him. When I finally had nothing left to give, I dropped my face against Seth's shoulder and tried to catch my breath.

Seth chuckled against my ear and then his mouth was pressing kisses wherever he could reach. I found enough energy to lift my head and kiss him the way he deserved and then I used all my strength to lift him high enough so that he could get his hands free of the coat hook. With his wrists still bound, he dropped his arms around my neck as his tongue searched out mine. I was too sated to worry about the contact because my only concern was staying inside of him as I maneuvered us so I could sit on top of the closed toilet. I could feel my own semen dripping down my dick as I made love to Seth's mouth but I made no effort to pull free of him.

None whatsoever.

CHAPTER 20

SETH

I tried not to check the clock for the hundredth time as I willed my eyes to stay shut. But my curiosity won out and I glanced at the nightstand and groaned when I saw it had only been five minutes since I had last checked the time. One a.m. More than twelve hours since Ronan had fucked me into near oblivion. And nearly just as long since he'd spoken to me.

We'd ended up kissing for a long time in the quiet bathroom but when the cooling come had become distracting, Ronan had slipped from my body and untied my hands. I'd hoped that he would kiss me again, but he'd quietly cleaned himself up, so I'd done the same and the silence continued as we'd gotten dressed. Once we'd returned to my office, the coolness had persisted and Ronan had actually left the office with an excuse that he needed to make a call and didn't want to disturb me.

When I'd kissed Ronan after his declaration that he wouldn't allow anyone to ever touch me the way Abernathy had, I'd known things might end up this way. I'd tried to prepare myself for it but it still hurt, especially as Ronan's distance grew as the day went on. The drive home had been so rife with tension, that I hadn't tried to draw

Ronan out like I had on our previous commutes. And when we'd gotten home, he'd made an excuse about needing to relieve Hawke and I hadn't seen him since.

Ronan had run again even though he hadn't left the property.

As I flopped over to my other side so I was facing the glass doors that led out to the balcony, I heard my door click open. Since Bullet whined excitedly for a few moments before settling back down on the floor on the other side of the bed, I felt only excitement, not fear. And I realized that was how I'd felt a lot of the times these past few days since Ronan had moved back in. Besides the visit to the Mercer Island house, I hadn't had that same sense of panic and anxiety that often overcame me as I made the drive down to the office or as I prepared to deal with the countless people I would have to interact with throughout the day. Even when I'd been in meetings that Ronan wasn't permitted to attend, I hadn't felt the same level of tension I was so used to.

I didn't move as Ronan came around the bed. There was enough moonlight filtering through the glass doors that I could see him put something on the nightstand just before he sat down on the bed next to me. I had no doubt that he knew I was awake but instead of leaning down to kiss me, he just stared at me for a long time. I rolled onto my back and pushed the blanket down so my upper half was exposed and then I tugged my shirt up just a little. Ronan took me up on my invitation and spread his hand across my belly. I couldn't make out his features but I didn't really need to...I could feel what he wasn't saying in his touch.

His palm traveled up my chest and dipped beneath my shirt to stroke my skin. I kept my hands fisted at my sides so I wouldn't inadvertently end what was happening between us. As frantic as our coupling this afternoon had been, this seemed different. Ronan seemed different.

Ronan continued to explore me and when his hand shifted to push the blanket completely away from my body, I sat up just enough so I could pull my shirt off. My intent was to lie back down so he could continue to do what he wanted to me, but Ronan grabbed my arm and held me there, our bodies close but not quite touching. He held my gaze for a long time and then he leaned in and kissed me. It was slow and sweet and his tongue only teased my lips instead of surging between them. I couldn't stop myself from twining my fingers through his hair as he tormented me with the drugging kisses. When he finally did take my mouth completely, I groaned and pressed against him. I barely managed to avoid wrapping my other arm around him, but it didn't matter because he used his weight to press me down on the bed. His lips began burning a path down my neck and I barely managed to whisper, "My ties are in the closet," before another moan escaped me.

Ronan leaned back just a little to study me and I cursed the fact that I couldn't see his eyes. Not that it really would have mattered, since reading Ronan wasn't an easy thing. It was only a few seconds that Ronan watched me for, but it felt like a lifetime before he settled his mouth back over mine. But instead of getting up like I thought he would to get a tie, he lowered his body until it was covering mine and I wanted to cry at how good it felt to have his weight on me again.

I didn't like the feeling of Ronan's shirt against my hot skin, so I threw caution to the wind and reached down to grab the hem. He let me drag it off of him but then his lips were crashing down on mine again. Joy went through me that maybe I was finally going to be able to touch him the way I wanted, but my hopes were quickly dashed when Ronan grabbed my hands with his and raised my arms so they were stretched above my head. He used one of his hands to hold both of mine down and then he took complete and utter control of me, my body...everything. His hand dipped into my sweats and began teasing my cock as I squirmed in his hold. The contact wasn't enough because he was flicking the pad of his thumb back and forth across my slit before running it along the ridge of the flared head.

"Ronan," I bit out between the kisses he tortured me with.

He didn't answer with words, but he knew what I was asking because his hand closed around my cock and he began dragging up and down it without hesitation. His other hand still held me in place, so all I could do was twist and buck against him in an effort to get closer. His teeth nipped at my lips as he eased off the intense, deep kisses and then he was kissing anywhere he could reach that didn't require him to let go of my hands. I could feel my orgasm starting to build so when Ronan released my dick, I let out a sharp, "No!"

But Ronan's mouth swallowed down my protest and then he muttered, "Leave them there." I knew what he meant, so when he released my hands, I didn't move them. I watched Ronan get up and strip his own sweats off. I could see his cock hanging heavy between his legs and I wanted to taste it so badly that I actually licked my lips. Ronan groaned and I had no doubt he knew what I was thinking.

My pants were stripped off of me and I quickly separated and raised my legs in invitation. Ronan's eyes stayed on me as he grabbed what I now realized was a bottle of lube from where he'd placed it on the nightstand earlier. I felt my mouth go dry at the sight of him stroking the thick liquid over his dick a few times and my hungry hole twitched in excitement. Ronan put some more lube on his fingers and then he was positioning himself between my legs. I wanted to tell him to hurry, but when all he did was coat my opening with some lube before placing the crown of his cock there, I wanted to shout out my happiness. Because even though there was more discomfort when he didn't prepare me with his fingers first, I'd discovered this afternoon as he'd pushed into me while he'd taken me up against that door, that I loved the intense burn. But even more, I loved knowing Ronan couldn't wait...that I'd stolen the control and patience he needed to get me ready.

And that in itself made me ready.

As Ronan began to press his thickness into me, I wished like hell my headboard was like the iron one in Ronan's room because I needed something to hold onto as the fire in my body threatened to consume me.

"Don't stop!" I shouted when I felt Ronan withdraw a tiny bit. But he pushed back into me just as quickly and I bit down on my lip when I felt my hole collapse and open fully to accept him. Ronan used his arms to bend my legs up and back in on myself and then he was leaning over me and taking my mouth. His hands sought out mine, but instead of holding them above my head, he drew them down so they were next to it and then he linked our fingers. His cock continued to work in and out of me in shallow thrusts and when he finally slid in as far as he could go, I let out a muffled cry of pleasure. With my legs pressed so high and close to my own body, it felt like Ronan was touching every part of me.

He held me like that as my body adjusted to his and then he began a slow, steady thrusting motion that nearly stole my breath. And he never once stopped kissing me. For the last two times that our coming together had been frantic and quick, I knew this time would be different. Ronan was making love to me in a way he hadn't been before. Every move, every touch, every kiss was about more than just pleasure...it was his way of telling me the things he couldn't say. We weren't friends. We weren't lovers. We weren't two men bound by terrible circumstances. In that moment, we were connected in a way that only the two of us could be. Nothing existed beyond us. And while I knew it wouldn't solve all the problems between us, I knew in that moment that he loved me. I also knew I was done being quiet.

"I love you so much, Ronan," I managed to whisper against his lips. The words caused Ronan to still above me and inside of me and I didn't need to see his eyes to know my declaration had caught him off guard. He didn't say the words back and I hadn't expected him to. What he did do was tighten his hands on mine just before he surged into me, his finesse gone. His mouth took mine without mercy and I gladly welcomed his weight as his body sank farther down onto mine. My ass felt like it was on fire as Ronan pistoned in and out of me and the tingling sensation in my limbs began to spread. Electricity shot up my spine when Ronan suddenly shifted just a little bit and struck my prostate. I let out a hoarse shout as the pleasure engulfed me and then he did it again. The orgasm washed over me in waves as Ronan nailed my gland over and over again and I felt my release scorch us both, as Ronan's tight abdominal muscles grazed my sensitive cock with every powerful thrust.

I felt Ronan's hands tighten on mine like a vise and he ripped his mouth from mine and clamped his teeth down on the spot between my neck and my shoulder as his climax hit him. Liquid heat burned my insides as he came and I let out a ragged moan as a series of quaking aftershocks rocked through my body. It seemed like Ronan's orgasm went on forever before he finally settled and became like a dead weight on top of me. His cock pulsed inside me several times as his body jerked every now and then, and I could feel his sweat slickened skin burning mine wherever we were touching. My legs ached from the position he continued to hold me in but I didn't actually want him to move. It took several minutes for my breathing to slow.

Ronan finally released his hold on my hands and shifted his arms so I could lower my legs. I wrapped them around his ass but kept my hands where they were because my gut was telling me that as amazing as what had just happened between us had been, it was exactly the thing that would send Ronan running again and even one wrong touch from me would bring that eventuality to head much sooner.

I guessed it was a good five minutes before Ronan moved and I couldn't stifle a whimper as his cock pulled free of my sore body. As Ronan shifted, I felt his wet dick brush my thigh. The perverse need to taste him ran through me again, but I stayed where I was as Ronan moved until he was once again sitting on the edge of the bed.

"Stay here tonight," I whispered desperately, and as I watched, his bent frame seemed to hunch in on itself. It wasn't a good sign.

"You know I can't," he said softly and then he was reaching for his sweats and pulling them on. I sat up and flicked the light on the nightstand on. The muscles of Ronan's back called to my hands as he leaned his elbows on his knees but I crossed my arms so I wouldn't reach for him. I had no doubt it was my declaration of love that had him folding in on himself as if in pain.

"You let me touch you sometimes," I finally said. As much as I hated needing to push him, I was feeling raw and vulnerable. I'd been certain only a few minutes ago that Ronan felt the way I did, but his sudden need to get away from me had me doubting myself.

Ronan ran his fingers through his hair. "It's not about you," he answered, his voice weary.

"Are you sure about that?" I asked. "Because I think it is."

Ronan made a move to get up but I leaned forward and grabbed his arm. I settled my hand on the now rigid muscles of his abdomen.

"Is it when anyone tries to offer you comfort or just me?"

CHAPTER 21

RONAN

My hands were shaking so hard that it took me three tries to get the door leading from the kitchen to the patio unlocked and open. The cool night air should have felt good against my skin but it didn't. Nothing felt good. I didn't even have the aftereffects of my mind-numbing orgasm to take the edge off, because every ounce of pleasure that had still been rolling through my body as I'd pulled free of Seth's tight body had been obliterated when he'd touched me...and when he'd given voice to one of my darkest secrets.

A few of the men I'd tied up and fucked after Trace died had had the balls to tell me the reasons they suspected I wouldn't let them touch me, but they'd all had the same train of thought...that it was a control thing. The men who worked for me hadn't ever commented on my aversion and I doubted most of them had even noticed since their interest in me and mine in them was about the job and nothing more. Mace's young lover, Jonas Davenport, was the only man I suspected who knew how deep my need to avoid physical contact was.

Except Seth.

But he'd seen what others hadn't. And he was exactly the person I'd wanted to hide the weakness from most.

I love you so much, Ronan.

Fuck, I couldn't even deal with that yet.

I'd managed to stop by my room long enough to clean the proof of mine and Seth's release from my body and drag on a pair of jeans, but I hadn't thought to grab my gun because I'd been too rattled by what had happened with Seth. But I couldn't risk running into him again so I hurried through the door and began striding across the patio.

"Running again?" I heard a voice off to my right say and I turned to see Hawke sitting on the single step that led from the study door to the patio.

I ignored the comment and asked, "What are you doing here?"

I hadn't seen or heard from Hawke much since I'd moved back into Seth's house other than to get reports and swap shifts with him so he could go back to his motel and rest while I did perimeter checks throughout the night. But his presence meant he likely suffered the same issues with sleep that I did. And considering the brutal way his wife had died, I wasn't surprised. I'd seen what the monsters that'd taken her from him had done firsthand. Only, Hawke hadn't had the pleasure of watching her murderers die like I had gotten to witness with Trace's.

I'd relieved Hawke almost as soon as Seth and I had gotten home and I hadn't expected him to return until morning. Of course, I hadn't expected to find my way into Seth's bed again just twelve hours after I'd slaked my need on him in his office.

"Figured you'd be preoccupied tonight," Hawke said. There was enough light from the full moon to see the silver of his gun that he had resting in his hands.

My agitation overrode my common sense as I said, "That the only reason?"

I didn't need to see Hawke's eyes to feel his chilly gaze settle on me. "You really want to do this?" he asked coldly. "You'd rather pick a fight with me than be with him?" he said as he glanced up at the other side of the house where Seth's bedroom was. It was far enough away that he wouldn't hear us unless we started yelling. "To be loved like that twice in a lifetime, Ronan? Do you even know what a lucky son of a bitch you are?" Hawke asked with a shake of his head. "What the fuck are you so afraid of?"

"He doesn't love me, Hawke. Not really. Fuck, he doesn't even really know me!"

"And whose fault is that?"

I shook my head in frustration. "So what, I'm supposed to go back to being the good doctor? The man who saves lives instead of takes them? I'm supposed to pretend the last six years never happened?" I snapped. "I'm supposed to overlook the fact that he's my dead fiancé's little brother? That I'm the reason his brother is even dead in the first place?"

"If the fact that he was Trace's brother really bothered you, you never would have touched him," Hawke said, his voice irritatingly calm. "And if you want to keep playing the martyr and pretend what happened to Trace was your fault, then fine. But damn well leave him the fuck alone then," Hawke bit out, his anger finally rumbling to the surface. "Because if you'd open your eyes for one goddamn second, you'd see that that man loves you in a way that all the shit from your past won't change. Can you say the same thing about Trace?"

I was on Hawke before I could stop myself, but he easily side-stepped the blow I'd intended for him. He grabbed me and shoved me back against the side of the house and before I knew it, his forearm was pressed against my neck, threatening to cut off my air supply. Hawke held me there for a moment but never increased the pressure on my neck and despite knowing how lethal he was, I never felt a moment of true danger. He finally shoved away from me. "I'm sorry," he said. "I shouldn't have said that."

I managed a nod but I couldn't get his last question out of me head. *Can you say the same thing about Trace?*

"Can you hang out here for a bit?" I muttered as I rubbed at my throat. Hawke nodded and I pushed past him and began walking across the patio. I snapped out of my reverie long enough to notice the barking coming from inside the house and I turned to see Bullet pawing at the kitchen door. I sidetracked and opened it and then followed the dog down towards the beach. As I began crossing the lawn, I glanced up and saw Seth watching me from one of the windows in his room. Much like the day I'd arrived. And like that day, he turned away from me.

I ignored the urge to go back up to his room and lose myself in his body again and made my way down to the beach. The full moon cast the entire back yard in an eerie glow that matched my mood. I'd been itching for a fight with Hawke just so I wouldn't have to feel any of the emotions Seth's words had called forth, but now I was stuck with Hawke's words instead.

I had no doubt that Trace had loved me but I'd always had a feeling that my love for him was just a little bit...more. There wasn't one thing I could put my finger on that had made me feel that way. Maybe it was the fact that he hadn't ever pressed me for details on my childhood. Maybe it had been that he'd never bottomed for me, even after I'd asked him to. He'd simply told me he didn't do that, hadn't ever done it with anyone and that was it. Conversation over. I hadn't really cared that he'd relegated us to the roles we'd played in the relationship, but his flat out refusal to even consider letting me know him in that way had left me feeling like he didn't completely trust me.

Not like Seth trusted me.

I came to a stop as the realization hit me. I was doing to Seth what Trace had done to me. I'd taken everything Seth had given me but all I'd given back was the pleasure my body could give his. I knew Hawke was right...Seth was all in. He'd meant the beautiful words he'd said to me, that he'd whispered against my lips as our breaths, our bodies, our souls had connected. I'd loved Trace but I couldn't deny that what Seth and I had just shared had shattered me in a way that I'd never experienced with Trace.

Guilt rushed through me and I didn't even make it to my log on the beach before I sank to my knees. A chill went through my bones but it wasn't from the cold. I'd suffered after Trace had been taken from me but I'd lived. I'd survived. But I knew in my gut that I wouldn't survive it if I lost Seth. I was in love with him. Plain and simple. And yet it wasn't. I'd been in love with Trace, but with Seth... God, I lived and breathed for Seth.

Bullet pushed against my hands with his cold nose and I sank down on my ass as he practically crawled into my lap. I wrapped my arms around his big body and buried my face against his fur. I couldn't help but wish it was Seth I had my arms wrapped around… that I could accept the comfort he'd been offering from the first time he'd followed me down to this very beach after our encounter in his bathroom. But I couldn't have Seth that way. Not because I didn't want him but because I knew Hawke was wrong about one thing – there was no way Seth could love me enough to overlook all the things I'd done since I let his big brother die.

∼

I hadn't expected Seth to wait for me the next morning like he usually did, especially since I'd overslept and was running ten minutes late. But he was sitting patiently at the kitchen table, the travel mug he'd bought from a coffee shop that we frequented on the way home from the office sitting in front of him. He looked as bad as I felt and I had no doubt he hadn't fared much better than me in the sleep department.

"Would you mind driving today?" Seth asked as I reached his side. I wanted so badly to lean down and tip his head back for a kiss, that I actually fisted my hand behind my back in a desperate hope the move would somehow prevent me from grabbing him. I took the keys with my other hand.

"Sure," I managed to say, though my voice sounded raspy.

I hadn't returned to the house until almost four in the morning. I hadn't seen Hawke but I'd known he was around somewhere. I'd glanced up at Seth's window as if expecting him to be standing there waiting for my return. He hadn't been.

It wasn't until we were on the ferry that I finally broached a subject I'd needed to speak with Seth about, but that I'd put off after the awkwardness that had occurred after I'd fucked him in his office bathroom the day before.

"I'd like to come to New York with you," I said, though I kept my eyes on the approaching mainland. Seth and I were standing in our usual spot on the upper level of the ferry.

"Okay."

It was the answer I'd wanted but the tone in his voice made my heart sink. Dejected, dull…lifeless.

I'd done that to him. He'd done nothing but give and I'd shit all over that because I was too much of a fucking coward not to give him back what he deserved.

"You told Dr. White it was a chartered jet."

Seth nodded. "Stan knew I wouldn't be comfortable on a commercial flight so he suggested it. He said we could take it as a business expense but I'm going to pay for it myself. Stan's flying out a couple days earlier…he's got family out there."

We were both silent for a while. I hated that Seth wouldn't look at me. I hated that he wasn't the same Seth he'd been just twenty-four hours ago. Laughing, joking, making fun of the fact that he kept kicking my ass at Tetris.

"Seth, about last night-"

"You don't have to explain, Ronan. I shouldn't have pushed so hard."

"Seth…"

"Please, Ronan, don't. Okay?" Seth whispered, his voice thick with what I suspected were unshed tears. "Just don't."

I forced the knot in my throat down with a hard swallow as I watched Seth turn away from me and head for the stairway that led to the lower level where the cars were. I waited a few minutes and then followed. I didn't speak to him again and once we arrived at his office, I used an empty cubicle nearby to check my email and make a decision on which security firm to go with. When I went to Seth's office to check on what he wanted to do for lunch, his assistant informed me that he was meeting with Stan and that he wouldn't be available for the rest of the afternoon.

I busied myself with looking at the latest information Daisy had sent me, but for the first time that I could remember, I struggled with making any decisions about how to move forward with the case she had outlined. It was as straightforward as they came. The man had been accused of killing two little girls after abducting them from their homes in the dead of night. He'd escaped prosecution on the first case because the witness lineup had been tainted by an overzealous detective. He'd been convicted of the second murder, but had escaped from custody while being transferred to prison. Daisy had managed to find him after pictures of him and one of the victims surfaced on the Deep Web – the arrogant fucker had posted the pictures himself in a private chat room for pedophiles that Daisy had hacked. She'd then used the IP address to find his location. Ironically, he was less than an hour's drive from Whidbey Island, which meant I was the closest operative besides Hawke to take him out. I knew what needed to happen but what was bothering me was the fact that I didn't want to do it myself. Not because the idea of killing the fucker bothered me in any way... no, my reasoning was much more personal than that.

"You ready to go?"

Seth's voice startled me. I glanced at the clock on my laptop and saw it was well past the time we normally left the office. I nodded and shut my computer down.

As we made our way to the elevator, I debated whether I should try talking to Seth again about the night before, but he made the decision for me when he stepped onto the elevator car behind me and promptly moved as far away from me as he could get. My stomach sank when I realized that would be his reaction if and when he found out what I did for a living these days.

I followed Seth off the elevator but nearly slammed into him when he stopped suddenly in front of me. I immediately looked around to see what had frozen him in place, at the same time that I stepped around him to shield him. My gun was drawn by the time I searched out what he'd been looking at. Seth's car sat exactly where we'd left it, but all four tires were flat and even from where we stood, I could clearly make out the words spray painted in red along the side of the car.

Cocksucker.

I searched the rest of the garage for any signs of life but there was no one. I knew whoever had vandalized the car couldn't have done it long ago or someone would have reported it by now. I took Seth's hand in mine as I approached the car and tested the paint. Sure enough, it was still wet.

I heard a muffled wheeze behind me and saw that Seth was struggling to draw in air. I knew he was hyperventilating because his whole body was shaking and he was shockingly pale. "Baby, look at me," I said as I tucked my gun in my waistband and put my hands on his face. "Hold your breath, okay?"

Seth shook his head violently.

"I know it's scary but I need you to do it."

After a few more unsuccessful attempts to draw in air, Seth did as I said and held his breath. I counted slowly and methodically before I told him to release it. I promptly repeated the process and continued to do it until I saw the color start to return to Seth's face.

"Better?" I asked.

Seth managed a nod but he was still shaking as his eyes skirted back to his car. "Hold on to me," I said as I took his hand in mine while I reached for my phone with the other one. I led Seth back to the elevator as I waited for the police to pick up. Unlike our elevator ride down to the garage, Seth refused to leave my side and he was gripping my hand with both of his. Once I had given the police the building address, I hung up the phone and turned to Seth and pulled him into my arms. He went willingly and I didn't feel my own body relax until he finally wrapped his arms around me.

It took several hours to talk to the police and arrange to have Seth's car towed to a mechanic after the police finished dusting it for prints. The officer had questioned us in the garage near the car which had made Seth edgy again, but I'd managed to keep him settled by holding on to his hand. When the officer had asked what we wanted done with the car, Seth had been adamant about not wanting to ever see it again. It was a clear indication that though he was holding it together, he was struggling to do so.

I'd called Hawke to tell him what had happened because I wanted him to be on alert in case whoever had vandalized the car decided to go after Seth at his house. The officer had been certain it was just kids messing around and I hadn't bothered to correct him. The vandalism wouldn't be much more than a blip on the cop's radar…to me it was yet another warning that Seth was being targeted.

It wasn't quite dark by the time we arrived back at Seth's house. Seth hadn't said a thing once we left the city and he'd folded in on himself once he'd collapsed in the passenger seat of the rental car that I'd had brought to his office. Several people had seen the commotion in the garage as they were leaving work for the day and many of them had been Seth's employees. The cops hadn't bothered to cover up the vile word scrawled on the car so there was no way for Seth to escape the humiliation of it all. Even Stan had come down to investigate and console Seth. And then he'd announced to everyone within hearing range that he was expediting the process of having a security firm come in and monitor things.

I wanted to punch the fucker in the throat.

Since I'd forgotten to grab the opener for the gate from Seth's car before leaving, I had to enter the code into the keypad. The gate opened and I drove through but I waited until I was sure it had closed behind us before driving up to the house. I knew the security for Seth's house would be next on my list. As big as the property was, there were just too many points of entry for someone to access the grounds. Putting a fence around it was the first line of defense, but he'd need some other security measures as well. If I had my way, he'd hire himself a couple of full time guards to monitor the property.

Because I wouldn't always be around to watch out for him.

Hawke was sitting on the steps leading up to the house when we arrived. Seth finally realized we were home and got out on his own, but he seemed stiff and uncomfortable as he made his way to the door.

"You okay?" Hawke asked, his voice surprisingly gentle as his eyes met Seth's.

Seth nodded. I could hear Bullet barking inside excitedly and it was on the tip of my tongue to ask Hawke why the dog was inside when Seth said, "I'm just going to let him out."

Hawke carefully grabbed Seth by the arm before he could reach for the door. "Just a second, Seth."

"What?" Seth asked. "What is it?"

Hawke's eyes shifted to mine and I went on alert. I could tell he had something he needed to say. "It's okay. You can tell us both."

Seth seemed confused and he took a few steps back so he was standing next to me. We watched as Hawke rose. As he stood, he grabbed a plastic baggie that had been sitting on the step next to him. "I found these down by the gate a little while ago."

Hawke handed me the bag and I sucked in a breath when I saw what it was.

"Is that...hamburger meat?" Seth asked.

Hawke merely nodded, though his eyes remained on me. I used my fingers to maneuver the baggie to separate one of the chunks of meat. I barely held back a string of curses at the sight of the green pellets that greeted me.

"What...what is that?" Seth asked as he leaned over to get a better look.

"It's rat poison," Hawke responded.

Seth snapped his head up. "What?"

I handed the bag back to Hawke. "It was meant for Bullet, Seth."

Seth seemed confused for a moment and then he shook his head. He automatically started towards the door but Hawke stepped in his path and grabbed him by the shoulders. "He's fine, Seth. He was with me the whole time. He never ate any of it."

Seth managed a shaky nod and Hawke released him. "Why?" he asked. "Why would someone do that?" Seth looked at me. "I don't have any neighbors so his barking couldn't have bothered anyone. And he never leaves the property..."

Hawke saved me from having to answer and I was supremely grateful because I struggled with having to tell Seth the truth.

"Whoever it was wanted Bullet out of the way so it would be easier to get to you."

It took a minute for Seth to comprehend Hawke's words and he sank down onto the steps. "Oh God," he whispered. I moved to sit down next to him. His breathing was sketchy but he hadn't escalated into a full blown panic attack yet. "You were right," Seth murmured as he looked at me.

"No one touches you, remember?" I said firmly. Seth studied me for a moment and I knew he was remembering my words from the day before when Abernathy had gone after him. He finally nodded and then stood and headed for the door.

"I should go get dinner started," he said numbly.

"Keep Bullet inside," Hawke said. "I want to check the grounds again. You should probably keep him on a leash for the next few days when you take him outside."

Seth managed a nod and then he was pushing into the house.

"Fuck," I snarled as soon as the door closed.

"It was close, Ronan. Bullet saw the meat before I did…if he wasn't as obedient as he is, he would have eaten all of it before I could have stopped him. I wouldn't have even known what it was."

I scrubbed my hands over my face in a vain effort to get control of myself.

"Any idea who's behind this?" Hawke asked.

I shook my head. "There are a couple guys it could be. His piece-of-shit therapist, but I'm not sure he has the balls to pull this off. He had a run-in with this union president asshole yesterday. Only the guy didn't have a problem with Seth until the news about the possible sale of the company leaked a few days ago…And I don't believe for a second that the mugging or Bullet getting shot was a coincidence."

"I think we should bring some more guys in. The property is too big to maintain a completely secure perimeter with just one person."

I nodded. "I want you to come with us to New York the day after tomorrow. I don't think the threat will follow him there, but I want someone else watching his back besides me."

"No problem."

"Thanks," I muttered as I went up the steps. I had my hand on the door when I turned to face Hawke. "Daisy has a case. The guy's only about an hour away-"

"I'll take care of it," Hawke said instantly. "Just go be with him."

Relief flooded my system, but I wasn't sure if it was because Hawke was giving me an out to ending another life or if it was because he knew I needed to be with Seth tonight. I nodded and turned my back to him. "Thank you," I said softly as I opened the door. I didn't wait to see if Hawke said anything back.

Once inside, I checked the kitchen for Seth but it was empty. I didn't bother checking the rest of the lower floor for him because I suspected where he'd gone. I was right when I opened his bedroom door. He was lying in the middle of his bed with Bullet next to him, his big body pressed up against Seth's front. Seth's eyes were open, but I wasn't sure if they were really seeing anything. His hand was buried in Bullet's fur. Bullet looked at me and thumped his tail but didn't move from Seth's side.

Because he knew what Seth needed.

And for once, so did I.

I went around the other side of the bed and toed off my shoes before climbing on the mattress and lying down next to Seth. I shifted my position so my front was pressed to his back.

"I can't," Seth whispered. "Please, Ronan...I can't."

I knew what he was talking about and shame went through me that he thought that I would take advantage of him while he was this vulnerable.

"I know," I whispered just before I placed a kiss on the back of his neck. I wrapped my arm around Seth's waist and shifted forward until there was no space between our bodies.

"I have a confession to make," I said to Seth.

I felt Seth tense against me. "What is it?"

I remained quiet for a moment before taking a deep breath and saying, "I've been letting you win at Tetris."

It took Seth a moment to catch up and then he relaxed in my hold and let out a little laugh. "Liar," he chuckled.

The insertion of levity seemed to work because Seth reached down to take the hand I had pressed against his stomach and drew it up to his chest. He linked our fingers together and then turned his head to look over his shoulder at me. I leaned down to brush my lips over his but kept the kiss brief.

"I won't let anyone hurt you," I whispered. "Ever."

"I know," Seth responded, his eyes on mine. He turned his attention back to Bullet but his next words stole my breath. "I love you, Ronan."

CHAPTER 22

SETH

"You okay?"

I managed a shaky nod and tried to unclench my fists where they were bunched in my lap. The jet was in final preparations for take-off, so I knew I hadn't even gotten through the worst of it yet. The layout of the luxurious plane was such that some of the seats were actually the size of loveseats and they faced the middle of the plane rather than the front of it. I'd chosen one of the benches so Bullet would have more room to lie at my feet. Ronan was sitting across from me on another bench and Hawke was closer to the back of the plane.

I hadn't had any issue with Ronan's suggestion that we leave for New York a couple days ahead of schedule. And while I didn't like the feeling that I was running away from something, I knew I was too close to breaking down completely after what had happened in the parking garage at my building and the second attempt on Bullet's life.

After Ronan had crawled into bed with me, we hadn't talked much because my mind and body had started to shut down from the stress. But feeling Ronan's warmth at my back had helped ease the sense of cold that had settled over me and I'd managed to fall asleep at some point. Ronan was gone by the time I woke up the following morning, but Bullet had still been in bed with me. It had been well after ten in the morning when I'd woken up and found Ronan working on his computer in the kitchen. I'd been torn between the need to leave the house and go to work just to prove to myself that I still could, and spending the rest of the day hiding out in my room like I wanted to. Ronan hadn't pushed me either way, but it was his whispered words from the night before that had me making a decision.

I won't let anyone hurt you. Ever.

I *had* believed Ronan when he said that. So I'd asked him to take me back to the office. I'd been too on edge to actually get any work done, so we'd only stayed for a little while. The hardest part had been going down to the garage to get the rental car. I hated that I'd been forced to seek out Ronan's hand yet again, but I'd known if I didn't have him to ground me, I wouldn't have been able to move forward.

It was over dinner the night before that Ronan suggested we leave for New York the following day. Ronan and I had played video games after dinner, but my heart hadn't been in it and I'd excused myself early so I could go to bed. A part of me had hoped that Ronan would come to me again like the night before but he hadn't. I knew it was for the best because despite Ronan's words that no one would ever hurt me again, I knew he was wrong. Because he was the one hurting me. Every look, every touch was a reminder of what I would be losing when Ronan decided to walk away from me again. I *had* been wrong about Ronan's feelings the night we'd made love and I'd confronted him afterwards about his unwillingness to let me comfort him with my touch.

It was in that moment that I'd finally come to accept that I couldn't fix whatever was broken inside of Ronan. I'd thought by giving him every part of myself that it would be enough, but it wasn't. It never would be. Ronan had and always would love only one man. A man I couldn't compete with and didn't want to.

The jet jerked over some kind of bump on the tarmac and I barely managed to swallow the whimper in my throat. I'd been on planes before, but I'd been so young then that being on them had been more about the excitement of going anywhere other than home. I hadn't yet understood the concept of mortality or how one simple twist of fate could change everything.

Bullet sat up and put his head on my lap. I managed to unclench one of my hands long enough to drop it on his head, but as the jet began racing down the runway, I felt my panic start to rise. Bullet whined but it was Ronan who got up from his seat and moved across the jet to sit down next to me. I saw the single flight attendant flash him a disapproving look, but I doubted Ronan noticed or even cared. His hand forced mine open so he could link our fingers and then he was drawing my body against his. In one way, it was exactly what I needed. In another way, it was exactly what I didn't.

My second declaration of love had been ignored just like the first one, but I really hadn't expected anything different. I'd sensed that I wouldn't have much more time with Ronan because he had continued to withdraw from me emotionally, even as he physically kept me close. And once several more men had arrived to watch the house, I'd felt like it was the beginning of the end. Because Ronan was only keeping his promise not to let anyone hurt me. He'd never promised me he'd stay with me.

Once the jet was airborne, I straightened so I was no longer pressed against Ronan's broad chest. I carefully tugged my hand loose and put it back in my lap. Ronan quickly got the message and got up to go talk to Hawke. I kept myself busy by massaging Bullet's ears but when he finally dropped back down to the floor of the plane, I had nothing to do but get lost in my own thoughts.

And I'd been doing way too much of that lately.

If I thought Seattle was bad in terms of congestion, New York was an absolute nightmare. Even being in the relative safety and quiet of the limo Stan had rented to pick us up from the airport, I felt like I was going to throw up at the sight of all the cars, bikes and people. The drive from LaGuardia to the posh hotel in Manhattan took a while because of the midday traffic. Bullet was between me and Ronan on the back seat and Hawke was sitting on the opposite side. Not a word was spoken, but the way both men kept scanning our surroundings had me on edge. Not to mention the sight of their guns sitting in their holsters.

I had no clue who might be after me or why. The mugging had scared me, so had Bullet getting shot. But I'd accepted them as terrible, but random, events. Knowing that someone wanted to hurt me was nearly crippling. Because it took me right back to the night of the home invasion that had killed my parents. And I felt as helpless now as I had then.

When the limo pulled to a stop in front of the hotel, Hawke got out first, then Ronan. I waited until Ronan told me it was okay and grabbed ahold of Bullet's leash and led him from the car. To my surprise, Ronan took my free hand in his. It both thrilled and irritated me because every time I felt like I had him figured out, he did something that just confused me further.

Once we were checked in and settled in the room, I escaped to the bedroom. I'd ended up booking an actual suite in the hotel so both Ronan and Hawke had their own rooms. Hawke left almost as soon as we arrived in the room. Other than our talk on the beach a couple of weeks ago after I'd made Ronan leave my house, I hadn't spoken much to Hawke. But I'd realized my first impression of him had been both right and wrong. I knew he was hard and unyielding, but he'd shown his compassionate side as well, especially when he'd been reassuring me that Bullet hadn't eaten any of the poisoned meat. I also knew that Bullet was a great judge of character and the fact that he spent nearly as much time with Hawke as he did with Ronan meant that for all his darkness, Hawke was a guy you wanted at your back.

A knock on the sliding French doors that closed the master bedroom off from the rest of the suite had me closing my eyes tiredly. "Come in."

I'd slept surprisingly well the past few nights despite everything that had happened, but I still felt worn out. I was worried what that would mean for my meeting on Tuesday. I needed to be at the top of my game, but the lack of control over what was happening to me just made me feel like a little kid.

Ronan slid the doors open and came around to face me where I was sitting on the bed. "How are you holding up?"

I managed a slight nod but it felt like a lie. My eyes were downcast so I didn't notice Ronan's hand until his fingers settled under my chin and tipped it up. "How are you holding up?" he asked again.

God, why could I hide nothing from this man?

I closed my eyes and shook my head.

"How about we go someplace nice for dinner?"

Shaking my head, I said, "I'm not really hungry."

"You need to eat, Seth."

I pulled free of Ronan's hold but didn't say anything.

"Why don't you get some rest and I'll check on you in a little while?" Ronan gave Bullet, who was lying at my feet, a quick pat and then turned to leave.

I knew it wasn't the time, but there was so much emotion churning in my belly that I just wanted some of the uncertainty to be over. "What are we doing, Ronan?" I said quietly. I was glad when Ronan didn't ask what I meant. Instead, he turned to face me. But he didn't answer me.

Frustration welled inside of me. "I can't do it anymore," I whispered. "I can't pretend that what we have is enough."

"What do you want, Seth?"

I let out a harsh laugh at that. The fact that he had to ask me that question was answer enough and I climbed to my feet. "I want what you had with him," I admitted brokenly. "No more, no less. I want all of you…I deserve it."

Ronan dropped his eyes and ran a hand through his hair. His silence was telling and I realized I'd had enough. I moved to the bathroom but stopped in the doorway. "After this is over, I need you to let me go."

I didn't wait to see what Ronan's response would be because I knew there wouldn't be one. He would fight to save my life, but he wouldn't fight for us.

And I didn't have the strength to fight by myself anymore.

CHAPTER 23

RONAN

The room Seth had booked was huge, but still felt too small to me. Of course, it hadn't felt that way until after Seth's heartbreaking words.

I want what you had with him. I want all of you.

The only problem with that was that Seth didn't know all of me. If he did, he wouldn't just be begging me to let him go, he'd be running from me as far as he could get.

I leaned the chair I'd snagged from the dining room back so the top of it was pressed against the wall behind me. I'd been out on the balcony for several hours now as I waited to see if Seth would make an appearance, but he hadn't. After he'd disappeared into his bathroom the night before, I'd hoped that if I gave him some time, he'd come out and I could find a way to try to put us back to where we'd been before I'd fucked everything up. At least when we'd been friends, Seth had smiled. He'd laughed and joked. And he'd reminded me so much of the younger version of himself, that I'd felt a little less guilty for leaving him three years ago. But the only time I'd seen Seth was when he let Bullet out of the room so I or Hawke could take the dog outside, or to get the breakfast I'd ordered for him this morning and left outside his room.

"Ronan?"

"Out here," I called to Hawke as I heard the front door open. I rocked the chair into an upright position and got up to go back inside. I was tempted to search out the alcohol that I knew would be in the mini bar, but I needed to be one hundred percent sober so I could be on alert for any danger that might come Seth's way. As much as I believed the threat was isolated to home, I wasn't going to risk Seth's life for anything. Not even the need to drown myself in my own pity party.

I met Hawke in the seating area of the main room and was surprised to see he actually looked agitated. In all the years I'd known him, he'd always been in complete control of himself. "What is it?" I asked.

"Daisy, she found something."

I automatically reached for my phone. "What did she find? She didn't contact me."

"Not about Seth. About Revay."

I stilled and then put my phone down on a side table. "She found them," I said quietly, unable to hide my surprise.

Hawke's wife's murder had remained unsolved for years, so one of the things I'd tasked Benny with from day one was trying to find ways to use the limited evidence the police had recovered in the murder to find the men who'd killed the young woman. I had no doubt that Mav had shared the information with Daisy in the hopes that she could find something new. As much as I'd wanted Hawke to get the break he deserved, I hadn't actually expected it to happen.

"What did she find?"

"A DNA match and a name. In California."

I nodded as I understood Hawke's urgency. "Go," I said. "Find them. And if you need anything…"

"I know," was all Hawke said. "But I need to know you and Seth are covered."

"I'll get someone out here by tonight. We're good…go."

Hawke hesitated and then he was stepping back towards the front door. "I already found someone," he said and then he opened the door.

My stomach dropped out at the sight of a man I never expected to see again.

Mace Calhoun.

The very man I'd thought I'd been helping when I recruited him after the brutal rape and murder of his seven-year-old son. The man Benny had used to try to take out Jonas Davenport in exchange for a quarter of a million-dollar payout.

As Mace moved into the room, Hawke gave me a questioning look and I sent him a quick nod. His relief was palpable and I realized how much I truly owed this man. He'd saved me in so many ways even while he'd been suffering through his own personal hell.

Hawke went to his bedroom, presumably to get his stuff together, leaving me and Mace alone. I hadn't seen Mace for several months – not since he'd asked me to keep an eye on Jonas and his other lover, Cole, while he went to bring Cole's father to Chicago where Cole had been shot while protecting Jonas from one of the men who'd put a contract out on him.

"You mind?" Mace asked as he motioned to one of the two plush white couches across from one another. I heard Bullet whining excitedly behind the sliding doors leading to Seth's room, but before I could go over to them and ask Seth if the dog could come out, Seth slid them open and Bullet darted through them. His eyes fell on Mace who was in the process of being checked out by Bullet, but if Seth was at all curious about the other man's presence, he didn't show it. His eyes met mine only briefly before he closed the doors again, shutting himself away from us…from me.

I went back to the seating area and dropped down on the couch across from Mace. Bullet had completed his exploration of the heavily tattooed man and came to plop his head on my lap. I let my fingers roam over his head as I studied Mace.

Mace was a larger guy like me, but that was about the extent of our similarities. His arms were covered from wrist to shoulder in tattoos and I'd seen enough of him during training exercises to know they continued along his chest and back. His dark blond hair was on the long side. The ex-cop had been one of my best men and had often worked cases involving crimes against children. I'd thought the jobs would cleanse his soul, but after Jonas accused me of using Mace's grief over the loss of his son against him, I'd begun to wonder if I'd just fed the darkness inside of him. The way I was just now coming to realize I'd fed my own.

"How are Cole and Jonas?" I asked.

"Good," Mace responded, his dark eyes studying mine intently. I felt like he was trying to get a read on me. We were both momentarily distracted when Hawke came out of his room, bag in hand. He gave me a quick nod and when Bullet ran up to greet him, he gave the dog an affectionate pat before leaving the room. I shifted my attention back to Mace and did my best not to show my discomfort at his presence.

I'd always kept my distance from all the men who worked for me. It wasn't because I was on a power trip or anything or felt the need to wrap myself in mystery. I had just been too focused on the job to care about building friendships with any of them. I dealt in death. It wasn't a "company picnic" kind of business.

"I never got a chance to thank you-" Mace began to say.

"Not necessary," I interrupted. Killing the men who'd abused and taken a hit out on Jonas had been a pleasure.

"Jesus, Ronan, would you just shut the fuck up and let me say what I need to say?"

I wanted to tell him no. Because it didn't matter. I'd done what needed to be done, plain and simple. Mace deserved a future with the two men he'd chosen to spend the rest of his life with. But I held my tongue.

"You already know I can't ever repay you for saving them both."

I managed to school my expression as I remembered the moment when I'd watched Cole take a bullet for Jonas. The whole thing had seemed to happen in slow motion as I'd rushed down the hall. Jonas had been screaming for Mace as a blood covered Cole lay prone before him. I'd pushed past countless people to get to Cole because in that moment, the doctor in me had replaced the assassin. I had saved Cole's life – it was true. And I'd saved Jonas's just hours later when the man who'd wanted him dead confronted him in an empty bathroom in the ICU of the hospital Cole had been taken to. I'd used my fingers to stem the blood of one man and used my gun to spill the blood of another. It was the first time I'd ever been the old Ronan and the new one.

"You saved mine too."

I began shaking my head but Mace put his hand up. "The thing Jonas said about you using me…we both know that isn't true. The only people who might have had a chance of saving me after what happened to my son would have been Jonas or Cole. I wouldn't have given up on ending my life for anyone but them…not my parents, not my ex, not you."

To my shock, I actually felt a shimmer of relief go through me. I'd found Mace by pure chance after his son's killer had come to my attention. I often researched how the surviving victims of my mark's crimes were doing…maybe because it made it so much easier to pull the trigger, maybe because I needed to know that the sin I was committing was truly justified beyond the victims who were no longer among us. I wasn't really sure. But learning about Mace had hit entirely too close to home. Because his guilt had driven him to try taking his life, much like mine had done to me. Hawke had saved me and I knew I could do the same for Mace. I'd met him just after he'd been released from the psych ward he'd been admitted to after he'd tried to commit suicide. After a brief conversation with the belligerent, bitter man, I'd known he'd try it again the first chance he got. So I'd killed the man who'd taken his son's life and offered Mace a chance to do for other kids what he hadn't been able to do for his own child.

"You gave me a reason to live. I could have walked away from you, the job, any of it at any point. I didn't because I needed it. Because it was all I had to keep me going, even if it was stealing little pieces from me bit by bit. Now I live for Jonas and Cole. I never would have had that chance if it hadn't been for you."

I was overwhelmed by the admission so all I managed was a brief nod. "Do they know you're here?" I asked.

"Cole and Jonas?"

I nodded.

"They know. And they're completely okay with it, Ronan. Like it or not, you're family to us."

I swallowed hard at that.

"Cole will be stopping by later tonight to spell me, if that's okay with you."

I felt pathetic for not being able to find my voice as I nodded yet again. As strange as being reunited with Mace and his lovers was, I would gladly accept the ex-cop and his Navy SEAL boyfriend's help.

"Hawke gave me some of the details. Can you fill me in on the rest?"

"Yeah," I finally said. My voice sounded shaky and uneven but I was glad that Mace didn't seem to notice…or that he was kind enough not to remark on it.

I took a deep breath and sank farther onto the couch as I began outlining the attacks on Seth, starting with the one that had happened the day I'd walked back into his life.

~

God, what the fuck was I doing?

I was in the process of debating whether I should go through with opening the door when a harried young woman trotted up to me. She glanced at me as I blocked the door and it took her saying, "Are you going in?" to get me moving.

I murmured an apology and opened the door for her. Before I could even decide if I should walk through it, another woman carrying a baby and holding a little boy's hand walked out and nodded her thanks.

I forced myself to enter the building, but felt my stomach clench as the woman I'd seen enter was walking through a doorway at the other end of the small space, a little girl in tow. "Bye, Jonas," the girl called as she waved enthusiastically.

"Bye, Alyssa! See you next week."

I managed to pull myself from my daze long enough to open the door for the woman again and once she was gone, I didn't hear or see anything. The decision to come see Jonas Davenport had been an impulse because when I'd asked Mace to keep an eye on Seth for a little while, my only intention had been to go outside and get some air. But Mace's visit had thrown me for a loop, as had his words about saving him. And then my last conversation with Jonas before I'd killed one of his attackers ran through my head. He'd thanked me for saving both Cole and Mace's lives. Right after he'd asked me that damning question that I could no longer adamantly answer yes to.

Did it work for you?

I'd always been sure that the path I'd chosen after Trace's death had saved me...had given me a new purpose in my life. But being with Seth...

God, I wanted *him* to be my purpose in life.

It was that realization that had caused me to get a cab and head to Brooklyn to see Jonas. Because it didn't matter what Mace said about me saving him. I needed to know that if I were to answer Jonas's question the way I really wanted to, would it change anything?

I forced myself to walk towards the back room where I knew Jonas kept the studio that he used to teach art to underprivileged kids whose schools could no longer afford art programs. I glanced at the art on the walls of the gallery which made up the front of the building. All of the artwork was on canvases and ranged from simple pictures of stick figures all the way up to more abstract-looking art with a wide array of colors and textures. Each canvas had a name on it and I could only imagine the pride each little boy or girl must have felt as they saw their art hanging on the spacious brick walls for all the community to see.

I saw Jonas as soon as I reached the studio doorway, but he had his back to me because he was bent over a canvas on a table in the center of the room. A little girl with mousy brown hair tied up in a tight ponytail was standing next to him, but her bright green eyes were on me. I guessed her to be seven or eight at the most. Her expression was blank as she watched me, but her small body was drawn up tight with nervousness. I saw her reach her hand up to tug on the end of Jonas's shirt.

Jonas automatically put his hand down on her shoulder as he turned but when he saw me, he froze and his mouth opened wide. "Ronan," he whispered.

It took him only a moment to recover, but that was probably because the little girl had pressed even closer to him. He automatically knelt down so he was at her level. "Natalie, this is my friend, Ronan." Jonas's eyes shifted up to mine. "Ronan, this is Natalie. She's one of my best students."

Natalie's eyes lit up just a little bit at that and she turned to look at Jonas. He brushed his fingers over her cheek. "Do you want to hear a secret about Ronan?"

The girl glanced at me and then nodded.

"He's a real life superhero," he whispered. I would have thought he was just saying the words to ease Natalie's uneasiness, but when he glanced up at me, I saw something I hadn't expected.

Not fear, not confusion as to why I was there. Just…happiness. No, that couldn't be right. He couldn't be glad to see me. He didn't even like me.

"Do you want to ask Ronan to help us hang your artwork?"

Natalie gave him a nod and I held my breath as she came right up to me and took my hand in hers. The feel of her tiny hand in mine, the cautious trust in her eyes, had a whole host of emotions churning through me.

I let Natalie lead me from the studio and followed her around one of the brick walls in the middle of the room. We ended up on the far side of the gallery near the window. There was an empty spot on the wall with a waiting nail. I expected Natalie to release me but she held on to me and when Jonas handed her the picture, she finally let go of my hand. But then she held both her arms up expectantly and even I knew what she wanted. I lifted her up and settled her on my hip and then stepped closer to the wall and helped her position the picture above the nail. She slowly lowered it until the string behind it caught and the picture stayed put.

"Good?" I asked.

Natalie studied the picture for a moment and then reached out to straighten it just the tiniest bit. She finally nodded and I set her back on her feet. I hadn't missed the fact that she hadn't said a word from the time I'd walked into the studio.

"Oh, Jonas, I am so sorry I'm late," I heard a woman say as she hurried through the front door. She had the same mousy brown hair as Natalie and she was wearing what looked like some kind of waitressing uniform.

"It's no problem, Sara," Jonas said as he accepted a hug from the woman. "We were just hanging up Natalie's art from today."

"Oh, honey, did you do that?" the woman gushed as she leaned down and hugged the little girl and then picked her up and moved closer to the painting so she could get a better look. To my surprise, tears welled up in the woman's eyes as she cast a glance at Jonas. "Oh, baby, it is so beautiful," Sara whispered as she hugged the little girl to her. The picture itself looked like many of the others and from what I could tell, it was a little girl's bedroom. There were two people on the bed, the larger one sitting on top of the covers, the smaller one beneath them. Both had lots of brown hair and the larger one was holding open a book.

"Natalie has already promised to let me keep this one on permanent display right here," Jonas said as he motioned to the picture. He focused his attention on Natalie. "You're going to make another one for your Aunt Sara next week, right?"

Natalie nodded and that earned her another hug from the emotional woman. "Okay, we should get going so we can stop at the store and get something for dinner. You ready?" Sara asked the little girl.

Natalie nodded and Sara put her down. The little girl immediately went to Jonas who dropped down and wrapped his arms around her. "See you next week, okay?"

Natalie nodded. To my surprise, she came up to me next and waited expectantly. I knelt down and tried not to react as she put her skinny arms around my shoulders. But I couldn't stop myself from putting my arms around her. Her thin body felt tiny and I released her the second she loosened her hold on me.

"It's a really good picture, Natalie," I said. The smile she gave me was like a punch to the gut and I was glad when she finally took her aunt's hand and followed her from the gallery.

"Thanks for that," Jonas said as he waved to the little girl as she walked past the window. "It's not easy for her to trust new people," he said sadly.

"What happened to her?"

"Her parents abused her pretty badly. Kept her locked in a basement for almost a year. They…they made her sleep in a fucking dog cage," Jonas muttered. The hatred in his voice was as unexpected as the swear word that crossed his lips. I'd known the instant I'd met Jonas in person that he was a gentle soul…luckily, something Mace had seen before he'd pulled the trigger.

"That's all she used to paint," he added.

"What?" I asked, not understanding what he meant.

"The dog cage. I give the kids a subject to paint about each week. You know, your family, your pet, your house…Natalie always painted a dog cage. Until today."

It took a lot to get a physical reaction out of me, but just the thought of the suffering the little girl had gone through…

"What was today's topic?"

"Your favorite part of the day."

Jonas gave the picture another glance and then began walking back towards the studio. "Her parents?" I asked.

"In prison. Turns out she wasn't their only kid…the other one wasn't so lucky. Sara had no idea her sister and brother-in-law had even had kids until the cops contacted her."

Once we reached the studio, Jonas began cleaning up all the various supplies. "We've been worried about you," he said, sending me a quick glance.

My first reaction was to ask why, but then I remembered Mace's comment about them seeing me as family.

"Mace tried to call you a couple times over the past few months just to make sure you were okay."

I actually felt guilty at that. "I thought he'd want a clean break…I thought you'd all want that."

"I guess the things I said to you didn't help with that," Jonas said with a sigh.

"Jonas-"

"I was wrong to judge you like I did. I let my fear for Mace cloud my thinking and I took it out on you. If you hadn't done what you did for him, for me, for all of us…" Jonas just shook his head as if the rest was too painful to even voice.

"You asked me a question in the hospital that day, do you remember?"

Jonas put down the paint tray he'd been cleaning up and nodded. "You said having an outlet for your hate worked for you and I asked if that were really true."

"I didn't see it then," I admitted. "I thought I'd fixed what was broken inside of me but all I did was bury it so deep that it couldn't touch me anymore. I became someone who wasn't broken. Someone who didn't feel, didn't care, didn't love or hate."

I sucked in a deep breath and forced myself to continue, but I had to drop my eyes to do it. "And I'm terrified that even if I can find a way to going back to who I was, what if I'm still so broken that even he can't fix me?"

"Is *he* the guy Mace and Cole are helping you protect?"

I nodded. It didn't surprise me that Jonas knew about Seth. I doubted the three men kept any secrets from each other. Not like I'd been keeping from Seth…that I was still keeping.

"Do you love him?"

I nodded again, not sure why it was so hard to say yes out loud.

"Does he love you?"

"He says he does."

"You don't believe him?" Jonas asked gently.

I shook my head. "I believe him, but he loves a version of me that doesn't exist."

"He doesn't know about what you do," Jonas said in understanding.

Humiliation coursed through me. I felt raw and exposed and weak and I fucking hated it. The need to escape was overwhelming. "You know what, I'm sorry…I shouldn't have bothered you with this."

I turned to go but Jonas easily caught up to me and stepped in my path. He didn't touch me which I was glad for. His touch wouldn't be devastating like Seth's, but I still didn't want it…especially now.

"Ask me, Ronan," Jonas said softly. "Ask me what you came here to ask me."

I shook my head but didn't move. When I finally lifted my eyes, I saw no judgement or ridicule in the young man's eyes. I drew in a deep breath and forced the words from my lips. "When you knew what he did, did it change how you felt about him? Even just a little?"

"No," Jonas said without hesitation. "No," he repeated firmly. No explanation. No reasoning. Nothing beyond the truth of that one powerful word.

I managed a nod. It was the answer I'd been expecting but it was the conviction with which he said it that had a glimmer of hope sparking deep inside of me.

"What's his name?"

"Seth."

I dropped my eyes again and realized I was tapping my fingers together. I bit back a curse and clenched my hand into a fist.

"Will you bring Seth to dinner tonight so we can meet him?"

I should have said no because I doubted Seth would want to go and I was feeling too much like an exposed nerve to deal with anything besides the anxiety of needing to find a way to tell Seth the truth…about everything. But then I remembered Mace's words about family and I realized that family was something Seth and I both desperately needed more of. At worst, Seth and Jonas were close enough in age that maybe they'd hit it off enough that Seth would have someone to talk to if he decided to send me packing.

"He has a dog-" I began to say.

Jonas laughed. "He's more than welcome. But just a word of warning…Casey kind of talked us into taking in a few foster animals."

I chuckled. Casey was Jonas's best friend and I knew from the research I'd done on Jonas after discovering Benny's failed hit, that the young woman and Jonas had run an animal shelter for years and that Casey Prescott continued to take in unwanted animals. The huge house she and her husband owned in the Hamptons had been turned into an unofficial sanctuary. It was no surprise that Jonas and his men had been sucked into the fold.

"I'll ask him," I finally said.

Jonas smiled brightly and stepped out of my way. "See you tonight."

I nodded and walked past him.

"Hey, Ronan?"

I stopped and glanced over my shoulder at him.

"Welcome back," he said with a smile. I studied him for another moment and then gave him a quick nod before I turned and left the gallery.

CHAPTER 24

SETH

I was numb by the time Ronan and I arrived back at the hotel after dinner at Jonas, Mace and Cole's townhouse in Brooklyn. I'd actually had a really good time getting to know Ronan's friends, despite my initial reservations about accepting the invitation. Before Ronan had left earlier in the day, he'd introduced me to Mace, but I hadn't actually spoken to the scary looking, tattooed giant of a man. I hadn't done much of anything since the night before when I'd begged Ronan to let me go. My request should have freed me to focus on the future.

It hadn't.

Because even in the years after Ronan had left me, deep down I'd believed he'd come back to me someday. He'd see that I could be what he needed.

But any hope I had left was gone. Especially after tonight.

The dinner itself had gone well and while Ronan had seemed tense at first, he'd relaxed enough to participate in the conversation here and there. It was my curiosity at seeing Ronan around people he seemed to knew pretty well that had me agreeing to go when he'd asked earlier in the day. Jonas, Mace and Cole had been welcoming, but it was seeing the three of them together that had me aching for something I couldn't have. I wouldn't have thought it possible for three men to be together in a relationship, but after having seen it for myself, I knew it worked for them.

While I guessed that Jonas wasn't much older than me, he'd taken me under his wing and by the time the evening was over, he'd given me his phone number and had programmed mine into his cell phone with the invitation to call or text if I ever needed anything or just wanted to talk. Then he'd wrapped his arms around me as Ronan had said his goodbyes to Mace. Mace and Cole had then kissed each other goodbye since Cole was coming back to the hotel with us. I'd been in the process of getting a goodbye hug from Mace when I saw Jonas say something quietly to Ronan and then wrap his arms around him. At that point, I'd felt the last little bit of my heart shatter into a million pieces. I'd managed to keep it together as Cole and Jonas kissed goodbye before we made our way down to the car, but I'd made sure to keep Bullet between me and Ronan on the back seat of the limo.

"You okay?" I heard Ronan ask as he closed the door behind us. I didn't see Cole so I could only assume he'd stayed in the hallway to keep a lookout for anything unusual.

"I'm fine," I murmured.

"Seth-"

Ronan's hand closed over my arm as he said my name, but any patience I had left fled.

"Don't touch me," I snapped as I yanked my arm away from him.

"Seth, what-"

"I want you to leave, Ronan. Now!"

Ronan was clearly confused, but I didn't give a shit and I turned my back to him and stormed to my room. I had barely closed the doors behind me before they were flung open again.

"What the hell is wrong with you?" Ronan asked angrily.

"You! You're what's wrong with me. Take your shit and get out. I'll hire a fucking battalion to watch out for me if it means I never have to see you again."

I could feel my anger giving way to crushing devastation and I wrapped an arm around myself to try to prevent the chill that was taking over my body.

Ronan took a step forward and I shook my head violently. "Get out!"

But my words had no effect on Ronan and he grabbed me by the arms before I could escape him. "Don't!" I cried, but it came out as a pathetic whimper.

"Seth, please," Ronan suddenly whispered, his voice sounding low and anguished. He tried to wrap his arms around me but I desperately lashed out at him. "Talk to me," Ronan pleaded. I knew tears were coursing down my cheeks, but I was too far gone too care.

"He hugged you," I managed to get out. "You let him hug you."

"Who? Jonas?" Ronan asked in surprise. "It didn't mean anything."

"Yes it did."

"No, Seth, I swear. He loves Mace and Cole."

Frustration surged through me and I shoved away from him. "You let him touch you, Ronan. And you damn well know I don't mean sexually."

I saw the moment Ronan finally understood what I was saying because he went pale and stepped back.

"One innocent kiss and you leave me for three fucking years," I yelled. "Then you come back and your only rule is that I can't touch you! And I followed it because I just wanted to be with you in any way that I could. One hug, Ronan. One fucking hug," I whispered brokenly. "You couldn't even give me that."

Ronan hadn't moved during my tirade and the blank expression on his face just hurt me more. "Get out," I said again and to my surprise, Ronan finally did it. I sank down on the bed and Bullet automatically came over and nudged my hands which were shaking violently. I used my sleeves to wipe at the trail of tears on my cheeks and tried to get my breathing under control. But I jerked upright when I heard a muffled shout and then a thud. I waited and heard what sounded like glass breaking. I hurried across the living room towards Ronan's room as more crashing noises resounded from the room. At the same time, Cole used his keycard to open the door.

"Everything okay?" he asked.

I couldn't speak because my heart was in my throat. I reached for Ronan's door but Cole got between me and it and pulled a gun from the back waistband of his pants before turning the knob. Panic shot through me when it didn't open, but I didn't even get a chance to say anything because Cole threw his weight against the door, causing it to crash open. As Cole was scanning the room for a potential intruder, I gasped at the damage. The lamp from one of the nightstands had been thrown against the wall, shattering the delicate glass base. Ronan's suitcase and the small table it had been sitting on were overturned and I could see that all the little decorative knickknacks on the dresser and small writing table were tossed onto the floor. I went around the bed and let out a muffled cry at the sight of Ronan sitting on the floor, his back to the wall and blood dripping down his hand. The remnants of the broken mirror that used to hang on the closet door were spread all over the place.

"Ronan," I said gently as I dropped to my knees in front of him.

Tears were coursing down his face and he was shaking his head back and forth.

"Here," Cole said from behind me and he handed me a towel from the bathroom. I placed it over Ronan's palm and applied pressure.

The room phone rang and Cole went to answer it. I kept my eyes on Ronan as Cole said, "Yeah, sorry about that. We were moving a couple of heavy suitcases around and a couple of them fell and knocked over a lamp. Please tell the people downstairs we're sorry about the noise."

Cole came back around the bed a minute later with a first aid kit in his hand. "Found this in the bathroom. There's probably not much in it."

I nodded and took it. "Can you give us a few minutes?" I asked.

Cole nodded in understanding. "I'll be out front if you need me."

"Ronan, can you stand up?" I asked. His silence was scaring the shit out of me...even more so than what he'd done to the room. He didn't answer me and I wondered if he even realized I was there. "Ronan, baby, please look at me."

Ronan's eyes finally shifted to me. "I didn't want to lose you," he whispered. "But I knew you wouldn't want me after I told you the truth."

I steeled myself because I knew in my gut what he was talking about. It was a subject I'd had to push from my mind over and over in the weeks following my conversation with Hawke.

Ronan is the one who needs you now.

"Ronan, look at me," I ordered gently. I waited until his focus was on me. "Nothing you tell me will ever change how I feel about you."

Ronan began shaking his head so I reached out to grab his chin gently with my hand. I was relieved when he didn't pull away from me. I leaned in and brushed my lips over his. "I love you so much, Ronan. That won't ever change."

He managed a shaky nod.

"Baby, there's a lot of broken glass around you. Can you stand up and sit on the bed so I can look at your hand?"

Ronan nodded and I kept the pressure on his hand as I helped him stand. We were both still wearing shoes so I didn't have to worry about his or my feet getting cut. I walked him around to the opposite side of the bed and sat him down. He hadn't destroyed the lamp on that side so I turned it on and carefully removed the towel. The bleeding had already slowed and I was glad to see the cut didn't look too deep. I didn't see any glass in it but I asked, "Does it feel like there's any glass in the cut?"

"No, it's okay. Just wrap it to stop the bleeding."

I hated how dull and lifeless Ronan sounded, but I did as he said and cleaned and dressed the wound as best I could.

"Do you want to lie down while we talk?" I asked.

Ronan shook his head. "No, I need...I need to be facing you."

I hated that he felt like he needed to treat what he had to say to me like a confession, but it was also a telling sign. Not only was whatever he was carrying inside of him about Trace's death really bad, he was also suffering from a heavy dose of guilt. I dragged a decorative armchair from the corner of the room and set it right in front of him where he was sitting on the bed. I sat down and took his hands in mine. I stifled the twinge of pain I felt as he pulled his hands free and settled them on his lap.

"I never wanted you to find out what really happened that night," he began, his voice breaking. "He wouldn't have wanted you to know what they did to him...he wouldn't have wanted you to have to live with it."

I swallowed hard. As much as I'd tried to prepare myself for this moment, I knew that such a thing really wasn't possible.

"There was this spot on the outskirts of the base. It was where the equipment that needed to be repaired was kept. At night it was pretty isolated so Trace and I used to meet up there when we wanted to be together."

"The army didn't know you two were together?"

"Don't Ask, Don't Tell was still in effect back then. We both would have been discharged if they'd found out we were gay. Trace didn't want to meet up that night because he was worried some of the guys in his unit had started to become suspicious, but I wanted to see him because we hadn't had a chance to be together since he'd proposed to me a week earlier."

Ronan used the back of his bandaged hand to wipe at his face. "Neither one of us heard them sneak up on us. There were five of them."

My heart sank as I realized what was coming.

"Two of them grabbed me. Trace was holding his own against the other three, but he gave up when one of the guys put a gun to my head...I was so scared that I didn't do anything. I didn't fight back, nothing."

"Ronan-"

"Don't, please. I have to get this out now or I never will."

I nodded.

"They started beating him and he let them. I begged them to stop but they just kept kicking and hitting him until he stopped moving. I thought the whole thing was over but then they came after me.

But they only hit me a few times. Then one of them pulled out a knife."

I stifled a moan as I remembered the cuts on Ronan's chest.

"He could barely talk but he kept trying to goad them so they'd go after him again."

"He loved you, Ronan. He would have done anything to protect you."

Ronan managed a nod. "It seemed to go on forever. Every time I thought it was over, they just tried something new. But then this one guy…the leader, he kept asking Trace how he liked taking it up the ass. And then he asked him if he'd take anything up the ass."

Ronan began sobbing and I pushed back from the chair and dropped to my knees in front of him and gently grabbed both his hands and dragged them to my chest and held them there.

"They raped him with a fucking pipe," he let out with a hoarse cry. I could feel my own hot tears streaking down my face and dripping beneath the collar of my shirt, but I ignored them and pushed to my feet. I sat down next to Ronan and dragged him up against my chest.

"I'm so sorry, Seth! I couldn't stop them! I couldn't save him."

"It's okay," I whispered as I dropped my lips to his head and just held him as tight as I could. His tears soaked through my shirt as he wrapped his arms around my middle and let out heart wrenching sobs. It took several minutes for him to quiet enough so that I could be sure he heard me when I said, "Tell me the rest."

He shook his head violently against me. I leaned down and skimmed my lips over his forehead. "I need to bear this burden with you, Ronan."

Several long seconds passed before he started speaking again. "Trace stopped moving after that, but he wasn't gone yet. They…they made him watch."

I felt like my insides were being ripped out with every word that fell from Ronan's lips. "He had to watch them do the same thing to you," I whispered.

Ronan nodded against my chest. "I kept wishing for it…death. For him, for me. After a while, I didn't feel anything anymore and I thought I was dead. I could see both of us lying like broken dolls in the sand. I saw the man who'd hurt Trace leaning over me, holding me down. I could hear his buddies laughing. I saw my body jerking and the blood pooling beneath me as the man who'd cut me used the pipe on me. I saw Trace's outstretched hand reaching towards mine. Close but not close enough to touch. And then it was over and they were gone and I knew he was gone too. Then death finally came for me too."

"What happened after that?"

"I woke up about a week later. They'd put me in a medically induced coma to give my body time to heal. They'd had to perform surgery to fix the damage the pipe had done. I was in the hospital for a month."

"Why did the army tell me Trace had died in a training exercise?"

"Because they didn't want the negative press. They told me they'd punish the guys who did it, but if I went public, everyone would know what had been done to Trace." Ronan shook his head. "I couldn't let them do that to him. It would have been like he was being violated a second time." I felt Ronan shift enough so that he could look up at me. "I didn't want you to know either."

I used my finger to wipe away his remaining tears. "I'm so sorry, Ronan," I whispered as I brushed my mouth over his. "I'm so sorry for what happened to you."

Ronan jerked and sat up, putting distance between us. But I still had my hands on his arms and either he didn't notice or he didn't care because he didn't move them. "No...I told you, it was my fault. I made him meet me. He couldn't fight back because he was defending me! I couldn't save him."

With every word, Ronan's whole body shook and he tried to put more space between us. But I followed and when he got too far away, I snaked my hand around the back of his neck and gently pulled him forward until our foreheads were touching. "I'm sorry for what happened to *you*, Ronan."

"Seth, don't-" Ronan whispered harshly. His fingers were biting into my arms but I didn't care.

"I'm so glad you survived. I'm so glad you came back to me."

This time Ronan didn't say anything; he just shook his head against mine and then let out a brutal, gut-wrenching sob. I knew the tears he'd shed before had been for Trace but these…these were for himself.

CHAPTER 25

RONAN

It took me several long seconds to process what the heavy weight on my chest was, but once I did, I was glad I was laying down because the night before came back to me in such a rush, that I was sure it would have knocked me to my knees if I'd been standing.

I hadn't understood the reason for Seth's violent outburst when we'd gotten back to the hotel after dinner, but once I'd seen my actions through his eyes, I'd understood that I'd pushed him too far. I'd hurt him too badly. And then I'd only wanted to hurt myself. So that was exactly what I'd done as soon as I'd seen my own reflection in the mirror. But it hadn't been enough and I vented all my grief and heartache on the rest of the room before giving in to the stunning realization that I'd lost Seth for good.

And then he'd been there before me and I'd known it would be my last chance. My only chance.

"Is this okay?" Seth asked, his breath gently washing over my skin where he had his head resting on my chest. His arm was wrapped around my waist and my arm was resting against his back. I didn't remember taking our shirts off last night after he'd held me for what seemed like hours. We were both still wearing the pants we'd each worn to dinner.

"Yes," I said, my voice sounding hoarse. I ran my hand up and down Seth's back and felt a sting of pain as I put too much pressure directly on the cut that slashed across my palm. The bandage was still in place, but I could see a little bit of dried blood on it. I lifted my hand and let my fingers trail through Seth's hair. "Will you come take a shower with me?"

Seth nodded against me and then lifted up and kissed me gently. He got up and climbed over me and then searched out my hand and led me to the bathroom. As he got the water started, I began unwrapping the bandage but Seth quickly took over the task and when he had the bandage free, he carefully placed a kiss on an uninjured section of my palm. While I checked the severity of the cut, Seth got undressed and then he was working on my pants. His seeking fingers quickly distracted me from the gash on my hand.

"Does it need stitches?" Seth asked.

The feel of Seth's hands roaming over my ass as he pushed my underwear and pants down had me asking, "What?"

"Your hand, does it need stitches?"

"No," I managed to answer, though what I really wanted to do was kiss Seth and beg him to keep touching me. But he finished stripping me and then led me into the shower. I only managed to steal a few kisses as Seth took his time washing me and by the time he'd finished, I was painfully hard. I reached for the soap to return the favor, but let out a muffled moan when Seth's hand closed around my cock.

"Tell me if you want me to stop," Seth murmured as he began to drag his hand up and down my length. I hated that he felt insecure enough that he needed to ask, but I knew it was my own fault. I went to reach for his cock, but remembered my injured hand. The left hand would be more awkward to use, but I could make do. But Seth beat me to it because not only was he jerking me off, he had his other hand on his own dick, matching the same pace he was using on me. Despite my tired body, the pleasure began to flood my limbs and I put my hands on the tiled wall behind Seth. I thrust against him so that our dicks were touching as he worked us both. His mouth parted as he began to increase both the pressure and the pace and I couldn't resist dipping down to steal into it. He moaned into my mouth just before he came and the second I felt his hot come splash against my own dick, I let out a shout and gave in to my release. Seth gently caressed me for a few more minutes as the high wore off and then I went about washing him as best I could with one hand.

Once we were finished with our shower, I dried off and began brushing my teeth but when Seth made a move to leave to get his own toothbrush, I grabbed his hand and pulled him back to me. I handed him my toothbrush and was glad when he took it without hesitation. I knew my neediness was off the charts because even the idea of being apart from him for the few seconds it would take for him to get his toothbrush was too much for me to handle right then. We didn't bother getting dressed since it was still early and after Seth rewrapped my hand, we went back to bed and Seth instantly snuggled up against me.

"Where's Bullet?" I asked.

"Cole texted a little while ago. He heard Bullet whining at the door so he took him outside."

It was humiliating to know that Cole had witnessed my meltdown, but there was nothing I could do about it. All I cared about was figuring out where I stood with Seth. Because he still didn't know what I'd become after Trace's death.

"Seth, last night...the thing with Jonas-"

Seth cut me off with a kiss. "Just sleep, Ronan," he said gently as he trailed his thumb over my cheek. "We have plenty of time to talk about everything." He kissed me again. "I'm not going anywhere," he said firmly. "I'm not going anywhere," he repeated, more softly this time.

I felt tears threatening as hope began to bloom in my chest. Did I really have a chance of getting everything I wanted?

"Sleep," Seth whispered against my lips. I nodded and closed my eyes. Instead of moving back to my chest, I felt Seth's mouth settle against the spot where my neck met my shoulder. For all the times I'd worried about how his touch would shatter me, I hadn't even once considered that his touch could actually start putting me back together again.

But that was exactly what he was doing...what he'd been doing all along.

~

It was almost noon before I woke up again. And when I didn't feel Seth's weight on me or his body pressed against mine, I jolted awake and sat up.

"Hey, I'm right here," Seth quickly said, his hand settling on my arm. I tried to catch my breath as I realized he was sitting cross-legged near my hip facing me. Seth kept soothing me with his touch. "I ordered us some room service," he said as he motioned to the food cart near the door. "I got you a BLT. You like those, right?" I nodded. Of course Seth would have noticed what I ate for lunch nearly every day while we'd been at his office.

"Did you eat?"

Seth nodded. "Do you want me to get yours?"

"No," I said. I noticed Seth was wearing his sweats, presumably to answer the door for the food. "Is Mace here?"

"Yeah, he's by the door."

"Good. Where's Bullet?"

"Cole took him home so we wouldn't have to worry about taking him out. He'll bring him back tonight when he switches shifts with Mace."

"I need to tell you how I know them," I said quietly. "I know you said it doesn't matter but I need there to not be any more secrets between us."

"Okay," Seth said.

"After I realized the army had lied to me about getting justice for

Trace, I lost it. I started taking pills and drinking, not caring what happened to me after that. And then I met someone who offered me a chance to get for Trace what the army wouldn't."

"Was it Hawke?" Seth asked.

I nodded. "How did you know?"

"He came to talk to me after I made you leave the house…after I locked you both out. He said you saved his wife. I asked him if he was helping you keep an eye on me because he owed you. He said something about not owing you anymore."

I dropped my eyes. My intent had been to keep Hawke's name out of it. We'd been careful about covering up the punishment we'd inflicted upon Trace's murderers, but I didn't want to put him at risk.

"Your secrets are safe with me, Ronan. His too."

It was then that I realized Seth had likely already figured out what I'd done. But he didn't know that I'd gone beyond just seeking vengeance for his brother. "The man who raped Trace was the first to die," I finally said, carefully watching Seth's reaction.

"What about the one who hurt you?"

The question caught me off guard. "He was the last. They're all gone. No one will ever find them."

Seth nodded.

"They weren't the only ones," I said. "I used the money you gave me to set up an underground organization that would let me go after men just like them."

Seth was quiet for a moment. "How many?"

"How many men have I killed?"

"How many lives have you saved?" Seth asked.

I shook my head. "Don't you get it, Seth? I'm a murderer. At least in the eyes of the law."

"How many?"

"I don't know," I said in exasperation.

"I do," Seth said. "Countless ones. Future victims, their families, the families of the victims. What I wouldn't have given to have someone like you stop the men who took my parents from me," Seth whispered.

"You're saving much more than just lives, Ronan. Trace would have been proud."

"Jesus, Seth. You can't just be okay with this."

"Why not?" Seth asked. "You see me as some naïve, innocent kid. But I have to spend the rest of my life wondering if the men who brutalized me and my parents are out there doing it to someone else. Yes, I'd love to see them rotting in prison, but justice can only do so much. If it's something you need to keep doing, it won't change anything between us. You save lives, Ronan. I don't care if you do it with a scalpel or a gun or both…as long as you keep doing it because that's who you are. That's who you've always been."

I was too overwhelmed to speak so I didn't. I just reached for Seth and pulled him forward. He straddled my lap as he closed his mouth over mine. I let him kiss me for several seconds before I gently pushed him back. "After what happened to Trace, I didn't like to be touched… not by anyone. Not sexually, not in passing, not in comfort. I wanted it with you…all of it. But I was also afraid of what it would do to me."

Seth's hands were holding the side of my head, his fingers rubbing the sensitive skin behind my ears. "What do you mean?"

"I can't explain it. I just…I was wrapped up so tight inside that I felt like I would just snap if you showed me any kind of comfort…like you would be forgiving me for something you hadn't known I'd done. I didn't deserve it…least of all from you."

"What happened to Trace-"

"I know," I said with a nod. "I know in my head that it wasn't my fault but my heart needs some time to catch up."

Seth nodded and kissed me. "I don't ever want to hurt you, Ronan."

"Not possible," I whispered. "You've been touching me from the moment I showed up at your house. Every word, every look, every kiss, smile…all of it. You were putting me back together long before I even realized it."

Seth's smile had something inside of me splitting open and flooding warmth to all my limbs. "I love you, Seth. You're my everything."

I saw Seth's eyes go bright with unshed tears and then he was wrapping his arms around my neck.

"I love you, Ronan."

Even though he'd said it before, I still felt a rush go through me. I suspected that would be the case every time he said the words to me. And if I had my way, I would have a whole lifetime to prove my theory.

CHAPTER 26

SETH

My heart felt like it was going to pound right out of my chest as Ronan kissed me. Ronan loved me. I couldn't believe it was real and I was certain I would wake up at any moment and find myself back in my own bed trying to envision a future without him.

But if it was a dream, it was the best kind because I could finally feel Ronan's skin beneath my hands. I was still sitting on his lap and though I was wearing sweats, Ronan was deliciously naked and I took advantage of my newfound freedom and skimmed my hands across his shoulders and down his back. His muscles flexed and rippled beneath my seeking fingers and his skin felt almost unbearably hot. Ronan's own hands were busy stroking all over me, and I couldn't contain my moan of pleasure when his hands slipped inside my pants and curved around my ass. I could feel his erection pressing against me as his tongue relentlessly explored my mouth.

Ronan used his grip on my ass to begin dragging me over his rigid cock and I stopped my own caressing of his body to absorb the shock of pleasure that coursed through me as our dicks rubbed against each other. And then in one swift move, Ronan lifted me and turned us so I was on my back beneath him. I let my hands trail down his sides as he tore his mouth from mine and began kissing his way down my body. But as much as I was enjoying what he was doing to me, it wasn't enough and I gently tugged Ronan's mouth back up to mine and gave him a quick kiss before saying, "I need to touch you."

A tremor of self-doubt went through me as he studied me and a terrible fear that I'd pushed him too hard assailed me. But before I could take back the words, he was rolling us so I was sprawled across his chest. His hands were on my upper arms, pressing little circles into my skin as his hungry eyes settled on mine. There was no fear or revulsion there, no need to escape or hide. All I saw was proof of the words he'd said to me.

I love you, Seth. You're my everything.

I leaned down to kiss him and this time it was slow and sweet. I took my time tasting him before placing soft kisses all over his face and jaw. I reveled in his musky flavor as I licked the corded muscles of his neck before making my way lower. My hands explored every part of him and when I got to his chest, I smiled at the feel of his chest hair beneath my fingers.

"What?" Ronan asked with a smile.

"It's been driving me crazy for weeks," I said as I nuzzled the spot between his nipples before looking up at him.

"What has?"

"Wondering if it would be as soft as it looked." I ran my fingers through the hair and said, "I'm not as well-endowed as you."

Ronan smiled and tugged me up for another kiss. "I think you're perfectly endowed."

I laughed and sat up so I was straddling him once again. I let my hands roam down his arms, beneath his armpits and down his sides before sliding them back up his chest. I ignored the rigid scars that met my seeking fingers. I would have plenty of time later to start to deal with the terrible things that had been done to Ronan and my brother.

"Shit," Ronan moaned when I tweaked one of his nipples. I did it again and then leaned down to taste it with my tongue. The man was undeniably sensitive there because as soon as I latched onto the turgid flesh with my teeth, he bucked up beneath me and put his hand on the back of my head. I gave his other nipple the same attention before scooting down his body so I could take in the rest of him. I'd felt his six-pack against me on more than one occasion, but there was nothing better than testing the firm, curved muscles with my fingers and my hands. But I didn't linger because there'd been another part of him that I'd been wanting to explore for a very long time. I glanced up to see Ronan watching me intently. His hands had maintained some kind of connection with me the whole time I'd been exploring him. Right now, they were resting on my thighs.

I knew what to expect when I touched Ronan's stiff flesh, but I hadn't had a chance to watch him when I'd touched him there before, so that's what I did as I tightened my grip on him and began dragging up and down his length. Ronan kept up the eye contact, but his lips parted and I could feel his muscular thighs twitching beneath me. I used my thumb to trace the flared head and gently pressed into his slit. I was rewarded with a sharp, indrawn breath and then a bead of fluid welled up the second I removed my finger. I grabbed it with my thumb and more instantly appeared. The more I stroked Ronan's dick, the more fluid began to leak from the head and I used it to lubricate my up and down motions. I increased the tempo as my other hand skimmed over his lightly furred balls. They were heavy in my hand as I rolled them back and forth. Ronan's breath had continued to tick up as I touched him, but when my finger brushed the soft patch of skin behind his balls, he let out a ragged moan. I did it again just to hear the proof of his pleasure and then I moved my hand to rest on his abdomen as I finally did what I'd been aching to do for so long.

I leaned down and tasted him.

His reaction was instantaneous. I'd only given him a single lick from base to tip, but Ronan thrust against me so hard that I was sure I'd lose my grip on him. Instinct had me wrapping my hand around his base before lowering my mouth to his crown and letting my tongue explore the taste of the fluid that was now glistening all over his flushed skin. I chanced a look up and saw that Ronan had levered up on his elbows so he could watch me. His eyes met mine and a fierce rush of power went through me. *I'd* put that look of pure need in his dusky gray eyes. I held his gaze as I closed my mouth around just the top of him. The lust in his eyes became almost feral, but he didn't reach for me and he didn't try to jam his dick down my throat like I thought he might. He just held there and watched me with open hunger as I worked more of him into my mouth.

I loved both the taste and feel of his smooth skin, but when my eagerness got the best of me and I took him too far down my throat, my gag reflex kicked in to remind me I had a lot to learn. But from the ragged grunts spilling from Ronan's lips, I knew my inexperience didn't bother him in the least. I switched over from exploration to pleasuring and began sucking on Ronan as hard as I could. I heard a muffled curse and I nearly smiled as Ronan finally began thrusting into my mouth. I had a tight enough hold on his base to keep him from ramming down my throat which was a good thing because I could tell Ronan was becoming more and more desperate as he fucked into me. My hope was to make him come in my mouth, but Ronan clearly had other ideas because his fingers wrapped around my arms and he jerked me up to his mouth for a scorching kiss.

"Now," was all he said as he wrapped an arm around my waist and sat up. I expected him to roll me beneath him, but he didn't. He just reached for the nightstand drawer and pulled out a small bottle of lube. I kissed and sucked every part of Ronan I could reach as he opened the bottle and slicked up his finger, but when he reached around me and sought out my hole, I nearly came on the spot. I knew I'd done a more than adequate job of turning Ronan on with my first blowjob because his finger pressed into me without any kind of finesse. It left my body only briefly for more lube and then it was plunging all the way inside of me.

"Yes," I whispered raggedly as Ronan massaged my prostate. But it was over too soon and within seconds, Ronan's thick cock was breaching me. The new position meant I had to bear down on him and I nearly bit into my lip as his crown held me open. The burn bordered on painful, but I loved it. I leaned down to slash my lips over Ronan's.

"Someday I want to see it," I said with a groan as another inch filled me.

"See what?" Ronan asked, his voice tight.

"The moment you take me," I said against his mouth. "It'll be just like this but there will be a mirror behind me that I can look into while I watch you fill me."

"Jesus Christ," Ronan snarled.

"Do you like that idea?" I managed to say. "Watching your hands holding me open while your cock pushes into me?"

The dirty talk was a clear turn on for Ronan because he began pressing into me without any kind of hesitation. "Fuck, yeah!" he snarled.

Ronan did exactly what I'd suggested and grabbed my ass with his hands and opened me. I didn't have a perfect view as I looked down over my shoulder, but it was enough. Just the sight of his big hands on me, his fingers biting into my skin had me jamming my hips down as hard as I could. Ronan and I both moaned as he sank all the way inside of me, but he pulled out just as quickly and rammed into me again. It would definitely be another fast and furious fucking but I was perfectly fine with that.

But to my surprise, Ronan only gave me a few more brutal thrusts before stilling inside of me. He moved his hands to my hips and then lay back down on the bed. His glassy eyes stroked over mine. "Ride me, Seth."

I understood what he meant, but it took me several tries to understand the mechanics as I awkwardly lifted myself before dropping back down. Ronan's hands on my hips steadied me, but didn't set the rhythm so I had to find it on my own. And then I realized why he hadn't. Because my body needed to decide what it wanted...or rather, it already knew but my mind needed to let go of the fear of doing something wrong. I settled on rocking back and forth over Ronan, adding a twist here and there that made something deep inside my ass spiral with sensation each time I did it. I found the rhythm I needed that kept the tingling sensation building and after a while, I began to pant as my body sought to drive the now spiking sensation even higher.

"Open your eyes," I heard Ronan order and it wasn't until he gave the command that I realized I'd closed them at some point. One of his hands was pressed against the middle of my chest and I was covering it with one of mine. His other hand was digging into my hip as I worked myself on him. I was desperate to come, but it wasn't until Ronan slammed his cock up into me that the building coil of need inside of me tightened unbearably. I kept up my own rhythm of twisting and rocking and somehow Ronan surged into me at the perfect time, every time. I lost the ability to speak as I rode the edge of my orgasm and I knew Ronan was in the same position. He suddenly surged upright again and wrapped an arm around my waist and then grabbed my legs, urging them behind him. I instinctively wrapped them around him as best I could and then Ronan crushed our mouths together. It took us just a few seconds to get back the same, perfect rhythm.

"Love you," Ronan suddenly whispered against my lips. "So fucking much, Seth."

I wrapped my arms around his sweat slickened shoulders. "Don't ever leave me again, okay?" I said desperately as my emotions took over.

"Never," Ronan promised softly and then he surged into me hard and I shattered as the coil inside of me snapped. I screamed Ronan's name as my orgasm swept through every part of me. I had absolutely no control as my body flailed against his. Ronan came at nearly the exact same moment and I felt his mouth seal over a spot on my shoulder, his teeth gripping me as his cock flooded my insides with the proof of his release. He kept thrusting into me over and over again and it wasn't until the intensity of my orgasm eased a little bit, that I realized at some point, he'd wrapped his hand around my dick. He released his hold on my wet cock and lifted his hand to suck my come into his mouth. The sight turned me on all over again and I began wondering how quickly I could get him inside of me again, despite the fact that he had yet to leave my body. And then he kissed me and I forgot everything else as I tasted myself on his tongue.

CHAPTER 27

RONAN

"What?" I snapped as Mace grinned at me for the third time in as many minutes.

"Nothing," he said.

We'd been sitting in the reception area of the office building that headquartered Seth's competitors for nearly two hours. I hadn't liked that I hadn't been allowed to accompany Seth to the actual meeting room, but I had been able to check the entire floor for any potential breaches in security. While the building housed hundreds of the shipping company's employees, the office we were in was designed for the executive staff and there were less than a dozen people on the floor. There was only one exit besides the main one near the reception desk where we were sitting and since it was a fire exit, it was armed to sound an alarm if opened. I'd had Daisy run security checks on all the men and women who would be in the meeting with Seth and since there'd been no red flags, I'd finally conceded and agreed to stay in the reception area while Seth conducted his meeting. Seth had gone a step further and had been texting me every fifteen minutes or so. And since many of the texts were explicitly suggestive about what he wanted to do to me as soon as he saw me again, I'd started shifting uncomfortably as my arousal had become harder to deny.

Apparently Mace had noticed.

Despite my obvious predicament, I began scrolling through Seth's texts again. I wouldn't have ever guessed the man would have such a dirty mind, but after his comments about wanting to watch me fuck him in the mirror, I should have suspected.

We'd spent all of Sunday in bed and had only stopped loving each other long enough for food, water and the countless showers we needed to wash the evidence of our pleasure from each other's bodies. I'd tried to slow the pace of our lovemaking down because I knew Seth's body had to be aching after the many times I'd slaked my need on him, but no matter how rough I was or how long I made him hold out for, he just wanted more of me. It was like he'd been making up for all the years we'd spent apart. But I couldn't fault him because I'd felt exactly the same way. I couldn't get close enough to him. I couldn't get enough of his taste or sound or smell. I couldn't get enough of the way he made me feel whole again.

Mace and Cole had continued to swap shifts keeping an eye on things for us and they'd kept Bullet overnight for us too. We'd finally forced ourselves out of bed on Monday. Mace had brought Bullet with him that morning and we'd taken the dog for a long walk in Central Park. The Seth I'd started losing my heart to three years earlier had started to return to me as the mantle of his insecurity and loneliness receded. We'd spent the whole day surrounded by people, but it had still just been the two of us. I'd been supremely grateful for Mace's presence as he followed us from a distance, because I hadn't been able to focus on anything but Seth.

We'd spent Monday night with Mace, Cole and Jonas and their small menagerie of animals. And for the first time, I'd truly felt what Mace had said…we were almost like a family. I'd been a little bit worried that there would be some awkwardness on Seth's part between him and Jonas, but there hadn't been. But the highlight of my night had been when I'd covered Seth's hand with mine at the dinner table in plain view of everyone. Seth's look of shock had been priceless. He'd clearly expected me to downplay what we were to each other in front of the other men. So I'd gone a step further and kissed him, hoping he finally got the message.

I wasn't running anymore...not from anything.

I glanced up from my phone to see Mace looking at me yet again. Never in all the years he'd worked for me had I seen the man smile. Now that was all I saw. And as much as it irritated me, I also liked it.

"Fuck off," I muttered.

Mace chuckled. "So if this deal goes through, would you guys need to move out here?" Mace asked slyly.

"Why? Two guys not enough for you?" I said with a smile.

"Hell, they're more than enough," Mace laughed. "You have no fucking idea."

I bit back another smile and focused on the text that appeared on my phone.

Be out in a few. Wrapping things up with Stan.

I was disappointed there wasn't a dirty note this time around, but glad to know I'd have eyes on Seth again soon. I saw a few people that I'd seen show up for the meeting start to come down the hallway and exit the office, so I knew it wouldn't be long before Seth came out.

My phone was on silent so I felt rather than heard the call coming in and I glanced to see that it was Mav. Since the receptionist had stepped away from her desk and there was no one else in the waiting area but us, I stayed where I was and answered the call.

"Hey," I said. I hadn't talked to Mav much in the days since we'd left Seattle, but he'd been sending me regular reports about the patrols that he and two of my other men were doing on Seth's property.

"We got them," Mav said in response.

I leaned forward and Mace instantly went on alert. I checked for the receptionist, but we were still alone so I put the phone on speaker and turned the volume down so only Mace and I would hear Mav talking.

"Tell me," I said quickly.

"We spotted her this morning-"

"Her?" I said in surprise.

"Yeah, it's a woman. Jennings saw her on the path from that access road next to Seth's house. She was trying to poison the dog again, Ronan. We found the meat on her."

Fuck. Thank God we'd brought Bullet with us.

"Who is she?" Mace asked after I remained silent for too long. I'd been caught up thinking about the devastation Seth would have felt if he'd lost his dog.

"Some lawyer," Mav said.

I stiffened at that. I only knew one female attorney in Seth's life.

"Says her name is Tabitha Brighton."

"What the fuck?" I snarled as I stood up.

"Ronan, she started saying a lot of shit when we questioned her. Like how she hadn't been the one who hired the guy who mugged Seth and shooting Bullet was an accident. She keeps insisting that some guy made her do it…that they were just trying to scare Seth so he'd be too afraid to leave his house again like before. She was also armed with a small caliber handgun."

Rage shot through me but Mace took the phone from me. "Did she say who the guy was?"

"She kept saying his name was Stan."

"What?" I croaked as I lifted my eyes to meet Mace's. I was moving a second later and shoved past the receptionist who came around the corner.

"Sir, you can't go back there."

I ran to the conference room and threw the door open, but my stomach fell when I saw it was empty.

"Sir-"

I grabbed the receptionist and barely managed not to shake her the way I wanted to. "Where the fuck are they?" I snarled.

The startled woman's eyes glazed over with fear and Mace stepped between us, forcing me to release her. His voice was firm, but he didn't put his hands on the woman.

"The two men that were in there" – he pointed to the conference room – "where are they?"

"Um…they went to lunch, I think."

"Lunch?" Mace repeated.

"Yeah. I went in there to ask Mr. Sadorsky if he wanted me to order him and Mr. Nichols something and he told me no."

"Mr. Nichols, did he look hurt or upset?"

"No," she stammered. "But I only saw him for a second because I spoke to Mr. Sadorsky at the door, not in the room."

My skin felt like it was crawling as I grabbed my phone from Mace's hand. I dialed Seth's number but there was no answer. I hit another speed dial and tried not to scream out my frustration as it rang three times before a woman's voice finally answered.

"Daisy, get me a GPS location on Seth Nichols's phone right now."

To her credit, Daisy didn't ask me why or balk at the fury in my voice.

"His number?" she simply asked and when I gave it to her, I heard her typing. It took several long seconds before she gave me the information. I hung up on her and looked at Mace.

"He's still in the building."

Since we'd both been covering the main entry and exit, I strode to the fire door and shoved against it. Raw panic settled in my gut when the alarm failed to sound. And for the second time in my life, I completely froze.

Mace snatched the phone out of my hand and dialed. I instantly heard Seth's ringtone but I knew in my gut that it wouldn't be that easy. We followed the sound down several flights of stairs, but when I saw the phone in front of the door that led to the parking garage, I couldn't stop the anguished cry that tore free of my lips.

CHAPTER 28

SETH

The first thing I noticed when I came to was the pounding in my head. It hurt like hell, but it was bearable. What wasn't bearable were my hands.

Because they were tied behind my back.

I tried not to panic as I struggled to get my bearings, but the coppery taste of blood in my mouth had me desperately trying to yank my hands free. I could feel that whatever I was tied up with was plastic and there was absolutely no give to it. I forced my eyes open and cried out when everything remained cloaked in darkness.

"Shut the fuck up!" a sharp voice yelled a second before someone kicked me in the stomach. I was already laying on my side, so the blow didn't knock me down, but the pain did have me folding in on myself. My sobs were muffled because of something that was stuffed in my mouth and tied around my head. My brain flashed back to the night I'd been in nearly this same position as masked men beat my father and mother before turning on me. The only difference was that I didn't have something over my head like I did now. The smooth material had me thinking it might be a pillowcase.

I tried to bring up my most recent memory, but the only thing that came to me was sitting in the meeting sending Ronan suggestive texts.

Stan had caught me staring at my phone on more than one occasion as the men we'd been meeting with spoke and he'd finally nudged me and sent me a dirty look when I couldn't hide the grin on my face as I imagined the expression on Ronan's face when he saw my suggestion that he bend me over the couch as soon as we got back to the hotel.

Stan.

An image of Stan pressing a gun to my side hit me hard and then everything came flooding back in a rush.

After the meeting had ended, Stan and I had remained in the conference room to wrap up and I'd told him that I'd already made the decision not to pursue the sale of the company or even discuss the possibility of a merger. The bottom line was that I wanted to run my father's company myself. And the merger hadn't been an option when I'd learned about all the safety and equal rights complaints our competitor was being investigated for.

I'd known Stan would be upset with me and I'd allowed him a few minutes to try and talk me out of it. We'd been interrupted by the receptionist knocking on the conference room door, but I hadn't heard what she'd said to Stan. Once Stan had returned to the table, he'd ripped into me about how I was making a mistake and that our company would go under if I didn't reconsider. But I'd been adamant and he'd finally relented. When we'd gotten up to leave, he'd told me that Ronan had asked the receptionist to have me and Stan meet him and Mace downstairs in the parking garage where they had the car waiting. I hadn't even considered questioning the change, nor had I thought it strange when Stan told me we could take the stairs because the fire alarm wasn't working.

But when I'd gotten my phone out at the bottom of the stairwell to let Ronan know we were there, I'd felt the cold metal of a gun pressed against my side. Stan had taken the phone from me and tossed it on the ground and then he'd ordered me to open the door. As soon as I had, a man waiting on the other side had hit me with something.

The pain in my body began to ease somewhat as I lay perfectly still and tried to quell my rising panic. I knew Ronan would come for me. I just needed to stay alive long enough for him to find me.

I could hear muffled voices, but couldn't make out what they were saying. But as heavy footsteps drew closer to me, the voices became clear and I knew without a shadow of a doubt that one was Stan's.

"I told you, I am not doing your fucking dirty work again," the stranger snapped.

"I'll double what I paid you last time," Stan said.

"No! The only thing that keeps me from going down for your shit is if your hands are as dirty as mine."

I felt a brutal grip wrap around my arm and then I was yanked to my knees. The covering over my head was ripped away and it took my eyes a second to adjust. But when I did, I froze. Because standing in front of me was Stan, the gun in his shaky hand pointed directly at me.

"I'm sorry," Stan suddenly whispered as his eyes connected with mine.

"What the fuck are you apologizing to him for?" the other man snapped. "Just fucking do it already." The stranger was in his early thirties and was wearing a pair of black jeans, a black shirt and heavy work boots. His hair hung well past his shoulders in greasy hanks and I could see several teeth missing as he railed at Stan. I didn't recognize him, but I let out a strangled cry when I saw the suddenly very familiar snake tattoo that went from his elbow to his wrist.

"You happy?" the guy snapped. "He's recognized me."

Tears began to streak down my face as it all came together for me. The man in front of me had been the same man who'd tortured me and slit my father's throat. And since Stan was in the middle of it all, it meant he'd had a hand in it.

"I'm sorry, Seth. I didn't mean for it to happen like that. You and your mom weren't even supposed to be there!" Stan was waving the gun around as he spoke. "I needed the money and your father...I knew he'd figure out that I'd taken it from the company. I loved him like a brother, Seth. But I was going to lose everything I had!"

"What the fuck are you explaining it all to him for?" the man yelled impatiently.

But Stan rattled on as if he hadn't heard the other man speaking. "I took care of you, Seth. I kept the company going for you. But...but you were supposed to sell it, not run it. My share of the profits wasn't enough...I needed the buyout to square away all my debts, to start over."

I wanted to scream at Stan, to yank free of my bindings and wrap my hands around his throat. He was talking to me like the more he said, I'd somehow understand and accept what he'd done to me...to my family.

"Then that bitch showed up at the office railing about me trying to steal her clients and I knew we could help each other. I told her I would convince you to keep her on as your lawyer if she helped scare you enough so that you wouldn't want to come back to the city...I knew if I could just get you out of the picture long enough, I could convince you to sell."

I knew Stan was talking about Tabitha Brighton and my heart broke for her father. Harry would be devastated to learn of his daughter's involvement.

"Jesus, fuck!" my father's murderer shouted. "Just pull the fucking trigger!"

Stan glanced at the man and his eyes went wide and his mouth began opening and closing as if he were trying to draw in more air. His gaze shifted back to me and he shook his head.

"I'm so sorry," he whispered again. "I don't have any other choice."

I shouted a ragged "No" against my gag as I realized I wouldn't have the chance to see Ronan one last time, to tell him again how much I loved him.

I closed my eyes and prayed to anyone who was listening to watch over Ronan so he wouldn't lose himself again and then I brought forth my last image of him. He'd pressed a sweet kiss against my lips right before I'd gone into my meeting this morning and then he'd whispered, "I'll see you soon" before he'd finally released me.

I waited for the gunshot but when it came, it didn't sound right. I opened my eyes, but couldn't take anything in because a heavy weight fell on top of me and I hit my head on the floor as I went down. I heard a crash and then shouting before several gunshots ricocheted through the air.

"Seth!"

I cried in relief at the sound of Ronan's voice and when my vision finally cleared, Ronan was moving towards me. The weight was lifted off of me and it took me a moment to realize it was Stan's dead body. A small, almost perfect circle stood out on the side of his head and there was just the tiniest trickle of blood streaming out of it.

"Seth, talk to me," Ronan whispered as he worked the gag free of my mouth. The plastic holding my hands together was cut free a second later and I realized it was Cole who'd done it.

"I'm okay," I managed to say as Ronan's fingers skimmed my face. The terror was etched in his features and I automatically put my hands up to encircle his neck. His pulse was pounding beneath my fingers. "I'm safe," I said. "You saved me, Ronan."

I could see Ronan was on the verge of falling apart, so I drew him down for a kiss and then wrapped my arms around him. He let out a sharp breath and then buried his face against my neck as his arms encircled me. His hold bordered on painful, but I didn't care. I kept whispering against his ear that I was okay. I noticed Mace enter the small building which I'd finally realized was a rundown cabin. In Mace's hand was a long, black rifle and I glanced over my shoulder and saw the bullet hole I suspected would be in the window. Mace had shot Stan, but I had no idea if Ronan or Cole had killed the other man who lay motionless on the floor not far from Stan, his chest riddled with bullet wounds.

"How did you find me?" I managed to ask once Ronan finally loosened his hold on me.

"Stan's second wife's family owns this cabin," Ronan said as he leaned back and began checking the injury on the side of my head where the man had struck me with something. "That's his stepson," Ronan said as he motioned to the dead man.

"He killed my father," I whispered.

Ronan stilled and pulled back from me just a little bit. "He's gone,

Seth. And we're going to find the others. They'll pay for what they did."

I managed a nod. "I knew you'd find me," I finally said when I tore my gaze from the dead man and focused on Ronan.

Ronan smiled and said, "Always" and then pulled me into his arms.

EPILOGUE

RONAN

Twelve days later

"Wake up, Seth."

"No," Seth grumbled as he burrowed deeper into my chest. "Too early," he mumbled. "It's Sunday," he added.

I glanced at Bullet who was sitting patiently on the floor next to Seth's side of the bed. "Okay boy, you're up."

"No!" Seth said a second before the dog jumped on top of him and began licking his face. Seth squirmed to get away from the wet tongue, but Bullet simply laid down on top of him and kept at it until Seth began laughing hysterically.

"Okay, okay, uncle!" Seth cried.

I chuckled. "Bullet," I said and when the dog looked at me, I patted the spot on the bed on my other side and the dog happily jumped over me and curled up against my back. I ignored the dog drool Seth was trying to wipe away with the bed sheet and leaned down to kiss him. "Morning," I murmured.

"Morning," Seth whispered and then he wrapped his arm around my neck and held me there as he thoroughly kissed me. My intent had been to get Seth up so we could go boating like we'd planned, but I quickly lost interest in the prospect as Seth made love to my mouth.

The kiss turned heated quickly and I was about to tell Bullet to take a hike when the dog figured it out for himself and jumped off the bed.

Seth rolled me to my back and began kissing his way down my body. He did what he often did which was give each of my individual scars his complete attention. It was something that had made me uncomfortable at first because I still struggled with the memories they brought forth. But like the day we'd gone to see his old house on Mercer Island, I'd realized Seth was giving me new memories to replace the old ones.

After Stan's attack on Seth, we'd spent a few days in New York to deal with the authorities and to give Seth time to heal from the concussion he'd suffered. Daisy had easily found the two men who'd helped in the home invasion. One had been a serial rapist who'd been convicted of murdering his ex-girlfriend shortly after Seth's parents were killed. The man had taken a plea and only served a few years in prison before he was paroled. There was no doubt in my mind that he'd been the one to rape and murder Seth's mother. Mav had gladly accepted the job and the man was dead before Seth and I even left New York. The second man was a different story. He'd been the younger brother of the rapist and had stayed out of trouble after serving two years in prison for drug possession. I'd given Seth a choice on that one and he'd said to let the young man be since he'd been the only one of the three men to actually try to stop the assaults once they'd started. But I'd told Daisy to monitor him.

I'd had the last several days to consider what and who I wanted to be going forward. I'd always thought I could only be one or the other, but Seth had made me realize I didn't have to choose. I hadn't just been Ronan, the doctor before losing Trace and I hadn't been just Ronan, the killer afterwards...I'd been a little bit of both with one just taking a more prominent role than the other. Seth had been right. I saved people. It was all I'd ever wanted to do.

While my organization would go on doing what it did best, I had no plans to pick up a gun again unless I absolutely had to. Mav had agreed to help me make decisions on the best way to handle all the incoming cases and my plan was to ask Hawke to deal with assigning the right man to the right job and pulling in new recruits who needed what Mace and I had needed so long ago.

I hadn't heard from Hawke since he'd left New York and while that had me worried, I knew it wasn't unusual. I'd been the same way, only now I had people who cared if I didn't pick up the phone or return a text. Hawke would get there someday too.

Seth had thrived once he'd returned to the office a few days after getting back from New York. He'd known he still had a lot of work ahead of him to regain his employees' trust and to get the company back on solid ground, but instead of trying to figure out how his father would have handled it, he focused on what he could bring to the table that would finally make the company his.

I hadn't been as certain as I'd wrangled with the idea of giving up the life I'd been living. The idea of returning to medicine was intimidating, but I also knew it was something that ran in my blood. I wasn't rushing into anything, but I had already started the process of figuring out what I needed to do to update my training.

"What are you thinking?" Seth murmured as he slid up my body and rested his chin on his folded arms.

"I'm thinking I want another new memory," I said. "A good one," I added. Seth understood what I meant and he traced his fingers over my lips.

"Tell me what you need," he said softly.

"You," I responded. "Every part of you."

It took a moment for Seth to understand what I was asking, but instead of resisting, he said, "Are you sure?"

I reached down to draw him up so his lips were hovering over mine. "Make me yours, Seth. In every way."

Seth ghosted a kiss over my lips and then settled his hands on the side of my face so he could hold me still for his next kiss. But it was so much more than that. It was him telling me what I needed to hear. That no matter what happened next, everything we had was perfect just as it was.

I'd toyed with the idea of asking Seth to make love to me after I'd come so close to losing him. The physical damage to my body hadn't been permanent, but I'd given up on the idea of ever letting anyone inside of me again because I simply knew I wouldn't be able to give someone that level of power over me. But Seth wasn't someone.

He was the only one.

And I knew he could take the pain of what had happened to me out in the desert and replace it with something beautiful.

Seth kissed me for a long time before he began working my body into a simmering pool of need. He and I had fucked in so many different ways, positions and locations, that I couldn't keep track of them all, but this would always be my favorite. This slow burn as we worshipped each other, as we healed each other.

I managed to hold it together as Seth took me into his mouth, but just as I was about to come, he pulled off of me and kissed his way back up my body. He took his time kissing me some more and then he started the process all over again. When he swallowed me down a second time, I begged and pleaded with him to let me come. But he was ruthless and pulled off of me with a pop. The lube was already sitting on the nightstand so when he grabbed it, I forced back the tension that shot through me. But Seth felt it anyway. I dragged him down before he could speak and I rolled him onto his back.

"I know you'll stop if I ask you to, Seth. I'm not going to keep quiet if I can't do this. I swear." Seth nodded.

I kissed him again and reached between our bodies to palm his dick. My own cock had wilted a little bit as my fear had started to inch up, but Seth was rock hard and pulsing in my hand. I teased him a few times like he had me and he let out a groan when I pressed my dick against his and began jerking us off together. My need came back quickly, so I only gave us a few tugs and then I rolled onto my back again. Seth crawled between my legs and gently urged me to lift and separate them. I automatically tensed up as his finger played with my hole, but when I saw Seth scoot farther down the bed, I nearly bit my lip as I realized what he was doing. It was something I'd done to him dozens of times.

I let out a ragged moan as his tongue licked my crease but it wasn't until the tip pressed against my hole that I nearly bucked off the bed.

Seth used his hands to separate my cheeks and pressed his whole mouth against me and then pressed his arms against my thighs to keep me in place. His tongue flicked at me repeatedly before he closed his mouth around my opening and sucked gently.

"Fuck, yes!" I shouted and I reached down to grab my own legs so I could spread myself wider for him. I hadn't ever been rimmed before since it wasn't something Trace had ever been into and the previous men in my life hadn't been interested in my pleasure. So nothing prepared me for the ecstasy that rolled through me. And when Seth stiffened his tongue and pushed it into me, I nearly passed out from the pleasure. He licked as much of my insides as he could reach before giving me a few more gentle kisses that kept me on the edge, but didn't drive me higher. When he reared back and reached for the lube, I knew I wouldn't be stopping him.

I knew what to expect when Seth's fingers began working into me and while there was no pain, I did have to struggle through a few moments of fear as my brain tried to send me back to the last time I'd been in this same position. But then Seth ordered me to open my eyes and I'd come back to the present and I'd relished the feel of him searching out and ultimately finding my prostate and gently massaging it.

"I'm too close," I said huskily to him as he increased the pressure on my gland. Under any other circumstances, I would have been fine with him getting me off and then taking me until I came again, but this time I needed him more than I needed the release.

Seth prepared himself and then leaned over me and kissed me. "I love you."

"I love you," I returned and then he kissed me again as his hand moved between my legs and positioned his cock at my entrance. He took me slowly and his mouth never left mine, not even after he'd bottomed out inside of me and stilled. My body adjusted quickly and the burning sensation that I had always loved in the past, rolled through me. The tingling quickly followed and when Seth began to move, my skin lit up deliciously. Every part of me that Seth touched sparked with sensation. With it being Seth's first time taking someone else, I'd expected him to fuck me quickly or struggle to find a rhythm that worked for both of us, but it didn't happen. Our coming together was as natural as it could be, as if we'd been doing it for a lifetime. There was urgency, but finesse. There was need but there was something else too...something only he and I would ever share.

I closed my hands over the back of Seth's arms as he continued to rock into me. His hand pressed between our bodies and wrapped gently around my dick and he began dragging up and down the sensitized skin at the same pace that he was fucking into me with. I had to stop kissing Seth as the need inside of me grew and I was forced to drag in more oxygen. I closed my eyes and pressed my head against the pillow, but the only place my brain went this time was the same place my body was...surrounded by Seth.

I came with little warning and as I cried out in blissful agony, Seth was there to drink down the sound. I felt his own release flood my inner walls as his free hand linked with mine on the bed. Seth groaned as his body finally took control and pumped into me over and over again, each slide of his dick causing aftershocks to roll through me.

He stayed on top of me and inside of me as he slowly brought me down with gentle kisses. I released the death grip I had on his hand and wrapped both my arms around him. I didn't need words to tell him what I was feeling.

When Seth did finally pull back from me a little bit so he could see my face he whispered, "I have a confession to make."

I stilled at that and couldn't help but wonder if he hadn't enjoyed what we'd done as much as I had. But when I saw the slightest hint of a smile, I automatically knew what was coming.

Because Seth was a terrible liar.

"Okay," I said. "What is it?"

"You suck at Tetris."

I laughed and kissed him. "I really have been letting you win."

"You have not," Seth said with a smile. But when he saw the seriousness of my expression, he said, "No way!"

I chuckled at his look of outrage.

"That's it, we're doing this," Seth said as he made a move to climb off of me. He groaned as his dick slipped free of my body and I quickly used the distraction to my advantage and flipped him on his back.

"Later," I said just before I kissed him.

It ended up being *much* later.

The End

Scroll to the next page for a Sneak Peek of Hawke & Tate's story

SNEAK PEEK

RETRIBUTION (THE PROTECTORS, BOOK 3) (M/M)

PROLOGUE

Hawke

*E*xcitement flooded all my nerve endings as I worked to pick the lock in front of me, but that wasn't a good thing. I needed the familiar numbness back. I needed to not feel anything at all.

Excitement in my line of work accomplished one of two things. It either left you open to making a mistake that could end up getting you killed, or it meant you were so far gone that you'd become as soulless as the men you'd been sent to rid the earth of. In my case, it was still the former, but I often wondered if there would be a point where I'd actually look forward to taking a man's life. Where I thought less about the life or lives I was saving in the long run and more about the satisfaction of finally having some of the power back that I'd lost so long ago…that had been stolen from me when they'd stolen her.

But unlike the countless lives I'd taken in the last decade for both the army and for the underground organization I now worked for, this kill *would* be about pleasure. I was going to enjoy watching the man's frantic eyes pleading with me as he desperately promised to give me what I wanted. And I'd let him believe up until the very end that he had a chance of walking away without a bullet in his brain.

He wouldn't. Nor would his partner. They would die the same way she had died. Slow and painfully. And they would suffer the way she'd suffered. They'd beg the way she'd begged. And I'd finally be able to keep the promise that I'd whispered in her ear as her heartbeat had slowed, the pauses between beeps on the heart monitor she'd been hooked to growing longer and longer.

I'll find them. I'll end them and then we'll be together again.

A sigh of relief went through me when I heard and felt the lock disengage. But as I reached for the knob, I heard the elevator open behind me and I yanked my tools out of the lock and hurried to the stairwell door that was just around the corner from the apartment I'd been about to enter. I didn't hear voices, but I could tell that there were at least two people heading in my general direction. And when I saw two men stop right in front of the door I'd been about to open, I felt a surge of energy rush through me. I'd hoped and prayed I'd find both of my wife's murderers at the same time, but it had been just that…hope. But my hopes were dashed when I realized one of the men wasn't old enough.

"Um, thanks for the ride," I heard the one guy say. His back was to me so all I saw was an average build and a head of thick, brown hair that had a little bit of curl to it. He was wearing a beat up leather jacket and a loose pair of jeans.

"My pleasure," the man with him murmured. He was about the same age as the first guy who I guessed to be in his mid-twenties. But whereas the other guy looked very blue collar, the guy with him was white collar all the way. His suit looked custom made for his tall, rangy body and I had no doubt the thick watch on his wrist cost more than my car.

Even from where I stood, I could tell by the first guy's body language that he was uncomfortable. But if the second guy noticed, he didn't care because he pressed against the first guy until the man had nowhere left to go since the door was at his back.

"I should get going," the first guy said. "I've got an early morning." Suit guy ignored the clear signals the other guy was sending and leaned down to kiss him. The brown haired guy turned his head away but that didn't stop suit guy from kissing the man's exposed neck. I couldn't say why the whole thing bothered me, but I didn't dwell on it. Brown haired guy deserved whatever he got because he was clearly the one who lived in the apartment...he was the man I was interested in, but for a whole other reason.

"I could use you again tomorrow night," Suit guy said as he took a whiff of the other guy.

"Yeah, sure," brown haired guy said, but he didn't move at all. He clearly wasn't enjoying the other man's attentions, but seemed reluctant to stand up to him.

"Okay, I'll see you tomorrow." Suit guy placed a kiss on the other man's cheek and then pushed back and strode away. I heard the elevator ding but my target didn't move right away. At some point, he'd closed his eyes and leaned his dejected frame against the door. He looked...done.

Rage went through me at the momentary pang of pity and that had me striding out of the stairwell as the guy turned to go into his apartment. I reached the door just as he was closing it. His startled eyes lifted to mine just before I used my booted foot to kick the door open, knocking him on his ass. I pulled my gun from my waistband as I strode into the apartment and slammed the door behind me.

"Please-" the man whispered but his words dropped off when I pointed my gun at him.

"Where is he?" I snarled.

The man put both his hands up. "Wh...Who?" he stammered.

I leaned down and grabbed the man by the hair and yanked his head back until he cried out in pain. "Don't fuck with me," I ground out.

"Please...please," he bit out as tears formed in the corners of his eyes.

I released my hold on him and pressed my gun against his forehead. He let out a choked sob, but I didn't care. I wanted so badly just to pull the trigger. But I couldn't. Because I didn't want to spend another day knowing that even one of the two men who'd raped my wife and left her for dead was still breathing.

"You want to play it that way?" I said calmly as I finally felt the familiar emptiness creep back into my veins.

I hauled the man up so that he was on his knees and then pressed the gun back against his head. "If the next words out of your mouth aren't his location" – I removed the gun from his head and pressed it against his groin – "this is where the first bullet goes."

The man was crying silent tears but he didn't say anything. He was shaking uncontrollably, but despite his fear, he remained silent and I noticed that even though he was crying, his eyes looked blank, like he was somewhere else. I ground my jaw in frustration and began searching for anything I could use as a gag. I didn't have a silencer but I could come up with creative ways to make the guy talk that didn't require a gun.

Before I could decide what to do next, I heard a knock on the door behind me.

I slammed my hand down over the man's mouth and yanked him to his feet. The move seemed to finally snap him out of his daze. "One word..." I warned quietly as I jammed the gun against his temple.

"Mr. Travers," came a woman's voice on the other side of the door. She began knocking harder. "Mr. Travers, I know you're in there. I saw you pull up out front a few minutes ago!" she shouted in irritation.

The man was frozen in place so I shoved him towards the door. I moved to the other side of the door jamb so that the person on the other side wouldn't see me when he opened it. But I kept my gun pointed at his head.

"Answer it," I ordered.

He shook his head violently.

"Do it!" I snapped.

"No!" he said in a harsh whisper.

The woman continued knocking. "Mr. Travers, we agreed to nine o'clock, no exceptions!"

"Answer it or I'll kill her," I threatened. "Get rid of her or you both die."

The man finally reached for the door and opened it a crack. "Mrs. Parks, I'm sorry-"

I nearly pulled the trigger when the door suddenly opened wider but it wasn't the woman who entered. A little boy no more than five or six years old squeezed through the narrow crack in the door. My instincts kicked in and I grabbed him and dragged him to me, covering his mouth with my hand before he could scream. The man at the door gasped, but the woman he was talking to didn't seem to notice that his attention was no longer on her.

"I'm sorry, Mr. Travers. We had a deal. You want me to watch him longer, you have to pay me for longer!"

I heard footsteps hurry off but the man staring at me in horror didn't move or even shut the door. "Please don't," he whispered as his eyes fell on the kid who was squirming in my grasp. And that was when I knew I had him.

I kicked the door shut and stepped forward. The man automatically stepped back.

"Where is he?"

"I swear to God; I don't know who you're talking about!"

"Your father!" I shouted.

The man was so caught off guard that he lowered his hands. "My father?" he stuttered.

The kid was furiously trying to escape me and it was a struggle to maintain my hold on him without hurting him. I also didn't know what the fuck to do with him – he hadn't been part of my plan. I hadn't even once considered the possibility that the younger of my wife's murderers might be a father. And no way in hell was I hurting a kid...I'd use him to get what I wanted, but I wasn't so far gone in my hatred that I'd actually follow through with my threats.

"I...I haven't seen my father in years," the guy said desperately. His eyes shifted back to the little boy. "It's okay, Matty. Daddy's here. Just be real quiet for a few minutes, okay," he said gently, his voice surprisingly even.

The boy quieted in my hold.

"No loyalty among murderers, huh?" I said.

"Murder?" the man whispered.

My fury was so intense that I released my grip on the boy and he ran to his father. "Get him here now!" I ordered.

"Jesus," the man cried as he grabbed his son and put him behind him. "You're looking for Denny!" he said.

"What?"

"I'm Tate. You're looking for my father and Denny, my brother."

ABOUT THE AUTHOR

Dear Reader,

I hope you enjoyed Ronan and Seth's story. They will be back in Hawke's story.

As an independent author, I am always grateful for feedback so if you have the time and desire, please leave a review, good or bad, so I can continue to find out what my readers like and don't like. You can also send me feedback via email at sloane@sloanekennedy.com

Join my Facebook Fan Group: Sloane's Secret Sinners

Connect with me:
www.sloanekennedy.com
sloane@sloanekennedy.com

ALSO BY SLOANE KENNEDY

(Note: Not all titles will be available on all retail sites)

The Escort Series
Gabriel's Rule (M/F)
Shane's Fall (M/F)
Logan's Need (M/M)

Barretti Security Series
Loving Vin (M/F)
Redeeming Rafe (M/M)
Saving Ren (M/M/M)
Freeing Zane (M/M)

Finding Series
Finding Home (M/M/M)
Finding Trust (M/M)
Finding Peace (M/M)
Finding Forgiveness (M/M)
Finding Hope (M/M/M)

The Protectors
Absolution (M/M/M)

Salvation (M/M)
Retribution (M/M)
Forsaken (M/M)
Vengeance (M/M/M)
A Protectors Family Christmas
Atonement (M/M)
Revelation (M/M)
Redemption (M/M)

Non-Series
Letting Go (M/F)

Printed in Great Britain
by Amazon